The
GIRL,
the DOG
AND THE
WRITER
IN
ROME

Also by
Katrina Nannestad

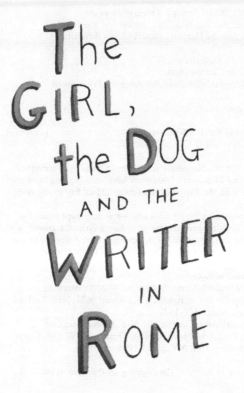

The GIRL, the DOG AND THE WRITER IN ROME

Katrina Nannestad

WITH illustrations by

Cheryl Orsini

ABC
Books

The ABC 'Wave' device is a trademark of the
Australian Broadcasting Corporation and is used
under licence by HarperCollins*Publishers* Australia.

First published in Australia in 2017
by HarperCollins*Children'sBooks*
a division of HarperCollins*Publishers* Australia Pty Limited
ABN 36 009 913 517
harpercollins.com.au

HarperCollins*Publishers*
Level 13, 201 Elizabeth Street, Sydney NSW 2000, Australia
Unit D1, 63 Apollo Drive, Rosedale, Auckland 0632, New Zealand
A 53, Sector 57, Noida, UP, India
1 London Bridge Street, London SE1 9GF, United Kingdom
2 Bloor Street East, 20th floor, Toronto, Ontario M4W 1A8, Canada
195 Broadway, New York NY 10007, USA

National Library of Australia Cataloguing-in-Publication entry:

Nannestad, Katrina, author.
The girl, the dog and the writer in Rome / Katrina Nannestad;
Cheryl Orsini, illustrator.
1st ed.
ISBN: 978 0 7333 3817 5 (paperback)
ISBN: 978 1 4607 0812 5 (ebook)
Nannestad, Katrina. Girl, the dog and the writer; 1.
For primary school age.
Friendship—Juvenile fiction.
Families—Juvenile fiction.
Rome (Italy)—Juvenile fiction.
Orsini, Cheryl, illustrator.

Cover and internal design by Hazel Lam, HarperCollins Design Studio
Cover illustrations by Cheryl Orsini; all other images by shutterstock.com
Internal illustrations by Cheryl Orsini
Typeset in Sabon Lt Std by Kirby Jones
Printed and bound in Australia at McPherson's Printing Group
The papers used by HarperCollins in the manufacture of this book
are a natural, recyclable product made from wood grown in sustainable
plantation forests. The fibre source and manufacturing processes meet
recognised international environmental standards, and carry certification.

For Carsten

Seeds

Freja sat on the grassy slope, as still as the granite rocks around her. The Norwegian wind was wild and gusty, and her curly hair flicked and whipped about her face like a mop caught in a tornado. Her nose wrinkled, but her body didn't move.

Not satisfied with teasing her hair, the wind started in on her scarf. The fringed ends flapped and flopped against her coat until the scarf came loose and drifted away from her neck. Still, Freja kept her legs crossed, her gloved hands pressed into the grass at her sides.

The wind howled with fury. The scarf gave a whippety-flick, slid across the back of her shoulders and took flight. Without moving her head, Freja followed its journey with her eyes. It sailed up into the air, where it snaked and wriggled in a cherry-red dance of freedom.

Aaw no! she thought. *I loved that scarf.*

But still she did not budge.

The wind blustered and whooped. The scarf flapped and wriggled a little higher before waving cheekily and soaring away to explore the vast expanse of the Arctic tundra.

Clementine, Freja's mother, whispered at her side, 'Never mind, my darling. I'll knit you a new one for your tenth birthday. An even better scarf — with twice as many fringy bits — and a beanie to match.'

Freja's smile flashed in the sunshine and her blue eyes sparkled, but she did not move.

The wind howled.

A lost puffin flew past.

The sun drifted westward and low.

Freja's nose and ears turned numb with cold.

The wind dropped.

And then, finally, they appeared.

Arctic hares. An entire family.

The mother came first, poking her pretty white face out between the rocks. She looked about. Her nose twitched. She blinked. Her long, black-tipped ears swivelled forward and to the side. Satisfied that the slope was free of predators, she lolloped slowly forth and was soon followed by her babies — five tiny grey leverets.

Freja gasped. She could sense Clementine smiling at her side, but dared not turn her head to see. Her insides bubbling with joy, Freja watched the leverets make their first journey ever into the sunshine and the wide-open spaces.

Five days ago, Clementine had discovered their nest — a mossy bowl lined with tufts of fur, filled with five fluffy grey babes — behind a rock.

'A basket of beauty,' Clementine had said when describing her find to Freja that night. The fire in their cabin had made Clementine's face glow to match her delight. 'Fur fairies wrapped in moss. Fluffy seeds that will sprout and grow into robust, leaping hares.'

'A whispered promise,' said Freja, 'of lolloping legs and powder-puff tails.'

'Yes!' agreed Clementine. 'A whispered promise. Like all babies. Like all precious offspring.' She smiled wistfully, her heart and mind seeming to drift to another place. Strange when she loved being in this one so much.

They had sat for hours each day, waiting to see the whispered promises come to fullness, hoping to be there at the moment when they had grown enough to creep out into the big, wide world of the tundra. And now here they were. Crawling. Hiccuping. Jiggling. Bouncing. Then, finally, when they had practised and copied their mother enough, leaping and bounding in fits and bursts.

All the while, Freja and Clementine sat silent and still. Watching. Rejoicing. Storing every tiny detail away in their minds.

Further and further, the leverets strayed down the grassy slope. Closer and closer they came until one fluff-bundle, more playful and intrepid than the rest, hopped a full circle around Freja. The others, emboldened by his success, wobbled and plopped over to investigate this strange-smelling outcrop. They tested Freja's pants and boots with the tips of their noses, then jumped back. A front paw reached out and patted her hand where it rested in the grass ... once ... twice. Two paws ventured onto her ankle with a snuffle and a swivel of stumpy, felted ears. Then, finally, one by one, the fluffy grey babes hopped, crawled and tumbled into her lap.

Freja's eyes widened. Her breath caught.

The babies wriggled and squirmed in the small bowl of her lap until they were squished and moulded together, like pairs of socks squeezed into a too-small drawer. They nudged noses, jiggled bottoms, licked one another's faces and, exhausted by their first great outing, yawned and fell asleep.

Freja's neck and shoulders tingled, and her face almost split with the width of her smile. 'Fur fairies. Fluffy seeds,' she whispered into the wind. 'Heaven.'

A shadow passed overhead, an eagle.

The mother hare sniffed the air. The black tips of her ears twitched. She sneezed, then made a series of grunting sounds. The leverets awoke and scrambled out of Freja's lap. The mother jittered and fussed, rounding them up, guiding them across the grass and through the gap in the rocks, where she would stuff them back into their nest, sheltered and safe from harm.

Freja took a long, deep breath of icy air and sighed. She turned her head towards her mother, expecting to see her own toothy smile reflected back at her. But instead she saw a tear, large and wet, slip from one of Clementine's eyes and roll, ever so slowly, down her thin cheek and onto her knee. And there, it made a small, dark shadow on the green fabric, strangely similar to that cast by the eagle on the grass.

CHAPTER 1
Perplexing people

Six months later, Freja found herself hiding beneath a table in London, safe and warm, sheltered from sight by the large striped tablecloth that draped to the floor. A leveret in a concealed nest! She had everything she needed to last out Mrs Thompson's visit — a rug, a cushion, a seal carved from spruce wood and a hefty book about hibernation.

The cloth lifted at one side and a plate slid towards her. Upon it was a soft-boiled egg and a piece of hot, buttered toast cut into four skinny soldiers. Freja poked her head out from her hidey-hole for a moment and smiled, all teeth and nose wrinkles. Her blue eyes sparkled beneath her wild mop of blonde curls. 'Thank you, Clementine,' she whispered.

Freja had insisted on calling her mother 'Clementine' since she was three years old and discovered a fruit by the same name. Both fruit and mother were deliciously sweet and zesty. 'Mummy' suddenly seemed a dull and inadequate word.

Taking one of the toast soldiers, Freja dunked it in the gooey egg yolk, nibbled it down to her fingertips and returned the uneaten stump to the plate. She repeated the ritual for the three remaining soldiers. Popping the crusts into the hollowed-out eggshell, she licked her fingers and wiped them on her tights.

The doorbell rang. Mrs Thompson, the lady who had just moved into the house next door, was ushered into the living room. Clementine made some light-hearted chit-chat about the weather, then pointed out the bathroom, the kitchen for making tea and the table in the corner, which, under no circumstances, was to be approached.

'Just my luck,' muttered Mrs Thompson. 'The child is not normal.'

While this was a rude and hurtful thing to say, it was, in fact, absolutely true. Freja Peachtree was *not* normal. She was an exceptional child. Although only ten years old, she had perched on clifftops with puffins, swum with seals, rubbed noses with reindeer and wrestled with Arctic fox cubs. She had lived in seventeen different homes, including a log cabin, a cave, a boat, a yurt, an abandoned church and an igloo. She knew all about the flight patterns of cold-climate bumble bees, the mood swings of walruses, the pooping habits of polar bears and the precise

way to scratch a moulting musk ox so that he wo
roll his eyes and croon with delight. She could swi ,
snorkel, ice-skate, ski and toboggan, and speak a
number of languages, including Swedish, Norwegian,
Finnish and French. But no matter how hard she tried,
she seemed unable to master the art of *fitting in with
others*. Unless, of course, those others happened to be
a lemming, a wolf or a beaver.

Freja's mother was none other than world-famous
zoologist Clementine Peachtree. Accordingly, Freja and
Clementine spent ten months of every year living in the
remote Arctic regions of the world, studying animals,
embracing nature. They spent very little time in the
company of human beings, except for each other.
It was a marvellous existence and one in which Freja
felt relaxed, happy and confident.

However, each and every year, they returned to
England for Christmas and the following two months
of deepest, darkest winter. There, Clementine delivered
lectures, collaborated with her colleagues at various
universities and gathered supplies for their next season
abroad. And Freja, poor little Freja, was plonked
into a world that contained very few animals and an
overwhelming mass of people.

Freja loved animals. They were, she thought, ever
so polite. Unless ill or frightened or wanting to eat her
for dinner, they usually approached slowly, cautiously
and with respect. They made time to watch, listen,
smell. And when, finally, they did make contact, it

was with lowered eyes, a gentle nudge, a tentative nibble and a readiness to retreat if they felt feared or unwelcome. Of course, there were those crowded situations where she and the animals could not help but rub shoulders — amidst a large herd of reindeer or a colony of seals, for instance — but even then, the animals were courteous. They simply pretended she was not there until a mutual comfort had settled upon them and everyone felt happy to gurgle, play or share a quiet cuddle.

With people, it was different. Forced. Rushed. There was no good-mannered staring, sniffing or circling during which Freja could gather her wits. No time to watch, listen or prepare an appropriate response. People ran straight at her, talking, telling her things she didn't understand, asking her questions she didn't know how to answer. It was overwhelming and Freja, so very often, longed to do what any frightened animal might do — run away and hide.

And sometimes she did.

In fact, in the last three weeks she had found herself tucked away beneath a train seat at her mother's feet, crouching amidst a flock of live sheep in an outdoor nativity display and hiding beneath a table. Just as she was on this occasion.

Mrs Thompson clucked disapprovingly, but Clementine's mention of the generous babysitting fees and the family-sized block of chocolate in the fridge seemed to quell her disgust.

'Well, I'm off now!' shouted Clementine from the front door. 'I'll be back in two hours, tops! Toodle-pip!'

'I'm not deaf, you know!' barked Mrs Thompson. But the shouted farewell was not for the babysitter. It was for Freja's benefit, a reminder that Clementine would not be gone too long, a 'toodle-pip' to carry her love.

Freja whispered, 'Toodle-pip, Clementine,' and waited.

The next ten minutes were critical. Freja knew that a babysitter who left her alone for these first moments would usually keep away for the whole tour of duty, either through laziness or understanding. She didn't really care which, as long as it happened.

Pressing an eye to a small hole in the tablecloth, Freja waited and watched.

Mrs Thompson was large and drab, with grey hair and blueish-white skin. An off-white petticoat hung beneath the hem of her skirt. Her shapeless legs ended in a pair of fluffy blue slippers. She sniffed, plonked a worn brown knitting bag on the floor, then shuffled around the living room. She read framed certificates and newspaper clippings, poked at photos, muttered at awards. She took the lid off a large jar containing a preserved owl chick and poked a pencil at the contents. She flicked carelessly through a stack of Clementine's beautiful sketches of bugs and birds. Lighting upon a test tube of lemming poo, she tipped several pellets into her hand, stared at them, sniffed them and —

obviously mistaking them for some sort of snack — ate them.

Freja clasped her hand over her mouth.

Mrs Thompson sucked her teeth, grimaced and proceeded to open and close every door and drawer she could find — the dresser, the linen cupboard, the writing desk, Clementine's filing cabinet.

'Oh no,' whispered Freja. 'She's a nosey one, a real snooper.'

That was bad news. Snoopers rarely left her alone. They wanted to find out what she looked like, why she was hiding beneath the table, whether they could coax her out. Sometimes they *did* coax her out, but then they seemed to regret the decision and would encourage her to hide once more.

'People.' Freja sighed and shook her head.

Mrs Thompson shoved the filing-cabinet drawer back in. A book fell to the floor. 'Boring scientists,' she muttered and kicked it away across the floorboards.

Freja gasped. 'What sort of person kicks a book?' she asked the wooden seal. The seal stared at her mournfully.

Freja pressed her eye back against the hole in the cloth and watched in horror as Mrs Thompson shuffled closer and closer, until all Freja could see was a fleshy knee, just centimetres away. She held her breath.

'Ah, what do I care?' the woman snarled. 'The child's probably as nutty as the mother. All that camping out in remote places, gawping at nature, eating seaweed and feathers. Might not even *be* a child. Could be a dog ... or a cat ... or one of those pot-bellied pigs that folk are so mad about nowadays.'

Freja stifled a giggle. She liked the idea of being a pig and felt a sudden urge to oink.

The knee and slippers retreated and there followed a series of sounds from the kitchen — kettle boiling, bickie jar being emptied onto a plate, fridge opening and closing. Finally, the shuffling returned to the living room and Freja watched as the lounge sagged and groaned under the weight of an ample bottom. Mrs Thompson gobbled and slurped, muttering through mouthfuls of biscuit about weird hippy people who didn't have the common decency to own a television. And then, suddenly, she began to snore.

'Goody,' whispered Freja. 'Safe.'

Lifting the tablecloth, Freja crawled out of hiding and stood before Mrs Thompson. The woman snorted, sucked on her hairy lips and settled back into the rhythmic snuffles of the deep sleeper.

'A walrus in powder-blue slippers,' Freja whispered. 'Not so scary.'

A loose thread hung from the sleeve of the babysitter's beige cardigan.

'A *moulting* walrus,' Freja whispered, then leaned forward to pull the thread free. It was a kind gesture, one that any itching, moulting animal would appreciate. But unfortunately, as so very often happens with knitted garments, the thread just kept on coming.

Freja pulled and pulled, and the sleeve of the cardigan unravelled further and further up Mrs Thompson's arm — almost vanishing to her elbow by the time the length of yarn came free.

Freja stared at the tangle of wool in her hands. She gaped at Mrs Thompson's sleeve, or what was left of it. Quickly, she scrunched the wool into a clump, shoved it into Mrs Thompson's pocket and dived beneath the table, where she read her book to the wooden seal.

One and a half hours later, Clementine returned.

'Freja,' she gasped. 'What on earth has happened to Mrs Thompson?'

Creeping out of her den, Freja explained, 'She stuffed herself with lemming poo and chocolate and Melting Moments and cups of tea, then fell asleep.'

Clementine sighed. 'I mean *this*.' She waved a bony hand towards Mrs Thompson's vanishing sleeve.

Freja blushed. 'An accident,' she whispered. 'A loose thread. I was just trying to help.'

Clementine dropped to her knees and stared into Freja's earnest blue eyes. 'That's very kind, my darling. I'm sure you meant well, but —'

'Oh, you're home,' mumbled Mrs Thompson. Her sleepy eyes drifted past Clementine and fell, for the first time, on Freja. 'Urgh!' she grunted, her mouth turning down at the sides. Her eyes narrowed as they travelled from Freja's wild mop of hair, down her cream smock and green tights, to the tips of her wooden clogs. Her gaze darted back up to the smock, the neckline of which was adorned with clusters of freshly picked holly. A small, finely woven wren's nest was pinned like a brooch to Freja's shoulder.

Freja shuffled a little closer to Clementine, half-hiding behind her legs. Her clothes had seemed like a marvellous choice when she dressed at the start of the day. The smock was floppy and comfortable, the bright green tights warm and jolly, and the clogs ... Well, clogs were marvellous whichever way you looked at them — dry and warm, easily slipped on and off, and able to make loud clomping noises as you walked, just in case you wished to scare away wolves and weasels. As for the titbits from nature, she and Clementine often used twigs, leaves, berries, flowers and feathers to adorn their clothes and hair. They made a light and cheerful addition to the heavy quilted coats and layered woollen garments they needed to wear in the Arctic, and had the added bonus of providing a little camouflage. But now, under the piercing gaze of the babysitter, Freja wondered if she had got it wrong. Failed at something else in the world of People Other Than Clementine.

Mrs Thompson shook her head, sucked some drool through her teeth and moaned to Clementine, 'You took your time.' Floundering around on the lounge, she reached into her cardigan pocket for a tissue and drew out a large, tangled clump of yarn. She frowned and her chin quivered. 'Why, that's ... that's ...'

'Wool,' Freja whispered.

Clementine's hand flew to her chest.

'Wool,' echoed Mrs Thompson. Then, noticing her ravaged cardigan, she gasped. 'My sleeve!'

A choking sound forced its way from her throat. She heaved her bulk out of the lounge and glared at Freja. Sweeping her knitting bag up into her arms, she stomped out of the house, slamming the front door behind her. The brass knob popped off and rolled around on the floor.

The house fell silent.

Freja bit her wobbling bottom lip.

Clementine flopped onto the lounge and patted the seat beside her. 'Freja,' she said. 'We need to talk.'

CHAPTER 2

An unsettling change of plans

Freja slumped down onto the lounge, expecting a lecture. Instead, Clementine placed a small package on her knee.

'Oh!' Freja cried and threw her arms around her mother's waist. 'I love boxes tied up with string!'

'I hope,' said Clementine, 'that you will love what's inside!'

Freja grabbed the end of the string between finger and thumb and pulled the bow out. The lid popped up and inside, in a nest of green tissue paper, lay a tiny grey hare crafted from felt. She nestled it in the palm of her hand, where she admired its stubby-fuzz ears, black-bead eyes and fine, short whiskers.

'It's a leveret!' said Freja. 'Just like the babies we watched throughout the summer.'

Clementine smiled. 'A delicious summer,' she said. 'Those babies grew so quickly, became brave and independent long before we were expecting it ... long before their mother was expecting it.' Her voice caught. 'But they were strong and healthy when they left the nest. They were well and truly ready to take on the world. Excited even. Because new beginnings are a wonderful thing. An adventure!'

Freja stroked the hare with one finger and waited. Something big was about to happen. She could hear it in Clementine's voice. Feel it in the air, like static electricity.

She placed the hare carefully back into its nest of tissue paper and retied the string. Cupping the box in her hands, she sat as still as a granite rock, staring straight ahead at a small rip in the wallpaper. She waited and waited.

'I'm afraid we can no longer go to Siberia in the spring,' said Clementine.

'Oh,' sighed Freja, fiddling with the string bow. 'That's disappointing.'

'Yes,' agreed Clementine.

'We'll still go somewhere with bears, won't we?' asked Freja. 'I *really* want to see bears again. Even a little bear would do.'

Clementine wrapped an arm around her daughter's shoulders and drew her close. 'Unfortunately, we won't be embarking on *any* new field trips this year.'

Freja's eyes grew wide. She clutched Clementine's arm with both hands. 'We're *not* staying here, are we? Not in stinky old London?'

'No, my love. I'm going to Switzerland.'

'Switzerland?' Freja was horrified. 'I know there are mountains and glaciers and snow, but it's nowhere *near* the Arctic Circle.' She shook her head, then blew a corkscrew curl out of her face with a disgusted blast of air. 'Switzerland,' she scoffed. 'If I said that, Clementine, you'd say, "Why, Freja! Have you lost your inner atlas?"'

Clementine laughed at Freja's perfect mimicry, but the mirth didn't quite reach her eyes. There was no wrinkling of crow's feet, no sparkling of iris. No real joy.

Clementine shifted uneasily beneath Freja's gaze. 'I have not lost my inner atlas,' she explained. 'I am going to Switzerland alone, and you, my dear child, will be going on a special journey to Hampshire.'

'Special?' Freja released her mother's arm. 'Not with Mrs Thompson? Oh, Clementine, how *could* you? After all we've been through together. I am doomed to be bossed about by a walrus with fluffy blue slippers and a frown like a —'

'I am sick,' her mother whispered.

The little gift box tumbled to the floor.

Freja stared at the spot where it landed, but she did not move to pick it up.

'I am sick,' repeated Clementine.

The three little words hung in the air like an Arctic chill.

'Chicken pox?' asked Freja, knowing the answer already. One's face and hands did not grow slowly thinner and paler from a bout of chicken pox.

Clementine shook her head.

'A cold? An ingrown toenail?'

Her mother's head shook again, a little slower this time.

'I'll stay with you,' said Freja. 'I'll look after you. I can make soup and cocoa, and I'm very good with money. I'll be brave. I'll go to the shops all on my own and buy food and medicine and warm pyjamas. You can even have my hot-water bottle with the fluffy polar-bear cover.'

'You can't stay with me,' said Clementine. 'I'm going to a special clinic in the Swiss Alps and they don't allow children. But thank you. It makes me very proud that you would be willing to do all that for me.'

'I'd do *anything* for you, Mummy Darling Heart,' whispered Freja, using the endearment that she saved for special occasions.

'Then do this,' said Clementine. 'Go to Hampshire. Don't be sad, but have a wonderful adventure so you can write exciting, happy letters that will cheer me up. And then, when I am better and come to collect you, you can be my guide around every hill, brook and forest, tell me all about the wildlife and show me how bold and clever you have grown in my absence.'

Bother! Trapped by her own words!

The bottom of their world had just fallen out and splattered all over her feet, and she longed to cry, to throw herself into Clementine's arms, sobbing. But a promise is a promise and Freja had just declared that she would do *anything* for her Mummy Darling Heart.

She inhaled deeply, the breath wobbling as it went down into her lungs. She bit her bottom lip and rubbed the heels of her hands against her eyes. Then, stalling for time, she slipped to the floor and retrieved the little gift box.

'The leverets!' cried Clementine. 'I almost forgot. That's why I gave you the felt hare. To remind you of the mother hare allowing her babies to venture into the big, wide world. All alone. Even though it seemed too early. Even though she was a little nervous.'

'I was there for them,' said Freja. 'My lap was a nest when they were weary.'

'A safe haven,' agreed Clementine. 'Like Hampshire will be for you.'

'But why Hampshire?' asked Freja. 'There aren't even any bears.'

'Hampshire has something better than bears.' Clementine gave a knowing smile. 'Hampshire has Tobias Appleby.'

CHAPTER 3
Who is Tobias Appleby?

'Who is Tobias Appleby?' asked Freja.

It was, of course, the most important thing to know at this moment.

'Tobias Appleby is …' Clementine looked up to the ceiling. 'Tobias is …' She scratched her head as though struggling to find the right words. 'Tobias is a very important person. A dear friend.'

Freja frowned. 'But I've never heard of him before.'

'He's very trustworthy,' said Clementine.

'Trustworthy?' echoed Freja. It was a rather cold description. School principals were trustworthy, but she didn't want to spend a holiday with one.

'He is thirty-two years old and very tall.'

Clementine, it seemed, was determined to tell only the things that did *not* matter. Freja pictured a tall school principal blowing out thirty-two white candles on a very plain-looking cake. The cake was not iced. It didn't even have cinnamon sugar on top. Clementine's words gave her nothing to hang her thoughts on and only cold places to store her feelings.

'Please tell me more,' Freja begged.

'Oh, my darling.' Clementine ruffled her daughter's curls. 'You know that we should always decide for ourselves — watch, listen, learn. Like we do with the animals we study. I don't want you to look at Tobias Appleby through *my* eyes when you first meet him. I want you to use your own eyes, your own heart. My hope is that you will make him *your* friend for the reasons *you* choose.'

'Why Tobias? Why not someone else?' But as soon as Freja said it, she knew why.

There was no-one else.

It had always been just Freja and Clementine. In London or abroad. In a crowded room or out on the vast, icy expanse of the Arctic.

And until now, that had been enough. Better than enough. It had been perfect.

But sometimes, it turned out, you needed more.

'He's our only choice, isn't he?' whispered Freja.

Clementine blinked. She looked extremely pale and tired. 'The only choice,' she agreed, 'but the same choice I would make if I had a million exceptional people to choose from. A *billion* even.'

'But why?' Freja nagged.

'Because he's special.'

Clementine jumped to her feet. She climbed up onto her desk and retrieved something that had been hidden at the top of the bookcase, stashed behind journals and cobwebs. She returned to the lounge bearing what looked like a miniature treasure chest, no bigger than a box of tea leaves. Using her sleeve to wipe off the dust, she handed the chest to Freja. 'Take this.'

Up close, the treasure chest was rather disappointing. The metal bracings were battered and rusty, the timber was dull and scratched, and one end was charred black, as though it had been toasted over an open fire. Perhaps it was a ruse, to make one think that nothing of value could be hidden inside when, truly, the contents were spectacular — jewels, rare coins, a treasure map.

Freja's picture of Tobias Appleby quickly changed from school principal into swashbuckling, seafaring pirate. A green-and-red parrot sat on his shoulder, nibbling at his gold earring. His wooden leg made a delightful knocking sound as he strode across the deck of his ship towards the cannon. It was a pleasing transformation and Freja's spirits lifted.

She tried to open the lid, but it was locked. 'Where's the key?'

Clementine shrugged. 'Ask Tobias. I got the treasure chest. He got the key.'

'So I can open it when I get to Tobias' house?'

'Oh, I don't think so!' Clementine seemed shocked at the idea. 'I am simply making you joint guardian of

Tobias' and my secrets in my stead. Just until I'm well again.'

'What secrets?' cried Freja. 'Clementine! That doesn't make sense!'

'I know, my love.' Clementine patted her daughter's hand. 'But one day, it will.'

'One day? *Which* day?' pleaded Freja.

'The day that Tobias decides is right.'

'That's just silly!' Freja slapped the arm of the lounge so hard that her hand hurt. 'Why should Tobias Appleby decide?' She took a deep breath and shouted, 'Who exactly is Tobias Appleby?'

Gently, calmly, Clementine took the treasure chest from Freja's lap. 'I'm going upstairs now to pack. This will go in your suitcase.'

'But *who* is Tobias Appleby?'

Clementine looked back as she headed up the stairs, her face strange and dreamy as she said in hushed, low tones, 'Tobias is ...'

Freja could not be sure, but as her mother disappeared from sight, it sounded as though she whispered one last word:

'Family.'

CHAPTER 4

A surprising arrival

Freja sat at the breakfast table the next morning, a bowl of baked beans turning cold at her elbow. Her tummy was a churning whirlpool of worry. In just one hour, Tobias Appleby would be arriving to fetch her away. Not only would she be separated from Clementine for the first time in her life, but she would also be left all alone with the mysterious Tobias Appleby. She had best be prepared.

Freja chewed thoughtfully on the tip of her pencil. She muttered a few experimental lines in her head, then wrote on a cardboard tag: 'Freja Peachtree, to be delivered to Myrtle Cottage, Elderberry Lane, Little Coddling, Hampshire.'

She held up the tag, read it out loud three times, then frowned. Names and addresses were important, certainly, and if she was travelling alone by bus or train, it would save her from having to talk to strangers; she could simply hold out the tag and keep her eyes averted. But Tobias would already know both *her* name and his own address.

She waved the tag thoughtfully in the air and smiled. *Hmmm. Tobias may know my name, but he doesn't know what I look like! I could tie my nametag to someone else and he would never know the difference.*

She wondered if she might be able to duck out to one of the local parks and convince an adventurous girl to take her place on the journey south. An adventurous *boy* might even do the trick … if dressed properly.

'No,' she said, slapping the tag down onto the table. 'Clementine might not notice the wrong child leaving, but she would soon notice that I was still here. Besides, I've promised to be brave and go to Hampshire.'

She stared out the window for a moment, then wrote on a second tag: 'ATTENTION! Extremely shy child.' But as soon as the words were completed, she realised that they were all wrong. 'Attention!' was a silly word to use. It demanded the exact opposite of what she was hoping to achieve. What she truly wanted was to be left alone, to *escape* attention. She sighed and pushed the tag away.

Freja shovelled a spoonful of cold baked beans into her mouth. It felt like she was chewing limpets plucked straight from their shells. She swallowed, shuddered and chomped her teeth three times in disgust.

'Chomp!' she yelled. 'That's it! That's sure to keep Tobias Appleby at bay!' Pressing down hard with her pencil, she wrote on a third tag in dark uppercase letters. Satisfied, she rolled her pencil across the table, pushed back her chair and ran to the coat rack in the hallway. There, she tied the tag to the second toggle on her duffel coat.

'THIS CHILD BITES!'

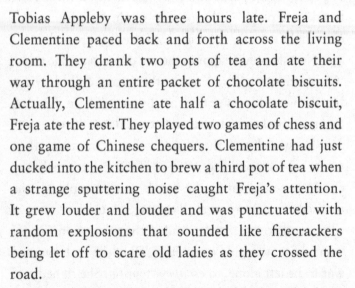

Tobias Appleby was three hours late. Freja and Clementine paced back and forth across the living room. They drank two pots of tea and ate their way through an entire packet of chocolate biscuits. Actually, Clementine ate half a chocolate biscuit, Freja ate the rest. They played two games of chess and one game of Chinese chequers. Clementine had just ducked into the kitchen to brew a third pot of tea when a strange sputtering noise caught Freja's attention. It grew louder and louder and was punctuated with random explosions that sounded like firecrackers being let off to scare old ladies as they crossed the road.

Freja pulled on her duffel coat and ran out the door. A green vintage motorcycle with a sidecar chugged past, black smoke billowing from its exhaust. Without warning, it swerved, lurched up the gutter onto the footpath, crashed through a white picket fence and came to a halt in the flowerbed at the front of Mrs Thompson's terrace house.

Freja clapped her hand to her mouth. Her eyes boggled as a ceramic fairy's head rolled across the footpath and toppled into the gutter. She felt an overwhelming urge to laugh.

A tall, thin man wearing an old-fashioned motoring cap and goggles stumbled off the bike. He muttered to his grey-haired passenger in the sidecar, 'Hmmm. Spot of bother. Must have tuned out for a moment. Didn't see that jolly curve in the road.'

Freja glanced back along the street. It was as straight as an arrow. She crept down the steps and moved a little closer.

The motorcyclist swiped off his goggles and cap to reveal emerald-green eyes and a mop of curly brown hair that was in great need of a trim. He stared at the broken fence and the squashed violets and tugged nervously at his ears. Freja wondered at the wisdom of this. The ears stuck out a little further than was necessary and although the tugging was probably not the cause of it, it certainly couldn't help.

Mumbling and sighing, he shrugged off his brown leather riding jacket to reveal a wrinkled sage-green shirt, a misshapen brown vest (inside out), a dark green cardigan worn through at the elbows and a pair of khaki flannel trousers that sagged and bagged like the skin on an elephant's bottom. The fringed ends of his long beige scarf were covered in thistledown and burrs. He might have been a bird-watcher gone wrong with all those browns and greens and frayed edges ... or a madman who'd been shut up in a zoo for several years and just escaped via the tiger's den. *He looks rather lovely*, thought Freja. *Not so very different from Clementine and me when we're camping out in the wild.*

Grabbing the handlebars, the man heaved the motorcycle backward out of the garden and turned it around. The passenger was now in full sight. It was not somebody's grandpa, as Freja had first thought, but a shaggy grey dog — an Irish wolfhound of prodigious proportions. The hound stared at Freja, yawned, then licked his long pink tongue luxuriously across his nose.

Freja giggled.

The man gave a start, seeming to notice her for the first time. 'Hello there, old chap!'

Freja blushed.

Holding out a gloved hand, the man said, 'Tobias Appleby at your service.'

'*You're* Tobias Appleby?' gasped Freja.

'I am indeed!' the man cried.

Curiosity outweighing her shyness, Freja moved a little closer and presented her hand. 'I'm ... I'm Freja Peachtree.'

'Freja Peachtree!' Tobias smiled and shook her hand with such enthusiasm that her teeth rattled. 'Freja Peachtree! The delightful daughter of Clementine Peachtree! Well, well, well. Fancy seeing you here!'

He rubbed his jaw and shook his head as though truly astonished.

The dog whined and flopped his chin on the seat of the motorcycle.

'But you were coming here especially to fetch me,' whispered Freja. 'Weren't you?'

Tobias frowned and then, suddenly, his eyebrows and arms shot upward. 'Yes! I *was* coming to fetch you! Which is why I am here, killing fairies and trampling gardens! Well, the killing and trampling were not part of the plan, but I am pretty certain that I was here to fetch something ... and if my memory serves me right, that something was a spiffing lass. You, in fact!'

They stared at one another for a minute or two, both blushing and awkward. Freja searched her mind for something sensible to say, but the best she could come up with was, 'I'm ten.'

'Marvellous!' cried Tobias. 'I used to be ten!'

Another long pause ensued.

The dog sneezed.

'Is he yours?' asked Freja.

'Absolutely!' said Tobias. 'This is Finnegan. He's just a puppy, really. Ten months old.'

The sidecar, built to fit a goodly-sized man, seemed barely to contain the puppy.

Tobias, noticing the tag on Freja's duffel coat, leaned forward and squinted. 'THIS CHILD BITES,' he read aloud.

Freja blushed once more. She would not have written such a label had she realised what a fine fellow Tobias was. She'd already managed to exchange a few awkward but friendly words. He'd even called her 'spiffing'! But now her stupid tag was going to ruin it all. Such a kind fellow would not want to associate with a girl who, were the label to be trusted, might at any minute bare her fangs and lunge at his throat like a rabid wolf.

I've messed things up again, thought Freja. *I'm hopeless with people.* She hung her head and kicked at a shard of fairy wing.

Tobias stood up straight and considered the words for a moment. 'THIS CHILD BITES,' he repeated, then nodded his approval. 'Well, that's jolly useful! Always good to have fair warning. And I dare say you would only bite when truly pressed. You don't look the type to run around snapping and snarling and biting willy-nilly. You appear thoroughly charming.'

Freja looked up hopefully.

Tobias continued. 'In fact, we should *all* come with warnings dangling from our toggles. Finnegan should probably have one that says, "THIS PUPPY LICKS." He's a habitual licker. Shows no restraint when it comes to his nose or the floor ... or *my* nose for that matter. And I should most definitely come with a tag that says, "THIS MAN DAYDREAMS," for I'm a *dreadful* daydreamer. I'm often staring into space, stumbling into babbling brooks and leaving pots of soup on the stove until they boil dry.'

A smile twitched at the edges of Freja's mouth.

'Truly!' Tobias declared. 'It's because of my daydreaming that I'm so terribly late in arriving. I was so busy holding a conversation with an imaginary mountain goat that I missed the turn-off to London. It wasn't until I passed a sign saying, "Welcome to Biggleswade" that I realised my mistake. We did an extremely rushed U-turn on the village green, didn't we, Finnegan? Scared the feathers off a rather large duck, I'm afraid.'

Finnegan grinned and dribbled.

'Yes, yes!' Tobias chuckled, running his hand through his tangled curls. 'There was also that embarrassing incident with the mud flying up from the rear wheel and splattering all over that poor woman. I remember, Finnegan. But, in my defence, it was a complete accident ... and I called out a hearty apology over my shoulder as we zoomed away ... and mud washes off, doesn't it? It's not as though it was beetroot juice or indelible ink.'

'Tobias!' Clementine was standing on the front steps.

'Clementine!' bellowed Tobias. He flung his long, gangly arms wide with joy and slapped Finnegan on the side of the head. Accidentally, of course, but that was little consolation for the poor hound.

Tobias bounded up the steps two at a time and threw himself at Clementine.

And as their arms wrapped around each other and their faces pressed cheek to cheek, Freja couldn't help noticing how happy, truly and deeply happy, Clementine appeared. Complete. As though she had just found something precious that had been missing for a long, long time.

CHAPTER 5

A face full of dog and tears

Freja skirted around the edge of the living room, half-watching, half-hiding. Clementine and Tobias spent a lot of time staring at one another, smiling, touching each other's arms and cheeks and hands. In between silences, they said mysterious things like, 'Remember the Faraway Fair?' and 'I wonder what became of Miss Frecklington?' and 'I eat a whole box of raisins every Easter, just because I can.' None of it made any sense to Freja. But to Clementine and Tobias, these simple remarks seemed to contain the seed of great, meaningful episodes of their lives, deep pools of emotion.

'Freja,' said Clementine, as though suddenly remembering a world beyond Tobias and herself, 'duck upstairs and grab your things. Then we will have tea and sandwiches and a lovely chat, the three of us, all together.'

Freja stepped over Finnegan, who lay by the fire licking the hearth, slid along the wall into the hallway and climbed the stairs. She stood in the middle of her bedroom feeling small, scared and alone. Clementine might be just metres away now, but soon she would be far, far away.

Lifting the flap on her satchel, Freja drew out the tiny felt hare and rubbed it against her cheek. 'It's an adventure,' she whispered. 'I must show Clementine that I can be brave.' She clutched the hare in her hand for a moment, then popped it into her pocket.

Shrugging her backpack and satchel onto her shoulders, she repeated, 'An adventure.' She heaved the suitcase into her right hand and tottered down the stairs, dumping her load by the front door. Creeping back along the hallway, she stopped and listened.

'So she's ... she's just like us,' said Tobias in hushed tones.

There was a long pause before Clementine said, 'Yes.'

'Does she know?' asked Tobias.

'No,' said Clementine. 'Please don't tell her ... Not yet. We'll know when the time is right.'

Freja's head spun. Her thoughts ran wild. *Like us? Does she know? Don't tell?* 'What does it mean?' she whispered. 'Are Clementine and Tobias —'

'Beasts!' Mrs Thompson burst through the front door, waving a broken white fence picket in the air. Squashing Freja into the wall, she galumphed along the hallway and into the living room, grumbling and growling.

Clementine, used to smoothing over Freja's muddles, stepped forward to make peace on Tobias' behalf. Unfortunately, Finnegan stepped forward at the same time. Or perhaps *lunged* forward would be a more accurate description.

Finnegan, while totally unconcerned by Mrs Thompson's threatening behaviour with the fence picket, was quite agitated by her fluffy blue slippers. He was, you see, a sight hound, the kind of dog who grows rather excited at the appearance of cats, rabbits and other fluffy things that move about.

It began harmlessly enough with a soft, deep growl at the back of his throat, but escalated every time Mrs Thompson moved her feet. And because she was outraged, she blustered, stomped and shuffled a great deal.

The blue slippers shifted to the left. Finnegan dropped to the floor and bared his teeth.

The blue slippers stamped to the right. Finnegan snarled and smacked his front paws on the floorboards. Once. Twice. Thrice.

The blue slippers shuffled forward. Finnegan scuttled from side to side like a crazed crab, snapping and barking.

The blue slippers hurried backward and Finnegan went in for the kill. Leaping at Mrs Thompson, he knocked her off her feet, snatched one of the slippers in his teeth and dashed upstairs.

By the time Freja reached her bedroom, the slipper was no more. Tufts of blue fluff drifted through the air, clung to the bedspread, littered the floor and stuck to the hound's large, wet nose.

On seeing Freja in the doorway, Finnegan whined, dropped to the mat and hid his head between his paws. Just like a scolded child.

Freja moved slowly, cautiously, across the room and sat down beside him. After a few moments, she rested her hand lightly on his back. Several minutes later, when sure that he was comfortable with her presence, she stroked his neck and whispered, 'I understand. I never quite know how to behave with people either. I get it wrong all the time. As a matter of fact, I did something very similar to Mrs Thompson's cardigan just yesterday.'

Finnegan lifted his head and blinked. He poked his wet nose into Freja's ear and she giggled.

'Perhaps,' she said kindly, 'we can help each other along. Learn from one another's mistakes.'

Finnegan licked her hand and grinned.

And Freja might have thought that this fine hound had understood every word she'd said, even agreed to the mutual support, had he not, at that very moment, leapt to his feet, bounded down the stairs and made a grab for Mrs Thompson's second slipper.

A great deal of time was needed to soothe Mrs Thompson's nerves. Clementine sat her neighbour on the lounge, brought her numerous cups of tea and fed her the sandwiches that had been made for their lunch. Tobias wrote a large cheque that was sure to cover the loss of slippers, fence, fairy and flowers, then paced back and forth, wringing his hands, fiddling with the knotted fringe of his scarf and staring, wide eyed, at Mrs Thompson's large, fleshy face and hands. He might even have muttered the words 'fearsome' and 'blubber' and 'lard'. Freja retreated to her hiding place beneath the table. Finnegan joined her and passed the time by licking every square centimetre of the floor, the underside of the table and Freja's gumboots.

By the time Mrs Thompson was sent on her way, Clementine's taxi to the airport was waiting outside, horn honking. Clementine, Tobias, Finnegan and Freja bustled out onto the footpath, a jumble of suitcases, warm coats, muddy paws and anxious feelings.

Freja stared at the motorcycle and wondered where she and her luggage were going to fit. But after five minutes and some serious shoving, coaxing, grunting, growling, snapping and an apologetic lick, she found herself wedged into the sidecar wearing a spare riding cap and goggles. Finnegan sat on her lap, bits of him spilling out all over the place. Freja's suitcase was tied to the rear of the sidecar. Her backpack and satchel hung off Tobias' shoulders.

'Oh, Clementine!' sobbed Freja, stretching her hand past Finnegan's enormous grey body. 'I ... I don't want to go. It's too soon.'

Clementine held her hand and smothered her face with kisses and something warm that might have been tears. 'You are in good hands, my love.' She stepped back and smiled at Tobias. 'The best hands.'

Tobias leaned out from the seat of his motorcycle and pecked Clementine on the cheek. Finnegan stretched up and sneaked in a cheeky lick.

Tobias kick-started the bike, yelled, 'Hold on to your hats!' and roared away from the footpath. He swerved back and forth across the street, narrowly missing the mailman on his bicycle, until he found himself somewhere towards the left of the road.

Freja shouted back over her shoulder, 'I love you, Mummy Darling Heart!' But an explosion from the exhaust drowned out her words and Clementine climbed into the black taxi without looking up. It felt as though her mother had just disappeared from the world altogether. Freja pressed her face into Finnegan's scruffy grey hair and sobbed.

CHAPTER 6

Carrots and crime

Freja awoke the next morning to a surprisingly warm and pungent breeze blowing on her face. She opened her eyes and found herself staring into a pair of big brown doggy eyes. Finnegan lay on top of her, blinking, waiting to be noticed.

'Hello,' said Freja.

The dog flicked his large pink tongue across her nose before resuming his warm, heavy breathing.

Freja scanned her surroundings without moving, just as Clementine had taught her to do in the wild. She found that she was lying in a pretty white bed, made up with pale blue-and-white striped sheets, a powder-puff eiderdown and a handmade quilt. The room was an attic nook, not much bigger than the bed. The sloped ceilings came all the way down to the floor, reminding

Freja of the tent that she and Clementine sometimes camped in during the summer.

'Clementine,' she whispered. All thoughts returned to Clementine. Freja's eyes stung and she sniffled.

Finnegan licked her nose again. Three times. Softly and lovingly.

Sunlight streamed in through a small, square window, blazing a trail across the quilt, along the bare timber floor and out the door. Wriggling out from beneath the huge dog, Freja stood up and stretched. She was still wearing yesterday's clothes. Tobias must have carried her from the sidecar straight to bed when they arrived last night. She hadn't woken for even a moment.

Leaning her forehead against the cold windowpane, Freja gasped. 'Oh, how lovely! Fields, hedgerows, a river, a forest.' She felt her body relax, as it always did when she escaped London and returned to a more natural world. Reaching into her pocket, she wrapped her fingers around the small felt hare.

Finnegan sprang from the bed and put his front paws up on the windowsill beside her. His heavy breath fogged up the glass. Freja giggled and wiped clear a patch through which she could continue to gaze.

Tobias dashed into the garden at the back of the cottage. His cardigan flapped about as he leapt and ducked and waved his arms in the air, acting out some sort of drama. A horse in the adjoining meadow followed along on the other side of a low stone wall, but Tobias didn't seem to notice his chestnut shadow.

Tobias stopped.

The horse stopped.

Tobias stared into space and tugged at his ears.

The horse craned her neck over the stone wall and nibbled at Tobias' sleeve.

Tobias spun around and laughed. Pulling a carrot from his cardigan pocket, he fed it to the horse and rubbed her nose. Then, turning away, he continued to dash back and forth, waving his arms in the air, thrusting his fists forward and, occasionally, yelling. The horse followed, despite the fact that she was struck across the nose twice as Tobias made sweeping gestures with his hands.

On his third crossing of the garden, Tobias stopped once more. This time, he pulled a notebook from his hip pocket and drew a pencil from behind his ear. He began to write apace, stopping every now and then to scratch his head with the pencil or feed another carrot to the horse. When all the carrots were gone, the horse contented herself with nibbling on Tobias' shoulder. The cardigan pulled and stretched and grew quite slobbery, but Tobias didn't seem to care ... or perhaps he didn't notice. He was completely absorbed in his notes.

'What on earth is Tobias Appleby doing?' asked Freja. 'He seems quite distracted. Rather mad, really.'

Finnegan whined and leapt back onto the bed.

'More importantly,' said Freja, '*who* is Tobias Appleby?'

Turning from the window, she crouched down before her suitcase, opened the lid and muddled through the clothes until she found the treasure chest that Clementine had given her two days ago. Placing it on the windowsill, she sat back down on the bed and stared at it. It really was a poor battered thing, quite small and ugly.

'*Who* is Tobias Appleby?' she murmured, scrunching her nose.

The treasure chest gave nothing away.

'Who *is* Tobias Appleby?' she repeated, turning towards Finnegan.

The Irish wolfhound did not reply. He was far too busy chewing on the corner of the pillow. This reminded Freja that it was a long time since she had last eaten. Her tummy rumbled.

Time for breakfast! Rolling across the bed, she headed out of the attic, down a steep, narrow flight of stairs and through the nearest doorway. But instead of the kitchen, she found herself in a cosy, cluttered living room.

'Wow!' she gasped. 'How ... how ... how terribly messy.'

An entire wall was covered in books, old and new, crammed upright, sideways and any-which-way so that not even an ant could find a gap in which to set up camp. In front of the bookcase stood a large timber desk crowded with an ancient typewriter, a stack of papers, ink pots, pencils, pens, a teapot shaped like a pineapple, piles of books, an old-fashioned telephone and three cups and saucers containing varying amounts of tea dregs.

Two green velvet wingback chairs, plump and worn, sat in front of a crackling fire. Perched precariously on the arm of one chair was a cardboard box labelled: 'LIBRARY BOOKS WHICH ARE SO TERRIBLY OVERDUE THAT I AM EMBARRASSED TO RETURN THEM.'

Freja giggled. 'Naughty but honest,' she said.

The floorboards were partly covered by a Turkish rug that looked rather grand, except for where it had been burned by cinders from the fire or stained with droplets of black ink. Every other spare surface was scattered with journals, books, partially chewed footwear, mail and scraps of paper bearing handwritten notes and diagrams. It was, in short, like standing in a museum or an ancient library through which a herd of musk oxen had stampeded. The overall effect was one of disorderly charm and Freja liked it very much.

She stepped forward to examine the telephone. It was black with a dial for the numbers, just like she'd seen in old movies. She reached out to lift the receiver, but was distracted by the pile of books on which it sat. Her hand froze mid-air as she recognised the name on the spines of the books.

'Tobias Appleby,' she read aloud. The back of her neck tingled with excitement.

Grabbing the edge of the desk with both hands, she bobbed down so that her eyes were level with the books. '*Three Cursed Pharaohs* by Tobias Appleby!' The tingle ran down her back. '*Lightning Strikes Twice* by Tobias Appleby. *A Mousetrap in Moscow* by Tobias Appleby. *Rome's Reward* by Tobias Appleby.'

She stood up and gasped. 'Why, Tobias Appleby is a writer!'

Lifting the telephone, she grabbed the book at the top of the pile, *Three Cursed Pharaohs*. She flicked through the pages, reading a sentence here, a paragraph there. A smile stretched across her face and her eyes twinkled. It was better than she had imagined! Clutching the book to her chest, she felt a deep satisfaction in knowing that she had at least solved one part of the puzzle.

'Why, Tobias Appleby is a writer,' she whispered. 'And his specialty is crime!'

CHAPTER 7

Bickies and Licks

'Morning, old chap!' Tobias sang out from where he was standing at the stove. 'I'm afraid Finnegan has started without us. Burnt toast and jam is his thing. And there's always plenty of that around. Especially the burnt toast.'

Finnegan sat on a chair at the head of the table, his nose deep in a jar of jam, slurping and guzzling. The tablecloth in front of him was scattered with crumbs.

Freja crept through the kitchen door, wondering just how long she had been lost in the opening chapters of *Three Cursed Pharaohs*. She sat down beside the hound. Tobias passed her a plate with a soft-boiled egg and piece of hot, buttered toast cut into four little soldiers. Just the way she liked it.

'Thank you!' she whispered. She dunked her first soldier into the egg yolk, nibbled the toast down to her fingers and popped the stump back on her plate.

'Pleasure!' cried Tobias. Sitting himself down at the opposite side of the table, he gobbled toast while staring at the ceiling. Between slices, he poured a cup of tea, stirred in copious quantities of milk and sugar, sipped it, spilt it and muttered to himself. Halfway through chewing his third slice of toast, Tobias dropped it and banged his hands down on the table. 'That's it!' he shouted. 'The ravine! Carl Benziger is hiding, lurking, snivelling in the ravine!' He leapt out of his chair and darted from the room. A moment later, the typewriter could be heard *clackety-clacking* in the living room.

'The ravine?' asked Freja. 'What ravine?'

Finnegan grinned and dribbled jam onto the tablecloth. He leaned forward, stole Tobias' deserted egg from his plate and gulped it down, shell and all. He sneezed at the pepper, coughed up a piece of shell, then started in on Tobias' sweet, milky tea.

Breakfast over, Freja crept back into the living room and stood, half-hidden, beside one of the wingback chairs. Tobias sat at his desk, typing. Fingers tapping, elbows flapping. Lost in a whirl of words.

And then he stopped. His hands hovered over the typewriter for a moment, then dropped to his lap.

He sighed, stared at the pineapple-shaped teapot and pushed himself back from the desk. His chair rattled and rolled on its worn wheels until it hit the bookcase and fell over sideways, with Tobias still in it! Three books fell from their shelf onto his head. Sweeping them aside, he leapt to his feet, crying, 'Aha!' He set the chair right, wheeled it back to the desk, sat down and resumed typing.

Freja stuck her head around the side of the wingback chair and said, 'I might have a little look around now.'

Tobias didn't reply.

'If that's okay,' she added.

Tobias typed on, oblivious to her presence. A different child might have been upset, felt neglected or lonesome. But Freja, who *loved* to be left alone, was delighted. She tiptoed away, feeling like things were growing more and more bearable with every passing hour, and spent a quiet morning exploring her new home. Finnegan shadowed her wherever she went, blinking, dribbling and licking random objects.

First, Freja made a lap of the garden, poking at woodpiles, climbing a winter-bare apple tree, cracking the ice on the birdbath with a stick and rubbing her face against the warm, musty neck of the chestnut horse. Back inside, she found very little beyond what she had already seen. The first door she opened revealed Tobias' bedroom, a dark chamber that smelt like soap and old books. The second door led to a pale green bathroom. The third led back to the kitchen, where she discovered a comfortingly large supply of baked beans, jam and biscuits — both cream centred *and* chocolate coated.

Finnegan sat down in front of her and placed his paw on her arm.

'What is it?' asked Freja, tilting her head to one side.

Finnegan tilted his head the same way and dribbled on the floor.

'I'm sorry,' said Freja. 'I don't understand.'

But she soon did. Finnegan trotted to the open cupboard door. 'Boof!' he exclaimed and poked a large jar of cherry jam with his nose.

'Jam?' asked Freja. 'But you have just gobbled a whole jar for breakfast!'

'Woof! Boof!' Finnegan sat by the cupboard. He grinned and swept his shaggy tail back and forth across the floorboards.

'I think,' said Freja, 'that one jar of jam a day might be all a dog needs. Even a super-sized Irish wolfhound.' She pushed the door shut with her foot.

Finnegan's ears drooped and he whimpered.

'I'm sorry,' said Freja. 'But even puppies must show some restraint.'

Finnegan blinked slowly, three times, then threw back his head and howled. 'Oooooow!'

'Shoosh!' hissed Freja, looking over her shoulder towards the door. 'What will Tobias think?'

'Oooooow!' howled Finnegan, eyes closed, nose to the ceiling, mouth tightened to a little 'o'. It was a pitiful sight, a harrowing sound.

'Shh-shh-shh,' whispered Freja, wrapping her arms around his hairy grey neck. 'There, there!'

But Finnegan howled on and on and on.

Freja was now quite frantic. What if Tobias thought she had done something cruel to his beloved puppy? Scolded or kicked? What would he think of her? What would he do?

'Ooooooow!' Finnegan mourned as though his heart was about to break in two.

'Bickies!' cried Freja. 'How about some bickies?'

The howling stopped. Finnegan's chin dropped. His eyes sprang open. He licked his nose and grinned.

Freja opened a packet of Jam Whirlies and held them out. 'Just one,' she said. 'I'm not really sure if you're allowed to —'

Finnegan knocked the biscuits from her hand, scoffed them all down and finished by licking the crumbs off the floorboards. 'Boof!' he said and swiped his tongue back and forth across Freja's face.

'You're welcome,' she muttered.

Satisfied, the dog trotted off, tail in the air, along the corridor and into the living room. He flopped in front of the fire and spent the rest of the morning licking the hearth stones and snoozing with his nose tucked into one of Tobias' slippers.

There was no use crying over spilt milk — or gobbled bickies — so Freja followed Finnegan to the fireside. Lying down with her head resting on the dog's shaggy grey back, she continued to read Tobias' crime novel. *Three Cursed Pharaohs*, written for adults, was *totally* unsuitable for a child, but Freja loved it. While most of the animals Freja encountered were gentle and shy, she had also seen her share of hunting, fighting, violence and death in the animal kingdom. Reading Tobias' novel, therefore, was not so very different from a season spent in the Arctic observing wildlife behaviour. Besides, she found it all so terribly informative, especially the kidnapping scene.

All the while, Tobias tapped away at his typewriter, stared into space or paced the floorboards, mumbling to himself and scratching his head with a pencil. He remained completely absorbed in his writing, oblivious to the small girl who had crept into his living room and his life.

CHAPTER 8
Marmalade and tears

At three o'clock, Tobias headed out for a walk. Finnegan leapt up from the hearth and followed, barking and tugging at the saggy seat of his master's trousers.

'But of course, Finnegan!' cried Tobias. 'Freja simply must come along too. That goes without saying.'

Freja grabbed her coat and scarf and slipped out the door after them. Tobias strode through the garden gate and into the meadow. He swooshed through the long, damp grass in his gumboots, heading towards the stone bridge that crossed the river. He didn't say a word and Freja had to run to keep up, but she did not mind. She preferred silence to the awkward questions or stern judgements that so often came her way. Besides, her face was tingling deliciously with the chilly fresh air and there was so much beauty to take in — the winter branches grabbing at the clouds as they whispered across the sky, the lush grass rippling in the breeze, the glossy banks of bracken with the strange leaves that looked like lace and teeth and serrated knife-blades all at the same time. She would remember it all, every detail, to share with Clementine when she sat down to write to her this evening.

Halfway across the stone bridge, Tobias stopped. 'I say, old chap, how about a game of Pooh Sticks?'

'I *love* Pooh Sticks!' cried Freja. 'Clementine and I play it all the time. It's her favourite game.'

'I know,' said Tobias.

'How do you know?' asked Freja. But Tobias had already crossed the bridge and was fossicking around the bank for what he thought was the fastest stick on earth.

When they had both found their ideal stick, they returned to the bridge. Hanging over the side that faced upstream, Freja sang, 'Ready, steady, go!' They dropped their sticks into the water, ran to the other side of the bridge and waited.

'There!' cried Freja as her stick floated into sight. 'I won! I won! My stick is the champion!' Just then, the stick caught in a tiny whirlpool and spun around and around in the same spot as though doing a victory twirl. Freja giggled.

They waited and waited, but Tobias' stick did not appear. 'Well, that's a jolly nuisance,' he said, tugging at his ear. 'It would seem the stick I chose is as bad at floating as me. I swim like a stone.'

Freja said, 'I swim like a fish. I've swum with seals and walruses. Seals are funny and friendly, but walruses are enormous — much bigger than you'd expect — and rather frightening. I can snorkel too.'

'You're jolly smart, you know,' said Tobias. He looked at her with such kindness and admiration that Freja felt tears well up in her eyes.

'Come along, old chap!' he said. 'Can't stand here all day waiting for my useless stick. Finnegan has just run into the forest after a rabbit and we won't find him before dark if we don't go now.'

Tobias strode off once more, muttering to himself. Freja ran after him and plucked up the courage to ask some burning questions about his crime novel she'd been reading, like, 'Do people *always* bleed a lot when their finger is chopped off?' and 'What's the quickest way to escape from the boot of a car?' Tobias did his best to answer in a clear and concise manner. By the time they had found Finnegan and returned to the cottage, Freja felt as though she had spent a surprisingly enjoyable and educational day.

That evening, however, things went south. They had just sat down to a simple supper of tea and toast when Freja began to weep.

Finnegan trotted to her side. He tried to cheer her up by licking her hand, her cheek and, finally, her earhole, but Freja couldn't stop the tears. She wept on and on, her face crumpled, her nose dripping.

She was, of course, homesick. Not for any particular place, for she had been moved about with more regularity than a morning-tea trolley in the corridors of a large office block between the hours of ten and eleven o'clock, and had no real place that went by the name of 'home'. Rather, she was homesick for Clementine, her darling mother. She was sad and soggy to the depths of her soul.

Freja did not, however, wish to admit such a thing. She had promised Clementine she would be brave, and a promise made was one that must be kept. Besides, Tobias had turned out to be a marvellous fellow — a font of fascinating and gruesome facts, and ever so kind. She did not want to seem ungrateful or in need of more attention. There was, therefore, only one thing to do. She would have to lie.

Tobias reached awkwardly across the table and patted her hand. 'What on earth is the matter, old chap?'

Freja poked at her toast and wailed, 'I don't like marmalade!' The words were false, but the tears were genuine and abundant.

'Oh my,' sighed Tobias, relieved that the problem was one so easily fixed. He gave both pieces of toast to a confused but appreciative Finnegan. Spreading two more slices with butter and a thick layer of blackberry jam, he passed them to Freja with an encouraging nod.

By now, the worst wave of homesickness had swept on by and Freja was able to force a smile onto her face.

By the time she had downed her toast, two glasses of milk and three chocolate biscuits, she was feeling quite robust once again.

Tobias relaxed and congratulated himself out loud. 'Disaster averted!' He put the kettle on to boil and took the teapot down from the shelf. 'We'll rub along just fine. This child-minding caper is not so difficult after all. Why, it's every bit as easy as making a cup of tea!'

And with that, he tripped on Finnegan's tail and dropped the pineapple-shaped teapot onto the floor, where it broke into a dozen pieces.

CHAPTER 9
Conversation and clouds

Three days later, Freja was reading, Tobias writing, when the clock struck two and fell off the wall. Tobias jumped with fright and toppled a cup of tea.

'Whoopsy-daisy!' Tobias leapt to his feet and used a nearby cushion to mop up the tea. Then he squashed the cushion into the large bottom drawer of his desk and rehung the clock. Glancing over his shoulder, he announced, 'I see what you're doing there, Finnegan!'

The dog stopped chewing on the hem of the green velvet curtains. He blinked slowly up at his master. Freja peeped over the pages of the latest crime novel she was reading, *Lightning Strikes Twice*.

Tobias planted his hands on his hips, his elbows popping through the frayed holes in his cardigan sleeves. 'We've talked about this before, young pup.

The *gumboot* is for chewing, but *not* the velvet curtains ... or any other curtains for that matter!'

Finnegan continued to blink at his master. He flicked his tongue across his big, wet nose and yawned.

'Yes, yes,' said Tobias. 'You are a very charming puppy, cute and just the right amount of silly. But *I* know that *you* know exactly what I'm saying!'

Finnegan dropped his shaggy grey head to the floor and whined.

'Gumboot!' commanded Tobias. He stamped his foot and shook his head, his hair flopping forward into his eyes.

Finnegan covered his face with his front paws and whimpered.

Freja's eyes grew wide.

'Gumboot!' Tobias repeated. He stomped across the room and grabbed an old black gumboot from the corner. Lifting it to his face, he eyeballed Finnegan, then began to chew on the rubber toe!

Freja dropped her book and giggled softly.

'Yum-yum-yum!' Tobias chomped and rolled his eyes as though the gumboot was the most delicious thing he had ever tasted.

Finnegan peered out from beneath his paws and whined.

'Yummy-yummy-yummo-yummikins!' sang Tobias, gnawing and tugging at the boot with even more enthusiasm.

Freja giggled a little louder.

Finnegan lifted his head, tilted it to one side and yawned again. Then, blinking defiantly at Tobias, he turned back to the curtains and resumed chewing on the frayed and soggy hem.

Freja fell back onto her nest of cushions and laughed until tears rolled down her face.

Tobias spun around. He took the gumboot from his mouth and dropped it on the floor. His eyes twinkled and wrinkled at the sides. 'I say, old chap! What a splendid cackle you have there. Like a happy hen splashing in a babbling brook. Simply marvellous.'

Freja blushed with delight. She sat up and wiped the tears from her eyes.

'Now what were we about to do?' Tobias scanned the room, stopping only momentarily to frown at Finnegan. He stared at his typewriter and tugged at his ears.

'Were we going to take a walk?' ventured Freja.

'Yes!' shouted Tobias, throwing his arms wide. 'Absolutely. Wind and clouds on the move! Don't want to miss the action. Pop your hands in your scarf. Wrap your neck in your mittens. It'll be brisk outside and we'll be sitting still for a long time.'

'I thought we were going to walk,' said Freja.

'Walk. Sit. Dream. Come along, old chap. Less talk, more action!'

Freja smiled. If only all instructions were as simple!

They walked, galloped, tucked bits of grass in their hair, tossed stones in the river and discussed the latest research Tobias had been doing on frostbite. Freja wondered how many toes you could lose before you were forced to walk with a permanent limp. Tobias told a very exciting story about a chap who was lost on a glacier, in a blizzard, and saved his thumbs from frostbite by sucking on them to keep them warm until he was rescued. They both wondered about polar bears and how they managed to keep their paws and claws and cute knobbly tails intact when they spent all their lives in ice and snow.

'Fat and fur, I think,' said Freja.

'And maybe they have central heating in their dens,' added Tobias. 'Or a cosy log fire.'

'Electric blankets,' suggested Freja.

'Thick, woolly bedsocks.'

'Hot-water bottles with fluffy covers shaped like seals.'

'And steaming mugs of cocoa to wrap their paws around and sip upon while listening to the BBC news on the radio each night,' added Tobias.

Freja's breath caught.

Was she scared? Was she sad?

No. It was something quite different.

Joy.

Excitement.

Pride.

For she had realised that she was, in fact, having a conversation. A relaxed and happy conversation with someone other than Clementine.

Still looking at the path ahead of them, she reached up and took Tobias by the hand. Not even the hand, really. Just two fingers. And only for a few seconds.

Tobias, bless his heart, pretended nothing had happened and they walked on, side by side, in companionable silence.

They came to a clearing in the forest that was carpeted with grass and dotted with clumps of bracken. 'Here!' cried Tobias. 'This is where I do cloud-dreaming.'

They flopped down on the ground. Finnegan stretched out between them, glad for a break in which he could chew on sticks and leaves and Tobias' bootlaces.

'If you stare at the clouds for long enough,' explained Tobias, 'they turn into animals ... and if you linger amidst the bracken for a further half-hour, a story about the animals will weave itself in your mind.'

So they did. They lay in silence — the girl, the dog and the writer. The sky came alive with tigers ... elephants ... aardvarks ... a scattering of mice. A herd of reindeer meandered along, just for a moment, trying to draw Freja back to memories of Norway and Clementine. But then an arrogant fat warthog barrelled into their midst, scaring them away. Freja watched and smiled and allowed the warthog to weave a tale about himself — a tale filled with spectacular and improbable acts of heroism and romance, which lasted until the sun sank low and the clouds turned from white to pink.

'Time to walk home,' said Tobias. 'Unless you'd like to learn a little something about frostbite first hand ...'

Freja shook her head and stood up.

'Home it is then!' Tobias glanced at her dirt-smeared face and the clothes she had worn both day and night since leaving London. 'And perhaps you could take a nice hot bath while I prepare our supper.'

But Freja didn't answer. The word 'home' had joined in her mind to another word that had been drifting about all afternoon: 'Clementine.' Suddenly, unexpectedly, the ugly homesickness, that deep longing for her mother, cut through her heart. Freja clenched her jaws and breathed deeply through her nose. She breathed in ... then out ... then in ... then burst into tears.

Finnegan bounded to her side. 'Woof!' he said and tried to lick the tears as they fell from her eyes and ran down her cheeks.

'Oh dear,' sighed Tobias, patting her awkwardly on the head. 'Whatever is the matter? Are you cold? Tired? Hungry? All three at once? Is it the bath? Are you scared of cleanliness?'

Freja sobbed and snuffled. She wiped her nose on the back of her mitten. How could she *possibly* tell the truth? It would be saying that Tobias' kindness was not enough. And it wasn't. But she felt that it should be.

And again, she was overwhelmed by how completely ill equipped she was for life in the big, wide world — life away from Clementine and the Arctic.

Freja sobbed and shook, grasping for any excuse other than the real one. 'I ... I ... I want a bubble ba-a-a-ath!' she bellowed.

Relief flooded over Tobias' face. 'Well, well, well. Let me see. I don't have any bubble bath ... but I do think ... no ... I am *certain* that a good dash of dishwashing liquid will work just as well.' He took her by the hand and led her home through the darkening afternoon, babbling on and on about bubbles and how simply marvellous they were for raising one's spirits and cleaning the grime from one's face.

Back at Myrtle Cottage, Tobias left Freja by the fire, sobbing into Finnegan's neck, while he dashed to the kitchen to find a bottle of lemon dishwashing detergent. By the time a hot and frothy soap-sudsy bath was run, the worst of Freja's sad and soggy mood had passed. She was able to force a smile onto her face, convincing Tobias that her woes really were of the small and easily mended kind.

And once she found herself sitting up to her neck in warm water and fluffy bubbles, staring at the giant Irish wolfhound who had decided that baths were meant for sharing, she really did feel rather happy.

CHAPTER 10

Tobias mingles in his own special way

Tobias drove like a maniac, his vintage motorcycle flying like a rocket one minute, chugging so slowly that they almost came to a standstill the next, then roaring off again for no apparent reason. Fast or slow, Tobias swerved from one side of the country lane to the other, splashing through puddles, side-swiping hedgerows, whooshing beneath low-hanging branches. Freja, seated in the sidecar, screamed, yelped and giggled. Finnegan, crammed onto her lap, revelled in the speed and the bumps, his tongue and ears flapping joyously in the wind. Every few minutes, he turned around to share his delight, licking Freja's face and lunging at the big, round cherry-red pompom on her beanie. It was the most thrilling fun Freja had had since she and Clementine rode on a sled pulled by huskies at the North Pole.

'Village day!' Tobias had announced that morning. 'You've been here a whole week and the bickie supplies are running dangerously low. Off to Little Coddling we'll go! Shopping. Errands. Ice-cream spiders and trifle at the tea room. Meeting, mingling, chatting.'

Freja, of course, did not like meeting, mingling or chatting with other people. But ice-cream spiders and trifle sounded ever so delicious ... and bickies *were* important ... Besides, Finnegan would be there. It was comforting to know there'd be a large Irish wolfhound behind which she could hide should the need arise.

The motorcycle roared over the last hill and they zoomed into Little Coddling at breakneck speed. The road curved to the left, but Tobias seemed drawn to the right. They clipped a street sign, ripped through a patch of winter crocuses, plunged down an embankment and came to a boggy standstill in the middle of a field. A flock of curious sheep surrounded them.

'Ever so sorry!' cried Tobias.

The sheep jostled and bleated.

'I'll be out of your way in a jiffy,' Tobias promised.

Freja giggled. 'They can't understand you, you know.'

Tobias climbed off the motorcycle. 'Of *course* they can! Why, just listen to them bleating and blabbering. "Ba-a-a-ad luck!"'

'Ba-a-a-ad driving!' bleated Freja.

Tobias chuckled as he heaved the motorcycle out of the bog, back onto the road.

They parked by the village common, where Tobias looked Finnegan in the eye and said in a clear and commanding voice, 'Stay!'

'Woof!' replied Finnegan. He blinked, licked his nose and leapt out of the sidecar. Without a backward glance, he trotted off to sniff at lampposts, car tyres, drainpipes and unsuspecting bottoms.

Tobias and Freja headed towards the grocer's. Freja was nervous and tried to conceal herself by walking close to Tobias, hiding in the floppy folds of his cardigan. She needn't have worried, however, for once they came into contact with the villagers, Tobias drew *all* the attention to himself.

'Hello, Tobias.'

'Good morning, Mrs Pargenter.' Tobias smiled and nodded. Then, turning to Freja, he remarked in a too-loud whisper, 'That woman's overbite is a marvel! How she manages not to swallow her own chin is beyond my understanding. And the amount of custard she has in her shopping trolley is *sensational*. Look! Perhaps eating solid food is a problem when one's upper and lower teeth refuse to meet at the middle.' He closed his eyes and muttered.

'What are you doing?' whispered Freja, tugging at his sleeve.

'Committing the details of lips, teeth, chin and custard to memory,' he explained. 'I might want to use Mrs Pargenter in a novel one day.'

Freja nodded. It was much the same as she and Clementine did when observing animals in the wild, except *they* committed the details to memory for the sake of research and a deeper understanding of nature ... and the animals never seemed offended.

Mrs Pargenter, on the other hand, was completely unnerved by Tobias' intense gaze and madman mutterings.

'Rude fellow!' she gasped and dashed away.

Tobias wandered around the grocer's, gathering apples and beans, milk and biscuits, cheese and crumpets, jam and oatmeal. All the time, he remarked loudly, enthusiastically, on people's distinguishing features — Jenny Sergeant's uneven gait ... the Vicar's slight lisp ... the fact that Charles Whitmore's left ear was a little bigger than his right. Freja didn't know whether to laugh, cry or be impressed by Tobias' acute powers of observation. In the end, she did a little of all three.

Halfway along the produce aisle, Tobias stopped and threw his arms wide. 'Helloooo, Mrs Indira!' he exclaimed. But by the time he had taken one step towards the woman, she had ducked behind a crate of oranges with her two small boys.

'Leave us alone, *please*, Mr Appleby,' the poor woman hissed. 'Sanjay is still having nightmares since our last meeting in the pet food aisle.'

Tobias ran his hand through his mop of hair, grimaced at Freja and tried to explain. 'But dogs truly *can* be trained to bite off —'

'Hush!' snapped Mrs Indira, and she hurled an orange at him.

In aisle three, Tobias sat down to better admire the unique qualities of Mrs Hawking's nasal hair and squashed a carton of eggs. At the deli, he stood for a full ten minutes, wondering aloud whether it would be best to hide a stolen ruby inside a bratwurst sausage or a wheel of camembert. And at the checkout, he was busy explaining to a teenage lad how a stick of celery could be used to break into a safe and failed to notice that he'd paid for his groceries with a chocolate wrapper and two old parking tickets. Mr Barnes, the store keeper, was so eager to see the back of Tobias that he accepted the payment without question and bid him a hearty goodbye.

Out in the street and the wintry air, Freja took a deep breath and looked up into Tobias' face. She thought she might see despair or at least embarrassment. Instead, she saw nothing but a dreamy smile and a twinkle in his eyes.

'I do *love* a good outing!' he cried, striding towards the motorcycle, arms laden with groceries. 'So many intriguing people. Always something new to observe. All fuel for one's writing. Chocolate topping and whipped cream for one's imagination.'

At the library, Tobias borrowed every book he could find on mountain climbing, including a fascinating little volume called *Gashes, Bruises, Slashes — An Illustrated Anthology of Life-Threatening Injuries*. While she waited, concealed by a bookshelf, Freja overheard a strange and disturbing conversation.

'It's true!' exclaimed a woman with a deep, husky voice. 'He really *does* have a child staying with him.'

A second woman with a high, squeaky voice asked, 'Who in their right mind would send a child to live with that mad writer?'

Freja gasped. They were talking about her and Tobias!

'Perhaps the *mother* is not in her right mind,' said Husky.

'Probably not,' agreed Squeaky. 'The child seems a little odd herself. Have you *seen* her? Wide, staring eyes. Feathers sticky-taped to the top of her gumboots. And a hat and scarf that look like they were stolen from a garden gnome.'

'Eccentric!' added Husky.

Freja ducked beneath the computer desk, lest the women should see her and scream with horror. She patted her cherry-red scarf and beanie, birthday gifts knitted by Clementine.

'Clementine,' whispered Freja, rubbing her stinging eyes. She took the little felt hare from her pocket and clutched it to her chest.

'Yes! Eccentric!' cried Squeaky. '*Just like Tobias Appleby.*'

There was a long silence that felt like it was full of something nasty.

'And that hair,' whispered Husky loudly. 'Feral and curly! Just like … well, *you know* …'

Freja peeped out from her hidey-hole and saw the women stroll past the Romance section, their eyebrows raised knowingly at each other.

'Come along, old chap, wherever you are!' called Tobias. 'I've just spotted Finnegan through the library door, with the front half of his body wedged down into a rubbish bin. There'll be trouble — and bad smells — if we don't rein him in.'

Freja gathered three feathers that had fallen from the top of her gumboots and crawled out from beneath the desk. She blushed as the two gossips stared at her. Springing to her feet, she ran from the library, relieved to be away from their confusing words and sizzling silences.

They extracted Finnegan from the bin. Tobias wiped gravy off the dog's face. Freja plucked squashed chips from his hairy grey shoulder.

'Come along, dog and child,' sang Tobias. 'Polly Wimple's Tea Room is waiting!'

Two lime spiders and a bowl of cherry trifle later, Freja felt full, warm and fuzzy. Tobias was sitting on the opposite side of the booth, pushing a blob of red jelly around the table with his finger. He muttered excitedly about squashed eyeballs and oozing goo. Finnegan had eaten three bowls of trifle and was moving his mouth, slowly, furtively, towards the pompom on Freja's beanie.

'Uh-uh!' Freja pulled away, wiggling her finger at the dog's nose.

Finnegan licked the finger in apology.

Freja poked her straw at the green froth in the bottom of her glass. 'Drinking a lime spider is like slurping up a magic cloud of happiness.' She sighed. 'It's fluffy, sweet, colourful and creamy, and the merry tingle lingers long after the last slurp is gone.'

At that very moment, however, the two women from the library strolled into Polly Wimple's. A gush of cold, nasty air accompanied them and blew the magic cloud of happiness away. Freja shivered and shrank down behind Finnegan's hairy body until they had passed.

Pulling one of her curly locks down before her eyes, Freja stared at it, then let it go. It sprang up and down, tickling the side of her nose.

'Tobias,' she whispered. 'Is my hair feral?'

Tobias froze, his finger submerged in jelly. He stared at her for a moment, then boomed, 'Absolutely!'

Freja gasped.

'In fact,' continued Tobias, his eyes wide and sparkling, 'yours is the most feral hair I have ever seen! It reminds me of wild storms at sea ... an octopus caught in a whirlpool ... a bowl of noodles tossed into the air ... an explosion in a factory full of corkscrews!

It is the most sensational, marvellous hair I have ever seen. A real crowd-stopper. You should be mightily proud of it and make sure to always keep it just as it is right now.'

How like Tobias, to take something troubling and turn it into something good.

'And by the way,' he added, 'have I told you how simply splendid that scarf and hat are? Like something one might have stolen from a garden gnome. Jolly exciting.' He grabbed the sides of his tattered brown cardigan and grinned down at his frazzled green vest. 'I haven't a tenth of your style, old chap!'

Freja beamed at him and, to show her appreciation, said, 'Please, before we leave, would you tell me all about squashed eyeballs?'

CHAPTER 11
The too-big lie

Two days later, a letter arrived from Switzerland. It was brief but meaningful, bearing Clementine's deepest love and three small treasures — a pressed edelweiss, a chocolate wrapper with German writing and a small, colourful drawing of a cow with a bell around her neck. They were snippets of Clementine's new world, something Freja could hang her thoughts on. Visions of a clinic with endless corridors and sterile white rooms faded from Freja's mind. Instead, she was able to picture Clementine eating chocolate and breathing fresh air while strolling through meadows full of flowers and fat cows.

'Delightful *and* delicious!' she sighed.

In the evening, Freja sat on the floor in the living room, pasting the new treasures in her scrapbook. The scrapbook was tattered from use, its pages bulging with objects she had gathered during her travels over the years — ferry tickets and food wrappers in different languages, feathers, pressed plants, her own drawings, Clementine's precise sketches, tufts of fur, shards of eggshells, photographs, seeds and a small but completely intact fish skeleton.

Freja had not taken the scrapbook from her satchel since arriving nine days ago. There had been no need, her time having been filled with crime novels, treks through the forest, cups of sweet, milky tea and Finnegan.

But here, now, her whole life with Clementine was laid out before her on the floor. Slowly, she turned the pages, staring at this picture she had drawn of a squirrel ... that tuft of fox fur she had found snagged on the bark of a tree ... those photos of their blissful summer in Greenland.

A hard lump formed in Freja's throat.

She tried to focus on the rhythmic *clackety-clack* of Tobias' typewriter, but it was no use. The lump in her throat grew until her neck ached and, soon, her eyes were stinging too.

Closing the scrapbook, Freja reached for *Rome's Reward*, Tobias' newly released crime novel and the only one she had not yet read. Leaning against Finnegan's hairy grey body, she folded back the cover. But before the end of the first page, her eyes filled with tears and the words washed away. She began to cry, ever so softly at first, but soon snuffling, gasping and — there was no other word for it — blubbering!

The typewriter stopped clacking. Tobias held his hands in the air for a moment and tilted his head to one side. He leapt up from his chair, strode over to the fireside and stared. His green eyes grew soft and sad. 'Why, Freja! You're sobbing again. What a shame!'

He dropped to the floor beside the girl and the dog and folded his long, gangly legs in a knot. Leaning forward, he squeezed Freja's shoulder awkwardly. 'There, there.'

Freja dived into his lap, wrapped her little arms around his body and buried her tear-drenched face in his vest. The vest was soft and woolly and smelt like comfort, love and old books. It was also being worn inside out *and* back to front, which helped her to feel a little bit happy amidst the gloom. Her sobs settled to gentle weeping.

Tobias seemed surprised by the close contact, but soon relaxed. He rocked Freja back and forth, whispering, 'There, there. Everything will be all right, old chap. Tobby is here and will keep you safe.'

Slowly, Freja's weeping faded to sniffs.

Tobias twiddled the golden curls at the back of her head and made up a jolly poem.

Mousey, mousey, needs a housey
Somewhere warm and dry.
Looky there! A head of hair!
A castle in the sky!

The hair was messy, curly, tressy
A tangled web of knots.
The mousey dived right in at once
And settled on the spot.

The little girl who owned the hair
Said, 'Welcome, little mousey.
I hope you'll feel quite safe and warm
In this, your brand-new housey.'

And so the mousey dwelt therein
Amidst the messy curls.
Warm and dry and safe at last
Atop the little girl.

By the end of the poem, Freja was smiling and quite eager to excuse her childish and needy behaviour. 'I'm so sorry, Tobias. I really am being a dreadful baby with all this sniffling. You've been very kind and I truly am having a satisfactory time here — even *happy* quite often. It's just that I ... I ...' Her heart began to race. The tears welled up and she was blubbering once more!

Freja looked around the cottage for inspiration, a convincing excuse. Her watery gaze skimmed over teapots, dictionaries, gnawed curtains and lumpy cushions, settling at last on the book she had been trying to read, *Rome's Reward*. It would have to do. She threw back her head and wailed, 'I WANT TO GO TO RO-O-O-OME!'

Tobias was stunned. And rightly so. This was certainly a step up from crying over marmalade and bubble baths!

'Hmmm,' he murmured. 'And here was I, thinking it might be slippers or porridge. Even something about Finnegan licking your face too often. This is not at all what I expected.' Still hugging Freja with one hand, he tugged at his ear with the other. 'But it's a jolly coincidence, that's what it is. Why, just this morning, I received a *third* letter from my publisher urging me to take a trip to Rome. My new novel, *Rome's Reward*, is coming out there in two weeks, you know. They want me to do some sort of promotion — a bookshop reading, I think. And now this ... you, crying for Rome ... extraordinary!'

Freja wiped her nose on Tobias' sleeve and whimpered.

'You really are a sad sausage, aren't you?' said Tobias. 'Want to go to Rome, eh? Well ... let me see ... we might ... yes, yes ... we might just be able to kill two birds with the one stone.'

Freja's little body shuddered.

'Buckle up, old chap!' Tobias held the girl at arm's length. 'If it's Rome you want, it's to Rome we shall go!'

Freja was completely shocked out of crying.

'I must admit,' Tobias trundled on, thinking aloud, 'I did enjoy Rome when I was there last. I was rather bogged down in my research and didn't really meet many people, but I did like the look and feel of the place. I do prefer to be home in Hampshire when writing, but I suppose I might just as well sit at a desk in an apartment in Rome as a desk in Myrtle Cottage. I'll still write every day and go for long, rambling walks. They'll just take me through ancient Roman ruins and crowded marketplaces rather than meadows and forests. And you and Finnegan will do your thing ... whatever that might be. Why, surely, our lives will barely change.'

Within the week, Tobias Appleby had packed three boxes and two suitcases of necessities, leased an apartment in the centre of Rome, sent his motorcycle and sidecar ahead by rail, locked up Myrtle Cottage, and was boarding an aeroplane with a ten-year-old girl and an enormous Irish wolfhound. Apparently, if you pay for the seat and make sure there are no stowaway fleas, a dog can travel first class with the best in the land.

And Freja, though stunned at what she had started, didn't have the heart to stop it once Tobias was on a roll. He was, after all, doing it for her, just to make her happy. How could one *possibly* repay such kindness?

She would repay, she decided, by going cheerfully along with the scheme.

Even though it meant another scary change.

Even though Rome was a city filled with people. Millions of people.

Even though every new move felt like she was being dragged further and further away from her old life with Clementine.

The jet engines roared to life.

The plane taxied along the runway.

Finnegan yawned and licked Freja's ear.

'Rome,' Freja whispered. 'What have I done?'

And her stomach lurched as the plane left the earth and soared up into the unknown.

CHAPTER 12
Pesky pigeons

'Good morning, beautiful Rome!' Tobias flung open the doors of the second-storey apartment, stepped out onto the balcony and tilted his face up into the warm Italian sunshine. He laughed and waved his lanky arms about like a conductor, all the while breathing deeply and sighing loudly. Freja knew exactly what he was doing, because in her own quieter way, she did the same thing each day. He was feasting upon this fascinating city — the sight of peeling green shutters against faded ochre walls; the music of church bells and shouted conversations; the smell of basil, garlic and wood smoke as the pizza ovens were fired up for the day.

Freja watched in delight as Tobias spun around, his green eyes sparkling, his cardigan flapping, his arms waving in the air. It was, she thought, a beautiful moment of joyous abandon. Except for one unfortunate fact. Tobias had forgotten about the open bottle of ink in his right hand. Jet-black liquid sloshed through his fingers, splashed onto the tiles and dripped over the edge of the balcony.

'*Santa Maria!*' roared a voice from below.

'Whoopsy!' Tobias grimaced and shoved the now-empty bottle into his trouser pocket. He wiped the ink from his hands onto his bottom. Stepping forward, he leaned over the railing and looked down into the cobbled street. Freja ran to his side.

Mother Superior Evangelista, a nun from the nearby convent, was frozen to the spot. She rubbed at a blob of ink on the front of her creamy white habit, turning it into a thick, ugly smear. She gasped, gaped at her blackened thumb and tilted her gaze upward.

Her eyes, upon meeting Tobias', widened then narrowed to two angry slits.

Uh-oh, thought Freja. *She recognises him. She knows it was Tobias who knocked her off her bicycle two days ago!*

'Tss!' Mother Superior hissed. '*Idiota!*'

Freja leaned in to Tobias. '*Idiota?*' she whispered. 'I think there might be a similar word in English.' The corners of her mouth twitched.

Tobias gave her a crooked smile, then looked back down at the nun. 'Sorry! Excuse me, Mother Superior!' He clutched his chest and grinned like a sick cat, but the nun continued to scowl.

'Maybe,' suggested Freja, 'she's waiting for you to apologise in Italian.'

Tobias nodded. 'Good idea, old chap!' Leaning further over the railing, he swept his arms wide and bellowed, '*Scusa*, Mamma Spaghettiosa!'

'Mamma Spaghettiosa?' shrieked the old woman. She stomped away, shaking her head.

Freja giggled. 'Spaghettiosa?'

Tobias let out a long, loud breath. He rubbed his forehead and ran his fingers through his hair. He patted his cheek, chuckled a little and scratched his nose. He clasped his chin and wondered aloud, 'Now what *was* it that brought me out here in the first place?' Each simple gesture spread the remaining ink on his hands further afield. Soon he looked more like a work-weary coal miner at the end of a twelve-hour shift than a successful crime writer living abroad in Rome.

Finnegan sauntered onto the balcony. He and Freja stood side by side, staring up at Tobias.

'Ink ...' muttered the absent-minded writer. 'Pen ... sunshine ...'

Finnegan cocked his head towards Freja and whined.

Resting her hand on the dog's back, Freja whispered, 'Give him time. He'll work it out sooner or later.'

'Ink ... pen ... *writing*!' Tobias cried, finally lighting upon the answer.

He ducked back inside and, moments later, a heavy oak desk came sliding through the French doors and onto the balcony. Tobias grunted, pushed and heaved until he was satisfied with its position, then straightened the items on top — his ancient typewriter, several medical journals, a tin of pencils and nib pens, a fresh pot of ink and a scruffy pile of papers weighed down with a teapot shaped like the Pope. He disappeared and returned once more, wheeling a large swivel chair he'd bought at a flea market three days ago. It was remarkably like the one he had in England, except more rickety, if that was possible. Placing the chair before the desk, Tobias gave it a complete twirl, then plonked himself down. He tucked a pencil behind one ear, threaded a clean sheet of paper into the typewriter and began to jab away at the keys.

Tobias had not typed more than three words when a large green-and-grey pigeon flew across the balcony and landed on the typewriter. Tobias swept the pigeon away with his hand. It flapped about in the air, then returned to exactly the same spot.

Finnegan barked. Freja giggled. Tobias moaned. They'd been in Rome long enough to know that where one pigeon lands, a dozen or more are sure to follow.

Within moments, the desk was a living, moving mass of green-and-grey feathers. Pigeons scuttled back and forth, fluffing their chests, bobbing their heads, pecking and cooing. Especially cooing.

'Go away!' cried Tobias ineffectually. 'I can't work with all this gossiping.'

'*Gossiping?*' asked Freja, creeping a little closer.

'Yes, gossiping,' said Tobias. 'Pigeons *love* to gossip. Why do you think they gather in such fussy clusters all the time?'

'I thought they were looking for food,' said Freja. 'Breadcrumbs ... or corn.'

'No, no, no!' Tobias waved his hand dismissively. 'They're blurting out their latest titbits of gossip. Then they'll fly off, each in their own direction, and share it with a whole new flock. And so the gossip will travel through Rome faster than if it was shouted from the balcony of the Pope's apartment in the Vatican. Listen.'

He pointed to one of the pigeons and spoke with a comical Italian accent: 'Signore and Signora Rappalino have been screaming and shouting at each other since sunrise.'

Pointing to a second pigeon, he said in a high-pitched Italian accent, 'Nobody argues like the Rappalinos.'

Pointing to a fat, scruffy pigeon, he boomed, 'Except for the Sciarras!'

Freja giggled again. 'You're right! They're *dreadful* gossips.'

Tobias nodded, then continued to speak for the pigeons: 'Young Bruno Bellini crashed his Vespa last night. Drove straight through the window of the Pope's favourite pizzeria.'

'The Pope eats far too much pizza.'

'Pizza never hurt anyone.'

'It hurt Signore Russo. Look how fat he got, then — *POOF!* — he exploded!'

'He didn't explode. He was hit by a train.'

'Same result.'

'Have you seen the new curtains Signora Sala has hung in her living-room window? Black with brown and yellow flowers.'

'Brown and yellow flowers?'

'Urk! That woman has no taste.'

'No taste at all.'

'*And* she has an enormous bottom!'

It really *did* look as though the pigeons were speaking the words as they fluffed and pecked and warbled about on the desk. Freja laughed until her tummy ached.

Tobias tugged at his hair and moaned, 'See, old chap? They gossip on and on and on, and even though one does not want to participate, one can't help getting sucked in. I'm now thinking all about poor Signore Russo and his five fatherless *bambini. And* Signora Sala's enormous bottom ...' He made a wide, circular motion with his hands. 'I haven't a thought to spare for the villain of my novel. Let alone the hero!'

Freja scrunched her nose. She disappeared into the apartment and returned a moment later with half a loaf of bread. The pigeons flapped excitedly into the air, wings and tail feathers brushing her face. She leaned over the railing and tossed chunks of bread down into the street below. With a whoosh of green and grey, the pigeons were gone.

Tobias lifted a feather from the table and tucked it

into his hair. He nodded to Freja, pulled his chair in to his desk and cracked his knuckles.

'I thought Finnegan and I might sneak out on our own today,' said Freja. 'I want to post a letter to Clementine, then we could explore a little.' She paused for a moment. 'Do I need to change before I go?'

Tobias spun around and stared. Freja wore her hiking boots, a crumpled cream blouse and a lumpy green pinafore. The pinafore was, in fact, Tobias' favourite woollen vest. Freja had taken a shine to it. She even wore it inside out and back to front as she had seen Tobias do three times out of four. Pinned to each of her shoulders was a sprig of olive leaves.

'Do I need to change?' she asked once more.

Her curly blonde hair shone like an angel's halo in the bright Italian sunshine.

'Why *ever* would you need to change?' cried Tobias. 'You look simply perfect, as always.'

Freja's face broke into a grin to match her golden halo — pure and bright. She waved, giggled and skipped into the apartment. Finnegan was right at her heels, a shaggy grey bodyguard. And as she went, she heard Tobias speaking with a deep, dramatic voice as he tapped away at his typewriter: 'Suddenly, from the dank, dark depths of the chasm flew a pigeon, flapping, cooing, shedding feathers and fear in equal measure.'

CHAPTER 13

Kindness and crowds

Freja and Finnegan trotted down four flights of stairs, across the courtyard where Tobias kept his motorcycle and through the heavy timber doors that led out into the narrow street.

Freja stopped, rested her hand on Finnegan's neck and took a deep breath. They had been in Rome for a whole week now. She and Finnegan had ventured out every day with Tobias, but this was their first time alone.

'I can do this,' she whispered.

'Woof,' said Finnegan. Not that he agreed. He just liked to reply when Freja spoke. She could have said, 'Six times nine is a thousand,' and Finnegan would have said, 'Woof!'

A pale blue Fiat puttered by, followed by a man on a bicycle. The cyclist clung to the handlebar with one hand and held a cone of strawberry gelato aloft in the other. He wibbled and wobbled, and the gelato fell out of the cone, landing on the cobblestones with a *splodge*. Unaware of the disaster, he rode on. Finnegan cleaned up the mess in three slurps.

'Good boy,' said Freja.

Finnegan licked his lips and wagged his tail. His left eye twitched a little.

'Brain freeze,' explained Freja, and she gave his head a warming rub.

Looking along the street to a café, she frowned. The waiters were setting out tables and chairs in the sunshine, ready for early customers.

'People!' she sighed. Her tummy tightened. It would be different exploring without Tobias. Tobias could always be depended upon to do or say something odd, thereby drawing all attention to himself. He was a wonderful companion for outings, for Freja rarely had to say a word. In fact, she was hardly noticed.

'Tobias and I are like a polar bear and an Arctic fox,' she told Finnegan. 'If an Arctic fox walked into a café, the waiter would be astonished. But if a *polar bear* and an Arctic fox walked into the café, the waiter would barely notice the fox. The polar bear would draw all his attention.'

'Woof!' Finnegan swiped his tongue across her cheek and grinned.

'Yes,' said Freja. 'I know. You'll be with me all the way ... and those waiters are busy with their work ...

and I really *do* need to post this letter ... and I would *love* to see some more of Rome. It's wonderful, despite all the people.'

Freja started along the cobbled street, making sure to stay pressed up against the wolfhound's comfortingly large body.

'*Ciao*, Goldilocks!' A tall, dark-haired waiter smiled and waved his tray at Freja.

Freja's cheeks burned and her legs turned to jelly. She grabbed a fistful of Finnegan's fur and looked around for somewhere to hide. The only place, however, was beneath a table and that was right next to the waiter.

'*Ciao, bella bambina!*' yelled a plump chef from inside the café.

Freja rushed on.

An old woman hung out from a window, two storeys above, beating the dust from her rug. She stopped and waved down at Freja, smiling. '*Buongiorno, bambina!*'

Freja swallowed and walked a little faster.

'*Ciao! Ciao, bella!*' cried the bartender from inside the next café. He lifted a glass in the air in a kind of salute.

'*Ciao, bella!*' cried another waiter.

Freja ran, stumbling over the cobblestones, until a tall, slim lady called out from the flower shop. 'It's a little golden angel running by!' She waved a large pink dahlia in the air, then pointed it at Freja. 'Your curls! The spirals! They are like fusilli pasta! Golden fusilli! Astonishing!'

It was all too much. Freja froze and her hands flew to her hair. Her messy, feral hair. Why hadn't she worn a hat?

'*Bella!*' cried the lady, stepping into the street. 'Do not cover your hair. It is *magnifico*! Golden fusilli is a beautiful thing.' She pointed to her own brown locks and frowned. 'We see this sort of hair all day, every day. Brown is so common in Rome.'

Freja dropped her hands to her sides and whispered, 'It's chocolate, not brown.'

The woman laughed. 'Chocolate! *Cioccolato! Delizioso!*' Her voice was deep, warm and musical. A kind voice.

'I think chocolate hair is beautiful,' said Freja. 'Especially *tidy* chocolate hair.'

The woman stepped forward and tucked the giant pink flower behind Freja's ear. 'A lovely flower for your lovely hair. You are a splendid girl.' She smiled and retreated into her store.

Finnegan poked his nose into the middle of the dahlia, then sneezed. Freja giggled. She touched the flower, glanced back at the cafés and apartments she had already passed, then walked on, her chin a little higher, her step a little lighter. She barely flinched when the next three waiters waved and cried, '*Ciao!*'

Two blocks along, the narrow street spilt into a wide, open place called Piazza di Spagna. It was one of Rome's most popular sites. The crowds thickened and Freja, much to her surprise, felt herself relax. She passed through a rabble of noisy nonnas, smelly backpackers, tortured artists, beautiful women, untamed toddlers, bellowing fruit vendors, bald-headed monks, strutting policemen and tourists in clumps large and small. It was like slipping into a giant seal colony where one was swallowed up in the press of blubber, the noise of barking, the smell of seawater and fish. One little girl with fusilli-feral hair would barely be noticed.

'As safe as a seal colony,' Freja whispered as she and Finnegan wove in and out through the warmth and colour and bustle that was Rome.

On reaching the centre of the piazza, Freja skipped a full loop around the pretty fountain with the boat in the middle. Finnegan galloped *through* the pretty fountain with the boat in the middle. He snapped at the jets of cool, clean water, sprang out and shook himself dry, all over a backpacker. Then, together, the girl and the dog stood at the base of the Spanish Steps, staring up at the twin towers of the Church of Trinità dei Monti.

'Spanish Steps,' murmured Freja. 'It's a terribly dull name for such a marvellous place.' For this wasn't just any old set of steps leading up the hillside. It was a collection of grand marble stairways and wide terraces. A work of art. A meeting place for friends. A sun-drenched wonderland.

Freja and Finnegan ran up the steps, stopping at the first terrace to catch their breath. An artist sat at her easel, sighing between brushstrokes. An elderly couple shuffled by, sharing a chocolate gelato and love.

'Woof!' said Finnegan, and he bolted upward. Freja followed.

At the next terrace, a group of preschool children ran back and forth, dodging their teachers, wiping their sticky fingers along the marble balustrade. A juggler tried to finish his performance, but dropped all of his balls. He cringed as they bounced down the steps towards the fountain. The children squealed and chased after them. Finnegan joined in the fun by barking and snapping at the ends of scarves, the tips of chubby pink fingers, as the preschoolers scuttled by.

'Come on, Finnegan,' said Freja, and she ran until she reached the top of the steps, where a wide, open terrace spread out to the church.

A group of nuns cycled by, voices cawing, black linen habits flapping in the breeze.

Freja giggled. 'A flock of crows wearing sandals and socks!' She leaned against the marble railing and watched as the nuns flapped away down the road. The sun felt warm and delicious on her back. 'Rome,' she sighed. 'It really is wonderful. Such a surprise for a city! Clementine would *love* it here.'

A lump sprouted in Freja's throat.

Clementine.

Always in her thoughts. But never by her side.

Not for weeks now.

Freja clutched at the letter in her pocket. She closed her eyes. 'I'm not going to cry,' she whispered. 'Not here. Not now.' But two fat tears forced their way out between her eyelids and dribbled down her cheeks.

And more might have followed, but a short burst of music tumbled through the air. Jolly and joyful.

'Woof!' said Finnegan, his ears pricking up.

Freja's eyes flicked open.

A second cluster of notes rollicked towards them.

'Boof!' said Finnegan, nudging the girl with his nose.

Freja wiped her sleeve across her eyes. 'Okay.' She rested her hand on the dog's neck and, together, they followed the music to the other side of the terrace.

'Look!' whispered Freja. 'It's an organ grinder and a ...' She wrinkled her nose. What was it?

Finnegan lowered his head and let out a low, cautious growl. The hackles on the back of his neck stood up.

'Oh!' Freja clasped her hands together. 'It's a *monkey*.'

The organ grinder smiled at the gathering audience, his thick black moustache stretching across his round face. He wore a battered straw hat, a billowing white peasant shirt and worn black trousers. At his side, on a small wagon the size of a pram, stood an antique organ. The brass pipes were polished to a shine, the timber casing was painted with a delicate flower pattern and the crank boasted a fine mother-of-pearl handle.

The monkey lounged on top of the organ, his legs and tail dangling over the edge. He wore a crimson fez on his head and a matching silk waistcoat with brass buttons. From their clothes and attitude, one might think the monkey was the master and the man the servant.

'*Ciao*, beautiful people! Welcome to Rome!' The man gave a sweeping bow. 'I am Giuseppe and this is Pazzo, the naughtiest monkey in Italy.'

Freja tucked herself between two plump nuns. She was half-hidden by their bottoms, but could still see Giuseppe and Pazzo.

Finnegan dashed forward from the crowd and barked. Giuseppe's bushy eyebrows wriggled, but Pazzo the monkey did not react. He just scratched his belly between the buttons of his waistcoat and yawned. As though everything — even this enormous, threatening hound — was too, too boring.

'Psst!' hissed Freja. 'Finnegan, come here!'

Finnegan slunk back to Freja, glancing nervously over his shoulder at the monkey.

When the crowd had grown to a good size, Giuseppe straightened his hat, cleared his throat and turned the organ handle. Cheerful pipe music tumbled across the piazza and he began to sing an Italian song, ''O Sole Mio'. His voice was surprisingly high and sweet for such a large man.

Freja wrapped her arms around Finnegan's neck and sighed. 'Isn't he wonderful?'

Giuseppe closed his eyes as he sang and Pazzo, completely lethargic and disinterested until now, began to misbehave. He pulled off his little red waistcoat and tossed it at Finnegan. He did a backflip on top of the organ, then another and another. Freja giggled. The tourists chuckled. The nuns tittered and pressed their hands to their chests. But Giuseppe was so lost in song that he didn't seem to notice. He continued to play the organ and sing of sunshine and love.

Pazzo, encouraged by the laughter, did three *front* flips, then stood on his head. His foot kicked Giuseppe in the face, but Giuseppe sang on and on.

Pazzo turned right side up again. He pulled his lips away from his teeth and grinned at the crowd. He bobbed up and down and scratched his bottom. Finally, tired of showing off, he sat down on the organ and picked nits from his belly and popped them into his mouth. By now, the crowd was roaring with laughter.

The final words were sung with a flourish. Giuseppe opened his eyes and frowned.

'You stupid monkey!' he roared, his voice no longer high and sweet. '*Stupido! Stupido!* What have you done with your clothes?'

Pazzo climbed down from the organ and pointed at Finnegan. The dog grabbed the waistcoat in his teeth and shook it from side to side. Freja prised it from his jaws and, blushing, handed it back. Pazzo gave her a teeth-baring grimace that she hoped was a smile, then blew a raspberry at Finnegan. The monkey tossed the vest to Giuseppe, hitting him in the face.

The crowd went wild. People were howling with delight, clutching their bellies, wiping tears from their eyes.

Pazzo climbed up onto Giuseppe's shoulder and stole his hat, then ran from person to person, collecting coins. If anyone refused to pay for their entertainment, the monkey jumped up and down at their feet, screaming, until they were shamed into opening their wallet.

As Freja placed a coin in the hat, she bobbed down and whispered, 'Hello, cutie pie.'

Pazzo froze.

Freja smiled and ran the back of her hand gently down his cheek.

The monkey sighed in delight, 'Oo-oo-oo,' and blew her a kiss. Spinning around, he squealed, yanked Finnegan's tail and returned to the organ, jangling the coins.

'*Bravo*, Pazzo! *Bravo!*' cheered Giuseppe. He took the hat and raked his fingers through the coins. 'Enough for our lunch. Maybe even a banana for you, naughty monkey.'

Pazzo jumped up and down on the spot, grinning.

Giuseppe tipped the coins into a little black money pouch, squashed his hat back onto his head and gave a dramatic bow to his audience. '*Arrivederci! Arrivederci!*' Pushing his wagon away down the street, he shouted back over his shoulder, 'Now, Pazzo, we must find a new audience to pay for our supper, our rent and, if business is good, a bottle of Rome's finest red wine!'

The crowd chuckled at this final snippet of theatre, then drifted apart.

Finnegan whimpered, baffled by the first monkey he had ever seen. He shuddered and pushed his head beneath Freja's arm. Furthermore, he refused to move until she had soothed his troubled nerves by stroking his neck, cooing gentle 'there-theres' and mentioning the most fortifying word he knew: 'Jam.'

CHAPTER 14
Café Vivi

Two hours later, Freja touched Tobias' sleeve. He stopped typing, looked to the right and stared.

'Hmmm,' he mumbled. 'Those sparkling blue eyes look ever so familiar. But what are they doing in the middle of my story?' He frowned and tugged at his ear.

Freja rested her hands on the desk and smiled.

'Finnegan,' he muttered, clutching at the first memory from the real world that floated into his brain.

'Close!' Freja giggled. 'I'm Freja. Remember? Finnegan is lying under the table, eating a jar of jam.'

Tobias bent down and peered at the large hound. Finnegan sucked in his tongue, grinned, then licked his master's boot.

'I'm hungry,' said Freja. 'Could we go out for lunch now? Please?'

'Why, of course we can, old chap! I'm rather peckish myself, now you mention it. And a stretch of the legs will do me no end of good.'

Tobias tugged the page from his typewriter and added it to the growing pile on the desk. He plonked the Pope teapot on top as a paperweight. Ushering Freja and Finnegan through the apartment, he grabbed his scarf and slammed the door behind them.

'Did you remember the key?' asked Freja.

'No,' replied Tobias.

'But how will we get back in?' she gasped.

Tobias leaned forward. 'Is that a bobby pin I spy in your hair, just behind that fabulous pink flower?'

Freja nodded, wide eyed.

'We'll use that!' he declared. 'You will recall that in my third novel, *A Mousetrap in Moscow*, Natasha Andronikov was not only a brilliant hairdresser, but a whizz at breaking into highly secure buildings. I did a lot of research into using various hair accessories to pick locks before I wrote that book. I am now quite adept at getting back into my own home without a key. Especially when accompanied by a spiffing lass who happens to be holding her hair in place with a bobby pin!'

Freja flashed him a smile, and they walked on down the stairs and into the street.

The lunchtime crowds were thickening. The cafés that Freja and Finnegan had passed earlier were now bustling. Waiters dashed back and forth between the outdoor tables, bearing giant pizzas, baskets of bread and bowls of tortellini. Wine and water flowed freely, as did the melodic conversation and laughter. Freja tilted her head to one side and listened. Already she was picking up a word here, a phrase there, the lilt and flow of the Italian language.

Tobias stared intensely, rudely, at people. 'Marvellous!' he cried. 'Noses, noses, everywhere. Never underestimate the power of a nose to reveal something important about a person!' He threw his hands wide to indicate the diners at the nearest café, but accidentally swept a wine bottle and two glasses from the tray of a passing waiter. The waiter was furious, but Tobias carried on, oblivious to the disaster. 'Just look at them! Noses twitching over the aroma of a carbonara sauce. Noses wrinkling in disgust at a fellow diner's manners. Noses flecked with small bits of tomato after a particularly enthusiastic slurp of spaghetti arrabiata.'

Finnegan's interest was more primitive. His big brown eyes roved from table to table, looking for dropped or unguarded morsels of food. On passing the fifth café, the pizza gods of Rome smiled down upon him. A young woman flew into a rage, leapt to her feet and stormed away down the street, teeter-tottering on her high heels. Her boyfriend raced after her, slapping his head and pleading for forgiveness. The pizza they had ordered lay alone and uneaten on their table. Finnegan — with the stealth of a ninja, the speed of a greyhound — dashed between the diners. Seizing the edge of the pizza in his teeth, he tugged it off the tray and shot back out into the street. By the time Tobias had committed seven different noses to memory and allowed his attention to return to the world at large, the pizza was gone. All that remained was a small pile of olives between the dog's front paws.

'Finnegan,' scolded Freja, but so gently and with such a sweet smile that the hound took it as a sign of approval. He blinked, licked his nose and dribbled on Freja's boot.

Tobias took one last glance at a pair of cavernous nostrils before they wandered down a street they had never explored before.

'Look!' cried Freja. 'Over there! Doesn't that café look pretty ... and happy ... and *pink*?'

Indeed it did! At the front of the tiny café sat a round pink table and two pink chairs. A pink-and-white striped awning hung out from the window and a cheerful pink sign with white writing swung above the door: 'Café Vivi.'

'Shall we have lunch in there?' Freja asked. But Tobias didn't reply. He was staring wistfully, admiringly, at a man with a nose the size of a turnip. Freja grabbed his hand and dragged him through the pink door.

Café Vivi was even prettier inside. It looked like a jumble sale in which everything had been dipped in pastel paints. Old tables and chairs, velvet lounges, squishy cushions, crocheted granny rugs, tablecloths, crockery, the walls, the floor, the counter and even the cash register were pale pink, powder blue, mint green, lemon yellow or white. Everything was well worn, loved to softness, yet looked perfectly fresh, positively delicious.

'It's like walking through a meadow of wildflowers in spring,' whispered Freja.

'Hmmm. It's certainly pleasing,' agreed Tobias. 'Soothing, subtle, sweet, sensuous.'

'Woof!' said Finnegan, although he was probably not agreeing so much as expressing his excitement at the smell of roasting meat.

Tobias peered over the shoulder of one of the diners. The plump woman and her even plumper friend were sipping red wine, chattering and nibbling away at their food.

'Fascinating!' gasped Tobias. 'Why, if I didn't know better, I would think you were eating Amazonian ghost fruit for lunch!'

The woman closest to Tobias frowned, a forkful of eggplant suspended in the air before her mouth.

Her companion threw back her head and laughed. 'Ridiculous!'

'No, truly,' said Tobias. Leaning forward, he spoke earnestly and rapidly. 'The Amazonian ghost fruit looks very similar to eggplant. It's a rare fruit found in an isolated region of Bolivia and can be incredibly useful. All you need to do is boil the skin for several hours, then reduce the resulting liquid to a concentrate, and you will find yourself in possession of a reliable tranquilliser. One teaspoonful mixed into a glass of water or a cup of tea will send a grown man into a deep slumber for at least twenty-four hours. Of course, more than a teaspoonful might have rather serious consequences, but that's the risk you take when playing with poison, isn't it, eh?' He stood upright, nodded and smiled as though he had just complimented them on their handbags. The women, not surprisingly, had suddenly lost their appetites. Their forkfuls of food were abandoned and their plates pushed away.

Freja poked Tobias in the side. 'There's a perfect table over there. In the corner, half-hidden by the wood fire.'

Tobias turned on his heel, took three steps and halted. His head flew backward as though he had been struck in the face. He let out a strange, high-pitched whimper: 'Oooh.'

'Tobias?' whispered Freja. But Tobias' feet were glued to the spot and he would not move. No matter how hard Freja tugged at his hand. No matter how many times Finnegan head-butted the back of his legs.

A young woman breezed out from behind the counter amidst a waft of delightful aromas — oregano, lemon, mozzarella and freshly baked bread. She was petite and olive skinned, with dark hair that fell to her shoulders in soft, shiny waves. She wore a pink apron with large white polka dots and looked as delectable as the tray of macarons she held in her hand.

Tobias gawped and began to mutter stupidly. 'Eyes! Two of them! She has two eyes!'

'Most people do,' whispered Freja, 'unless they're a pirate or a Cyclops or —'

'Beautiful eyes!' gasped Tobias. 'Deep chocolate pools surrounded by liquorice-thick lashes. And those lips! Her lips are plump and delicious, the colour of ... of ... what is that *sensational* colour?'

Freja thought she had elbowed Tobias into silence, but suddenly, unexpectedly, he shouted, 'RASPBERRY GELATO!'

The entire café fell silent.

Freja hid beneath the flap of Tobias' cardigan and giggled into his vest.

'*Ciao!*' sang the raspberry-gelato lips. 'Can I help you?'

Tobias froze again. He did not speak or move. He just stared at the pretty Italian woman and whimpered, 'Oooooh.'

Freja peered up into Tobias' face. He was being terribly odd. Somebody should probably take control of the situation, and it was not going to be Tobias or Finnegan. She took a deep breath, then whispered, 'We're hungry. We'd like to eat lunch, please.'

The waitress smiled and tilted her head towards the half-hidden table. Freja and Finnegan scuttled to the corner, where they each sat on a chair, but Tobias stayed put.

'I'm Vivi,' said the young woman, holding out her hand. 'This is my little café. I'm the waitress. And the chef. And the owner.' She laughed. 'I'm everything, I suppose.'

'Everything,' echoed Tobias. He took her hand in both of his and shook it with far more vigour than was normal.

Vivi stared at their joined hands — hers white with flour dust, his black with ink. She looked into Tobias' ink-stained face, tossed back her head and laughed once more.

'Oooh,' sighed Tobias.

'Pardon?' asked Vivi.

'What?' he gasped, as though awakening from a dream. He dropped Vivi's hand and allowed her to steer him towards the table where Freja sat giggling, peeping out from behind her menu. Finnegan licked the tablecloth.

'I'll have the pasta of the day, please,' whispered Freja. 'And Finnegan will have a bowl of sardines, a very big one, and perhaps two or three pork sausages.'

Vivi took a pencil from behind her ear and a notepad from the pocket of her apron. She wrote down the order and looked to Tobias.

Tobias gazed back at her, but did not order. Instead, he said, 'I tuck my pencil behind my ear too!' Then he launched into an animated — and totally inappropriate — description of the way in which a pencil could be used to hot-wire a car if one had the sudden need (or urge) to steal one.

When he was done, Freja smiled shyly at Vivi and said, 'Perhaps Tobias should have the pasta of the day, same as me, and a salad. *Grazie!*'

Tobias nodded and grinned. He drew in a deep breath and looked like he might be about to explain how a pencil could also be turned into a lethal weapon. But Finnegan interrupted by jumping to the floor and chasing his tail. He ran around and around, snapping and growling. When, finally, he caught his own tail between his teeth, the diners at the tables nearby cheered.

'*Bravo! Bravo!*'

'Well done, boy!'

'*Complimenti!*'

'*Fantastico!*'

Finnegan returned to his seat, where he settled down to chew on the breadsticks and then the bread basket. Vivi, laughing and shaking her head, disappeared into the kitchen to make their lunch. Disaster averted.

'She's pretty,' said Freja, 'isn't she?'

'Who?' asked Tobias.

Freja frowned. 'Vivi. The café lady.'

'Oh,' said Tobias. 'I hadn't noticed.'

Finnegan slumped his chin into the bread basket, put his paw over his nose and whined.

When Tobias had eaten spaghetti carbonara, a wild-rocket and parmesan salad, veal scaloppine, tiramisù and four strawberry macarons, all washed down with a glass of mineral water and two espressos, Freja managed to convince him that lunch was well and truly done.

'We could go for a walk,' she suggested. 'Explore some more of the city.'

'Yes, yes, I suppose so, old chap.' Tobias drew out his wallet. 'It's just so lovely in here. I feel like I could stay forever. I don't know what it is ...'

'You really don't know?' asked Freja.

Tobias stared at her, open mouthed. After much thought, he said, 'It's the colour, isn't it? The pale lemon walls, the powder-blue linen, the mint-green crockery, the pink velvet lounge. It's like sitting in a bag of marshmallows ... or floating on a cloud through which a rainbow has passed ... or flying with a flock of flamingos, bluebirds and canaries.'

'Hmmm,' said Freja, uncertain of what to say.

When Tobias had paid for their lunch, Freja crept forward and whispered, 'Thank you, Vivi. Your café is lovely.'

'I do hope you will come again,' Vivi replied. She did not look directly at Freja, but smiled while folding a pale pink serviette. '*And* your father.'

'Oh, he's *not* my father,' whispered Freja. 'Tobias is just ... just ... he's a writer ... and he's a little bit absent-minded, but he's ever so kind and sweet and ... well, he's just Tobias.'

The pretty Italian café owner, the little English girl and the scruffy Irish wolfhound watched as the writer walked out of the café, scratching his head and muttering to himself about his sudden mysterious urge to include pale pink macarons in the next chapter of his novel (even though it was set on an isolated mountain top in Switzerland) until he stepped straight into the path of an oncoming Vespa.

CHAPTER 15

The peevish priest

The girl, the dog and the writer wandered along the narrow cobbled streets, turning this way and that as the urge took them. There was no such thing as a wrong turn. Rome was a strange but pleasing mix of ancient and new, rough and slick. Everywhere was fascinating.

As they walked, Freja ran her hand along the buildings and walls, chanting. 'Peeling paint ... Damaged door ... Majestic marble ... Shonky shutters ... Glittery glass ... Burnished brass ... Luscious leaves ... Rusty railings ... Cracked concrete ... Lovely lady.' She stopped and stared at a picture of a beautiful woman. It was a mosaic, created with hundreds of tiny blue, white and gold tiles. They looked like jewels set in the middle of the stark concrete wall. Smiling, Freja ran her fingertips lightly over the woman's face and the golden halo of light behind her head. 'Oh! It's a picture of the Virgin Mary. And there's a little shelf at the bottom where someone has placed a vase of flowers — a gift! How sweet. Look, Tobias.'

But Tobias had not heard a word. He was skipping — actually *skipping* — to the other side of the street.

'A gelato shop!' He sighed and pressed his face against the window, like a small child.

When he drew back, his eyes were wide, his smile a goofy wobble. 'Would you like a gelato, old chap? I'd *love* a gelato. A pink one. A really, *really* pink one.'

'Yes, I would, thank you,' said Freja. 'But are you sure that *you* can fit one in? You did eat a huge amount of lunch at Café Vivi.'

'Café Vivi,' echoed Tobias. He grinned and drifted inside.

A glass counter ran the full length of the shop, displaying swirling mounds of gelato in seventy-two different flavours — everything from the light, fruity tang of mango, lime and passionfruit, through to the creamy, rich depths of toffee, hazelnut and dark chocolate.

'Oooh.' Tobias leaned forward, both hands splayed out on the glass. 'Raspberry gelato.'

'Grrrr,' said Finnegan. He nipped at the seat of Tobias' pants, bothered by his master's strange new behaviour.

The man behind the counter hovered, a gelato scoop in one hand, a waffle cone in the other.

Freja sidled up to Tobias. She whispered, 'I'll have chocolate gelato, please, Tobias. Finnegan will like strawberry because it tastes like jam.'

'Woof!' said Finnegan, delighted at the mention of jam. He dribbled down the glass counter.

'Righto!' Tobias threw his hands wide and cried, 'Raspberry gelato all round! *Grazie! Grazie!*'

The man looked from Freja to Tobias, shrugged and served three raspberry gelati. '*Tre gelati lampone. Deliziosi.*'

Finnegan gobbled his gelato, then galloped ahead of them, chasing cats, paper bags and the flapping laces on people's shoes. Freja and Tobias walked in silence, licking their gelato. At least, *Freja* licked hers. Tobias gazed longingly at his. He sighed, closed his eyes and pressed it slowly to his puckered lips.

'Did you just *kiss* your gelato?' asked Freja.

'Certainly not!' Tobias chuckled awkwardly, then tugged at his ear. 'What a strange thing to say!'

'It's a strange thing to *do*,' murmured Freja.

The air in the narrow street grew cool and damp. A few steps on, the sound of rushing water filled their ears. Freja looked up at Tobias and grabbed his free hand. They turned a corner and, unexpectedly, found themselves in a bright, open piazza, blinking at a giant cascade of water.

'The Trevi Fountain!' gasped Freja. 'Oh, my favourite place in Rome! I had no idea we were near here.'

'Nor did I, old chap.' Tobias scratched his head with the point of his cone. 'It's the way the streets curve and meander and jumble about to make way for the palaces, the churches, the old ruins. It's as though they *want* us to get lost. It's their job to lead us astray so that we see new places and return to our favourites unplanned.'

Freja beamed. This is what she loved about Rome — the glorious surprises, the never quite knowing what was around the next bend. It was, she felt, almost as good as discovering the nest of a snowy owl in an unexpected nook ... or seeing a bear cub a little too early in the season ... or returning to the beach after a swim and finding a seal pup sunbaking on your towel.

Freja and Tobias squeezed past tourists, a performing mime artist and couples sipping coffee at little round tables. They sat down on the steps at the edge of the Trevi Fountain and stared. Freja had been here twice before, but still it dazzled and delighted her. The fountain was enormous, stretching across an entire wall of the Palazzo Poli. Water gushed out and around giant marble sculptures of naked men and winged seahorses. It tumbled and roared over the rocks and into a wide blue pool, where it became still and calm at last.

Freja grabbed Tobias' hand and gave it a quick squeeze.

Tobias returned the squeeze and said, 'Still spectacular, eh?'

'Boof!' said Finnegan. He'd gobbled Freja's gelato while she wasn't looking and seemed very pleased with himself.

'I wonder if I can remember who the statues are,' said Freja. She tugged at her ear, but stopped when she thought of how Tobias' ears stuck out just a little too far. 'Let me see. The man in the middle is Oceanus. He's the spirit of the sea, which is why he's riding in a chariot made from a giant shell. Normal people like you and me don't get to ride around in chariots, you know, Tobias.'

'As if anyone would ever think *we* were normal!' cried Tobias. 'What a droll idea!' He threw back his head and laughed, untroubled by the fact that others might think him odd. Freja smiled a little. If only she could teach herself to feel the same way.

'Oceanus looks cross,' said Freja.

Tobias nodded. 'He might be annoyed at those naked fellows getting in the way of his chariot.'

'They're Tritons, aren't they? Messengers of the sea.' She frowned. 'I wonder *why* they're naked.'

'Well, it's obvious, isn't it, old chap? If you live in the sea, clothes aren't much use! They just get soggy and weigh you down. Quite dangerous, really.'

'Like swimming in gumboots and a heavy winter coat,' said Freja.

'Absolutely!' agreed Tobias. 'Think about it. How

many mermaids or dolphins have you seen swimming around in skirts and cardigans?'

'None!' Freja replied quite honestly.

'Exactly! Anyway, these Tritons might not know how to wear clothes, but they *do* know how to play a jolly tune on a conch shell. They blow in their shells to calm the waves or to whip them into a frenzy, depending on their mood. Having a happy day — smooth the waters. Feeling grumpy — whisk up some wild and woolly waves.'

'That doesn't sound quite fair.' Freja frowned. 'What if they're grumpy with their school teacher, or their brother, and they brew some wild, stormy waves that cause an innocent girl's boat to sink?'

'Aaah.' Tobias rubbed his chin and nodded. 'Yes, I see what you mean. But this is Roman mythology, not a fairy tale. Things are not always sunshine and roses, you know, old chap.'

'No,' whispered Freja. 'Not even in real life.'

A little pain stabbed her chest, reminding her, yet again, of the gap Clementine had left in her life. She reached into her pocket and wrapped her fingers around the felt hare. *Be brave*, she told herself. *For Clementine. For Tobias.*

They sat in silence, watching the fountain, until a group of tourists squashed into the space in front of them. They belonged to an organised bus tour and most wore red caps and green tracksuits that were far too tight. Tobias started muttering about bulging bottoms and overflowing waistlines, but, thankfully, was drowned out by the tour guide.

'The Trevi Fountain!' shouted the guide, pointing with a red umbrella. 'You should all toss in a coin, then go over to that there café for a gelato. We meet at the bus in five minutes before we head off to the Vatican for a quick prayer, then onto Florence by suppertime.'

The stunned tourists fossicked in their pockets, pulled out loose change and flung it into the pool. They nodded, patted each other on the back, then surged off towards the café.

Freja had a clear view once more.

'Uh-oh,' she gasped and leapt to her feet. There was a dog in the middle of the fountain.

And not just a quiet, little dog that might go unnoticed.

This was an enormous, shaggy grey hound, and he was galloping back and forth in the wide blue pool, splashing, barking and making a spectacle of himself.

'Finnegan,' sighed Freja.

A policeman blew his whistle and waved his arms. Finnegan barked and dashed towards him. But when the policeman grabbed for his collar, the silly dog retreated and jumped up onto the rocks. There he stood, halfway up the fountain, wet and bedraggled, barking and wagging his tail.

'You'd better do something,' gasped Freja, 'or he'll end up in jail.'

Tobias nodded. He stood up, but a priest wearing a long black robe stepped in front of him.

'Whoopsy! So terribly sorry,' said Tobias, stepping to the side.

The priest stepped to the side too. His biretta — a square black hat with a pompom on top — slipped to a jaunty angle upon his head.

Freja frowned.

'*Scusa, padre!*' cried Tobias, and he stepped the other way.

The priest followed, blocking his escape once more. This time, he clenched his fists and flexed his arm muscles so they bulged beneath the sleeves of his black robe. This no longer looked like an accidental muddling of paths. This was deliberate.

Freja stared up at the priest's face. A wide scar ran from the middle of his left cheek down to his chin. His dark eyes were narrowed to two little slits. His nostrils flared and there was a cruel twist to his mouth. This was not at all how she imagined a priest should look.

Tobias tugged at his ear. 'Hmmm.' He dropped his hand to his side and the priest's gaze followed.

'Uh-oh,' muttered Freja. For suddenly she noticed the ink stains on Tobias' fingers. Which in turn reminded her of the smears of ink that were still on his face, neck and trousers. Which in turn reminded her of the morning's disaster with the nun.

Tobias' thoughts must have been travelling in much the same direction, for he gasped, 'Ooh-waah! You, my dear priest, must be a friend of Mother Superior Evangelista! Let me explain —'

The priest grabbed Tobias by the front of his cardigan. He tugged him forward and snarled, 'I am Padre Paolo and I know who you are, *signore*. More to the point, I know what it is you are doing.'

Freja's neck prickled. This priest had the same wild look about him as animals when they were about to bite or scratch. *Uh-oh!* she thought. *Tobias is going to be punched in the nose ... or the teeth ... or both!*

Surprisingly, Tobias turned to Freja and winked.

Freja scrunched her nose and scratched her head, confused.

Tobias turned back to Padre Paolo. Taking a deep breath, he gave the priest a smile. Not a smirk or a half-baked affair like one might give to a traffic warden, but a full-blown grin that split his face from side to side and lit up his emerald-green eyes. It was sunshine on a plate. The priest, caught off guard, smiled a little in return and, in so doing, relaxed his grip.

At that very moment, Tobias flopped to the ground, twisting and squirming out of his cardigan as he fell. He dragged Freja to the ground and, together, they crawled away. They scuttled between Italian legs, Japanese legs, American legs, British legs, tourist legs from all over the world, while the priest stared stupidly at the empty garment in his hands.

Finding themselves out in the open, they sprang to their feet. Tobias whistled to Finnegan and he leapt from the rocks halfway up the fountain. Then the girl, the dog and the writer bolted. They zigzagged between sightseers, knocked over a stand of postcards, bit a poodle (just Finnegan) and darted back along the narrow cobbled streets. They turned corners, dashed up alleyways and circled buildings until certain they'd lost the priest.

'Tobias!' Freja gasped for breath, half-crying, half-laughing. 'That was just like a scene from one of your novels!'

'I suppose it was,' Tobias agreed. 'And you, old chap, conducted yourself admirably. You were quick thinking, fast footed and *terribly* brave.'

'I was chased by a wolf once,' whispered Freja. 'I climbed up a tree and waited for three hours until the wolf grew bored and wandered away. Clementine said it saved my life.'

'You're brilliant!' cried Tobias. 'A real-life heroine.'

'Woof!' said Finnegan, and he shook himself dry all over a passing businessman.

Freja wiped a tear from her eye, took a deep breath and smiled.

And as her eyes sparkled and her teeth flashed in the bright Roman sunshine, she realised, with a burst of pure joy, that she felt truly brave for the first time in her life.

CHAPTER 16

Nonna Rosa and Enzo

Freja sat at the dressing table in her bedroom, frowning at the battered little treasure chest. A pile of misshapen paper clips, safety pins and hairpins lay in front of her carved wooden seal. The skin on her thumb was red and raw.

Three days ago, on returning from the Trevi Fountain, Tobias had shown her how to pick the lock on their apartment door using her bobby pin. She'd practised all evening until she'd been able to do it with her eyes closed.

The first lock mastered, she'd turned her attention to the little treasure chest. Every morning, she'd spent at least thirty minutes bending wire objects into new and hopeful shapes, poking them into the keyhole on the treasure chest and twiddling them about. It had, however, remained firmly locked. Even when she'd bashed the treasure chest against the marble fireplace. Even when she'd kicked it across the bedroom floor and called it two or three nasty names under her breath.

This morning, Freja was feeling calmer, more hopeful. 'One last try,' she sighed, pulling a bobby pin from her hair. She bent it into an innovative new shape and stuck it in the keyhole. Slowly but firmly, she twisted it to the right and felt the pin catch on something. 'If only I can —'

'I say, old chap!' Tobias stood at the door. 'That's the treasure chest! The one that Clem and I dragged from —' He stopped abruptly, ran his hand through his hair and tugged at his left ear.

Freja leaned forward, hoping he might continue.

'Trying to pick the lock, eh?' Tobias chuckled. 'I admire your determination. You really are ever so much like dear Clementine. But it won't work. It's not that sort of lock.'

Freja blushed, bent the bobby pin back into shape and pushed it into her messy hair. 'I miss Clementine,' she whispered. 'I just wanted to —'

'Yoo-hoo! *Ciao!*' A woman's voice, Italian, called from the other room. 'Have you forgotten me, Signore Appleby?'

'*Sì! Sì!*' cried Tobias, running back into the living room. 'I *had* forgotten you! Completely and utterly!'

Freja crept to the door and peeped out. The guest was Nonna Rosa Esposito. Nonna Rosa and her husband, Enzo, ran Trattoria Famiglia, a nearby restaurant where the girl, the dog and the writer sometimes dined.

Nonna Rosa was old, short and plump. She had dark, soft eyes and grey hair pulled back into a bun. She stood inside the front door to their apartment, her hands folded across her white apron.

'I forgot all about you, dear Nonna Rosa!' cried Tobias. 'You see, I am terribly absent-minded! Just yesterday, I made a pot of tea with oregano instead of tea leaves. And this morning, I washed my hair with toilet cleaner. It stung my eyes *dreadfully*, but I do think my noggin is looking very clean!' He smiled and pointed to his hair, which looked as much like an overgrown mop as ever.

'*Sì! Sì!*' Nonna Rosa chuckled. 'Absent-minded. It is because you are the writer. Writers are always — how do you English speak it? Bunkers.'

'Bonkers,' said Freja, then she blushed because she had spoken so loudly.

'Ah, *bella bambina*!' Nonna Rosa smiled, her eyes twinkling at the sight of Freja, who was dressed in red from head to toe — red skivvy, red skirt, red jumper, red tights and red gumboots. Sprigs of red berries dangled and danced around the hem of her skirt.

'I have come to see if you would like to visit for the morning,' the old woman said.

'Alone?' Freja whispered.

'No,' said Nonna Rosa. 'The big, hairy dog will come too.'

'Woof!' Finnegan leapt to his feet and wagged his tail. Nonna Rosa was a good sort who always had a bowl of ravioli or a soup bone for a hungry hound.

Freja looked to Tobias for guidance, but he was staring at the ceiling, scratching his head with the point of his pencil. He'd already drifted away into the pages of his story writing. She looked back to Nonna Rosa.

'Enzo is driving me crazy!' cried Nonna Rosa, throwing her hands in the air. 'He is so lazy. All day long, he slouches behind the bar, talking, talking, talking with his silly old friends. I need someone sensible to keep me company ... someone to stop me from hitting him over the head with my frying pan.' Her words were harsh, but her eyes were soft and smiling.

Freja took a deep breath. *Be brave*, she told herself. *For Clementine ... For Tobias.* Nodding, she took Nonna Rosa's plump, warm hand and left the apartment. Finnegan was right by her side, grinning and dribbling.

Trattoria Famiglia was dark, cluttered and cosy. It felt more like Nonna Rosa's own dining room than a restaurant. The walls were hung with photos of her children and grandchildren and an enormous painting of the Pope. The beams across the ceiling were draped with bunches of plastic grapes, strings of fairy lights and clumps of real garlic.

'Pah!' grumbled Nonna Rosa, flapping her hand towards the bar. Enzo and his friends were drinking grappa, even though it was only ten in the morning.

Enzo was old, short and wide, just like Nonna Rosa. He had dark, merry eyes and fluffy grey eyebrows. The top of his head was bald and shiny, but grey hair grew in a frazzled fuzz around the sides of his head. As Freja walked by, he smiled and lifted his glass. '*Bella* Freja! *Buongiorno!* You are looking splendid today! Like a rosy red apple.'

Four old men turned on their stools, smiling. They all lifted their glasses and greeted Freja warmly.

'*Buongiorno!*'

'*Ciao! Ciao!*'

'Hello, beautiful girl.'

'*Ciao, bella.*'

But by the time they'd finished their greetings and drunk a toast to the beautiful child, she had vanished.

Overwhelmed by the rush of attention, Freja had crawled into a sheltered nook beneath one of the tables. She regretted it immediately and might have crept back out except that Finnegan had followed her, blocking her path.

'Nonna Rosa will be cross,' Freja whispered.

The dog licked her nose.

'At least *you* love me,' she sighed.

The dog licked her face all over, starting at her chin and working his way up to her forehead. He finished off with a deep, probing slurp to her ear.

Freja smiled. Finnegan always knew how to make her feel better. She lifted the edge of the tablecloth, stuck her head out and whispered, 'Psst. I'm sorry for hiding, Nonna Rosa. I got a fright.'

Nonna Rosa shrugged. 'Poor little *bambina*!' she shouted. 'I don't blame you. Five ghoulish old men. They are a terrible thing to see. I would be hiding beneath the table with you, *bella*. If only I was not so fat. If only my old bones were not so stiff.'

She stomped towards the kitchen, tossing a second scoffing 'Pah!' over her shoulder at Enzo and his friends.

Freja and Finnegan crawled out of hiding and slipped through the door behind her.

For three hours, Nonna Rosa and Freja worked quietly side by side, chopping vegetables for soup, stuffing figs with mascarpone, kneading bread dough and making fresh pasta. Nonna Rosa gave few instructions, but taught a great deal. Freja watched and copied, and when she needed a little more help, Nonna Rosa used her plump, old hands to guide Freja's in the way they should move.

'We cook with our eyes and nose and mouth and these,' said Nonna Rosa, wriggling her fingers in the air. 'The recipes are not so important — you can read them or make them up! The secret to cooking something delicious is choosing the best ingredients and touching the food in just the right way.'

Freja held up ten long, flat strips of freshly made fettuccine.

Nonna Rosa pressed her fingertips to her mouth and made a kiss. '*Bellissimo*, Freja! That is the most delicate fettuccine I have ever seen. Tonight, when my customers eat their fettuccine Alfredo, they will think they have stepped into the finest restaurant in Rome! You already have a good touch with your clever little hands.'

Freja smiled and draped the pasta over a rod that hung along the kitchen wall especially for this purpose. She wiped flour off the tip of her nose and giggled as Finnegan licked his way across the tiles, from one side of the kitchen to the other.

'Now,' said Nonna Rosa, 'I must take you home to the crazy writer before he misses you.'

This time, Nonna Rosa kept a reassuring grip on Freja's hand as they walked back into the restaurant. The old men were still sitting where they had left them three hours ago, laughing and slapping their knobbly hands on the bar.

'Look at them!' scoffed Nonna Rosa. 'Four silly old men perched on their stools, drinking grappa, eating walnuts and figs. Like a row of fat squirrels lined up on the branch of an oak tree. Useless! They think they are all so clever and amusing. If they were so wonderful to be around, their wives would not be sending them out, day after day, to *my* trattoria. The only time they go home is to eat their suppers and sleep. It's not fair, Freja. It's a cruel, cruel joke on poor, tired Nonna Rosa.'

'Don't listen to the old bat!' said Enzo. 'She's just cross because she has no friends and I have many. She's too grumpy. Gives too many orders. Nobody likes a bossy old goose.'

'I like her,' whispered Freja, pressing closer in to Nonna Rosa and her wide skirt.

Enzo tossed his tea towel over his shoulder. 'Of course *you* like Nonna Rosa!' he cried. 'That's because you are an angel. Just look at your golden hair — a halo of goodness. You are sent here today by God himself, to keep my nagging wife happy and to be her friend when no-one else will give the old bat the time of day.'

Nonna Rosa grabbed a breadstick from the nearest table and threw it at Enzo. He ducked behind the bar. The breadstick ricocheted off a bottle of wine and fell to the floor.

'Woof!' Finnegan pounced on it and gobbled it up.

The old men roared with laughter, rocking back and forth, clutching at one another's arms to keep themselves from falling off their stools.

Slowly, cautiously, Enzo popped up from behind the bar. He slapped his hand on the counter, shouted, *'Pazza nonna!* Crazy grandmother!' then burst into laughter.

And then Nonna Rosa and Freja joined in, laughing until tears ran down their cheeks.

CHAPTER 17

Books and dreams and nightmares

The next morning, the girl, the dog and the writer ran through the streets of Rome — boots clomping, tail wagging, map flapping. The bells of a dozen churches rang out across the terracotta rooftops. Ten o'clock!

'This is it, Tobias!' Freja looked at her map, gazed up at the pink building, then stared back along the narrow cobbled street. 'There's no sign, but this has to be it! Quick, or you'll be late.'

Squashing the map into her pocket, she pushed open the door. Orange paint flaked and crumbled through her fingers, falling onto the worn timber floor. She swept it away with the toe of her boot and crept inside. Finnegan and Tobias followed.

The large purple room in which they found themselves was bare, except for a crystal chandelier hanging from the ceiling. The scent of roses and dust loitered in the air. A cockroach scuttled across the floorboards and disappeared into a crack in the wall.

Freja looked back over her shoulder to see if, perhaps, they had entered the wrong building. Was the bookstore they sought on the *other* side of the street? Rome could be tricky to navigate — all those wonky alleyways, ancient ruins and slapdash maps.

An exotic bird swooped out of the darkness. It glided towards them, growing larger and larger, until Freja realised that it was, in fact, a woman. She was dressed in a silk kaftan of purple, pink and red. Snowy white hair hung to her waist. Her lips and fingernails were bright orange, and her arms jangled with dozens of silver bangles and beaded bracelets.

'Welcome! Welcome!' sang the woman in a voice as light and floaty as her kaftan. 'I am Delfina Eloisa Ventimiglia and this is my fabulous Libri e Sogni.'

'Libri e Sogni,' whispered Freja.

'Books and Dreams,' sighed Delfina Eloisa. 'But it sounds *so* much better in Italian.'

Freja looked around the bare space once more. *This*, she thought, *must be the room for dreams*.

Tobias stepped forward and introduced himself. 'Tobias Appleby, author of *Rome's Reward*.' He shook Delfina Eloisa's hand so that her bangles and teeth rattled in equal measure.

'Freja Peachtree,' whispered Freja.

'Woof!' said Finnegan.

'We are *all* here,' said Delfina Eloisa, sweeping her arm wide as if to indicate the empty room. 'We have been waiting eagerly for your arrival. We are very excited. Your last book, *A Mousetrap in Moscow*, was on my bestseller list for seven weeks. We *adore* a bit of crime here in Rome!'

Freja tugged at Tobias' cardigan sleeve. He bent down to listen.

'Is she bonkers?' whispered Freja. 'Is her store all dreams and no books?'

Tobias pulled at his ear and replied, 'Perhaps, old chap. She seems to be waving at imaginary readers. And I can't see a single book no matter how hard I strain my eyes.'

'Boof!' Finnegan bolted across the room and disappeared through a doorway, chasing after something which neither Freja nor Tobias had seen.

Freja's neck started to prickle. 'Finnegan?' she whimpered.

'Ah,' sighed Delfina Eloisa. 'He has seen Eufemia.'

'Eufemia?' Freja's shyness vanished in the face of her growing suspicions. 'Is Eufemia a dream? A figment of your imagination? A ... a *ghost*?'

Delfina Eloisa threw back her head and cackled. She spun lightly on her toes and floated through the doorway, calling over her shoulder, 'Come. Follow me and see the books and your fans and Eufemia.'

They drifted down a long, dark corridor, Freja

clutching Tobias' hand all the way, until they stepped through a pair of heavy velvet curtains.

'Thank goodness!' cried Freja. She smiled up at Tobias, relieved that they were, in fact, in a real bookstore, not a crazy hall of dreams and ghosts. Rome's delicious winter sunlight flooded down through a glass ceiling and fell upon thousands and thousands of books. There were books crammed into shelves, books covering the tops of tables, books spilling out of chests of drawers and books tottering in seemingly random piles all over the floor. It looked like a book sprouted and grew wherever a word was spoken, a story told, an idea born.

Squashed into the remaining spaces was a hodgepodge of sofas and armchairs — crimson, purple and orange. Every seat was occupied and, as they made their way further into this remarkable room, a spontaneous round of applause broke out.

'Ta-da!' sang Delfina Eloisa. 'See! See! They are very real, your fans. And very glad to see you.'

Tobias blushed and bowed. He dashed into the middle of the room, shaking hands and kissing cheeks. People spoke in rapid Italian and, although Tobias barely understood a word, he responded loudly and enthusiastically: '*Grazie! Grazie!* Sensational to be here. I adore Rome. Love raspberry gelato. What a magnificent nose you have there — white and lumpy like a blob of overcooked gnocchi! No! No! I haven't been to the Vatican this time. I've been there before, but haven't had the chance since returning to Rome. *Sì! Sì!* The pigeons drive me crazy.'

Freja ducked beneath one of the book-laden tables where she could avoid attention, but still see what was happening in most of the room. She was just making herself comfortable when she felt a gentle nudge in her back. Turning around, she found herself nose to nose with an Italian greyhound. She was tiny, black, skinny and ever so elegant. Beside her was Finnegan.

'You must be Eufemia,' whispered Freja. 'Pleased to meet you.'

Eufemia trembled from head to paw, but flicked her tongue across Freja's nose in greeting.

'Thank you,' said Freja. 'I know that took a lot of courage. I feel exactly the same way myself most of the time. I want to be friendly and to fit in, you see, but it's really scary. People are so complicated and I make such a mess of things. Animals are so much easier —'

'Woof!' interrupted Finnegan.

Eufemia turned her back on Freja and the two dogs lay down. Eufemia licked Finnegan's front paw gently, delicately, with her small pink tongue. Finnegan grinned, dribbled on her head, then licked the saliva off with one swipe of his enormous tongue.

Freja smiled and turned her attention back to the room. Tobias was still working his way around the crowd, springing from person to person. 'Impressive shoes you have there, *signorina* — as green as slime and as large as two canoes. And you, *signore*, look just like the crazy archaeologist in my first novel, *Three Cursed Pharaohs*! Doctor Harmony is as mad as a meat axe and your eyes have the same wild glint as his. Marvellous! Stupendous! Quite exciting to see in real life … although I'm not sure that I'd like to meet you in a dark alley at night-time!'

The poor man was gobsmacked.

Switching from English to Italian, Tobias babbled on with a string of nonsense: '*Lasagne ravioli spaghetti!*' he cried, sweeping his arms so wide that he knocked a pile of books and a stuffed pheasant to the floor. Unhampered by embarrassment, he continued singing out to the room: '*Scusa panini bambino gelati! Sì! Sì! Magnifico!*'

The Italians erupted into laughter.

'They love him,' whispered Freja. 'They love his craziness, his boldness, his energy, his silliness. But most of all, I think they love his kindness. He tries to please, even when he knows he'll get it wrong.' Freja thought about this for a moment. 'He's brave-kind,' she concluded and decided to remember the phrase. Perhaps it could help her. After all, what was the worst that could happen?

She thought of Mrs Thompson, the walrus in powder-blue slippers. She thought of the gossiping women in the library in Little Coddling. She shivered. But then she remembered Tobias soldiering on, even when Mrs Indira threw an orange at him.

'Brave-kind forges ahead even when others are mean,' she whispered. 'Even when the world is scary.' She reached into her pocket and found the tiny felt hare. 'The leverets' mother was brave-kind.'

The laughter died down. Delfina Eloisa Ventimiglia took Tobias by the elbow and ushered him to the front of the room. 'You, Signore Appleby, speak English,' she advised. 'I will translate to ensure that everything makes sense.'

Tobias wiped his hand across his brow and nodded. He picked up a copy of *Rome's Reward* and opened to the first chapter. He cleared his throat, took a deep breath and began: 'Crime —'

But at that very moment the heavy velvet curtains were whipped apart with a *swoosh* and into the room strode another customer. From beneath the table, Freja could only see his legs and feet. He had fine black leather shoes, polished to a shine. They looked expensive.

A rich man! thought Freja. She smiled, glad for Tobias, because such a customer might buy lots of books.

Delfina Eloisa floated towards the new guest, speaking melodic Italian, a greeting. But he ignored her. The feet turned towards Tobias, and a voice, Italian, deep and menacing, said, 'I know who you are, *signore*, and what it is you are doing!'

Freja's neck and shoulders prickled. She had heard those exact words before.

Crawling out from beneath the table, she peeped over the back of one of the chairs. It was Padre Paolo, the priest from the Trevi Fountain! She could only see the back of him, but she was sure. He had broad shoulders that strained against his black robe and the same square black hat with a pompom on top.

Tobias looked confused rather than scared. 'Well, of *course* you know who I am,' he said jovially. 'My name and photo are on the cover of at least fifty copies of my book, just over there!' He pointed towards the stack of books and, in so doing, caught Freja's eye. He shook his head, ever so slightly, and Freja bobbed down a little lower.

Finnegan, sensing Freja's fear, crept to her side. He growled softly, deeply.

'Furthermore,' said Tobias, 'you would be a real *dill* not to know what I am doing. We're in a bookstore and I am going to tell these lovely people all about my work. How I came up with the ideas before I put pen and ink to paper. How I researched all the gruesome details about blood and guts and explosions and severed body parts.'

Delfina Eloisa translated these last words and the audience chuckled. The priest, however, seethed.

'Uh-oh,' said Freja.

'Grrrr,' rumbled Finnegan.

'*Imbecille!*' snarled the priest. He pulled himself up to his full height, towering over Tobias. He held up his right hand and flexed his fingers.

This time, however, Tobias didn't wait to be grabbed. He sprang to the left, shouted, '*Grazie! Grazie! Arrivederci!*' and disappeared between the curtains.

Padre Paolo chased after him.

The audience gasped, then, one by one, rose to their feet and clapped.

'*Magnifico!*'

'*Drammatico!*'

'*Classico!*'

'Oh no,' cried Freja. 'They think it's some sort of performance, a scene from one of Tobias' novels.'

She jumped up from behind the chair and ran into the middle of the bookstore. 'No! No!' she shouted, waving her hands in the air. 'Don't cheer! It's real. The priest is angry because of the ink and Mother Superior Evangelista and the mess all over her habit.'

But even as she spoke, she knew that it made no sense to them. It barely made sense to her! Already the customers were trotting towards the trays of sweet treats — *cannoli*, *zeppole* and *cornetti*.

Freja bit her quivering lip, took a deep breath and beckoned for Finnegan. Together, they dashed from the bookstore, scrambled along the dark hallway, ran through the dusty dream room and tumbled out into the street. A Vespa zoomed by. Freja jumped back, pressing her body against the wall. Her heart thumped, her legs shook and her mind raced as she wondered what to do.

Finnegan paced back and forth, sniffing at the road. He barked, nipped at Freja's sleeve and bolted down the street. Freja slapped the palms of her hands against the wall and took off after him. She ran and ran, ducking in between people, stumbling over cobblestones, knocking gelato out of hands, apologising and all the while craning her neck to keep Finnegan in sight. It was easier to see once she reached the enormous, open space of Piazza Navona. It was long and wide, as big as three football fields placed end to end.

'Wow!' gasped Freja, slowing to a walk. 'Amazing!' She smiled as her gaze drifted around the piazza, taking in churches, palaces, apartment buildings, cafés and no less than *three* magnificent fountains.

But her heart sank when she spotted Tobias. He was running like an athlete, his long legs making great strides, but Padre Paolo was still in pursuit. Tobias stopped for a moment, ran his fingers through his mop of hair, then dashed around the nearest fountain, the Fountain of Neptune. The priest followed.

Freja stopped walking. She blinked, then gaped at the sculpture in the middle of the fountain. Neptune, Roman god of the sea, was wrestling with a giant octopus. He held his spear aloft, ready to kill. Fury filled his marble face. He looked like the angriest man on earth. *He looks*, Freja thought with a shudder, *like the priest.*

'*Idiota!*' Padre Paolo bellowed, slapping the back of one hand into the palm of the other.

Tobias had taken them on two full loops of the fountain and now they were back where they had started. All that separated them was the shallow water of Neptune's pool and a few marble figures — a mermaid, some seahorses and two fat, naked babies.

'It's not enough,' whispered Freja as she watched from a distance. '*Anyone* can leap over a fat, naked baby.'

Tobias hesitated for a moment. He tugged at his ear and looked from one side of the piazza to the other. There was nowhere to hide. No alleyway down which to duck and dodge and lose an enemy. No tour groups into which he could blend and vanish. Rome, normally so crowded and bustling, seemed strangely empty. Except for a nearby flock of pigeons. There were dozens of them, waddling hither and thither, pecking at a pile of breadcrumbs.

'Finnegan,' gasped Freja. 'We have to do something.'

But a waiter had dropped a calzone at a nearby café and the dog was lolloping towards it, leaving a trail of drool as he went.

Tobias pushed up his cardigan sleeves.

He stretched his neck, tilting his head to the left then the right.

He blew his nose.

The priest, confused, took a step forward, then retreated once more. He crouched low, muscles tensed, ready for action.

'Come on! Last chance, Padre Paolo!' taunted Tobias.

And he ran.

He ran. He galloped. He bounced. Straight through the flock of pigeons, waving his arms, shouting stupidly, 'SHOO! SHOO! SHOO! SHOO! SHOO!'

Feathers and confusion burst through the air. Hundreds of fat green-and-grey birds flew up around him, flapping, cooing, slapping each other with their wings. Padre Paolo followed Tobias into the feathery fold, but a pigeon slammed into his face. *THWACK!* He stumbled, cursed, swept the stunned bird aside and regained his balance.

A tiny green three-wheeled truck zoomed across the piazza. It drove straight through the flock of befuddled pigeons and Tobias leapt onto the back of it. He crashed amidst ropes, shovels and buckets of sand.

'Hooray! Hoorah!' Freja jumped up and down, clapping. 'Well done, Tobias! Hooray!'

The truck zipped away, across the open expanse of cobblestones to the centre of Piazza Navona. It disappeared behind the Fountain of the Four Rivers, a formidable structure of giants and rocks and sea creatures and gushing waters and a towering obelisk.

The priest stopped and waved his fist in the air. Then, conceding defeat, he flopped forward, hands on his knees, breathing heavily.

Finnegan trotted to Freja's side, licking the last cheesy traces of calzone from his lips.

'It's okay,' said Freja, resting her hand on his neck. 'Tobias is safe now.'

But she had barely spoken the words when the little green truck appeared around the other side of the fountain. It had done a complete loop and was now heading straight back towards them!

Slowly, Padre Paolo straightened up. He held his fists clamped at his sides and waited as the truck approached.

Freja's bottom lip began to quiver. 'How bad can it be?' she murmured. 'He'll probably give Tobias a good shake and tell him to keep the lid screwed on his ink bottle in future.'

The truck zipped by and the priest jumped aboard just as it turned out of the piazza. It gathered speed and disappeared into the distance.

Freja sniffed. She shuffled over to the Fountain of Neptune. She sat down on the cold marble edge. She didn't look at the mermaids or the seahorses, even though they were dancing joyfully through the water, just begging to be noticed. She didn't laugh at the pigeons as they landed at her feet and began to bob and gossip like the old men in Trattoria Famiglia. She did not even hum along with the bells as they chimed out from the Church of Sant'Agnese in Agone. In the past, she had thought the church bells of Rome beautiful, celebratory. But now they were the knells of defeat. Every dong sounded like another thump to Tobias' poor head.

'Woof!' said Finnegan, nudging her shoulder with his nose.

'I know,' sighed Freja. She stood up, ready to drag her feet home. 'At least I have a bobby pin in my hair. We can get into the apartment without Tobias and the key.'

'Woof! Boof!' said Finnegan. He nipped at Freja's elbow and trotted away towards the middle of Piazza Navona and the Fountain of the Four Rivers.

Freja followed wearily. 'Come back, puppy. We have to go home, in case Tobias —'

But Finnegan was now galloping, his tongue flapping out the side of his mouth. On reaching the giant fountain, he leapt up onto the marble edging, barked and belly-flopped into the water.

'Silly hound.' Freja sighed. 'We're in the middle of a disaster and all you can think of is taking a swim.'

But when Finnegan's head popped up over the edge of the pool, it was joined by another. This head was wet and bedraggled, but delightfully familiar.

Freja ran across the piazza, shouting and waving her arms. 'Tobby! Tobby! Tobby!' She didn't care that people were staring, laughing, pointing. Arriving at the fountain, she jumped up and down, blowing kisses across the water to Tobias. 'I thought he got you. I imagined all sorts of dreadful things. A bloody nose. A black eye. A lump on your forehead. A missing tooth right at the front of your mouth so that when you said "raspberry gelato", you would lisp and say "rathperry delato"! But here you are with your kind face and your twinkling green eyes and ... *and your pencil still tucked behind your ear!*'

The pencil was too much. Freja clasped her hands to her face, her mouth wobbled and she burst into loud, heaving sobs.

CHAPTER 18
To market, to market

'*Buongiorno!* Lovely morning for a swim!'

Freja peeped through her fingers and saw a pretty young woman dressed in white jeans, a pale pink sweater and a lemon-yellow beanie.

'Vivi!' cried Freja, wiping tears from her cheeks.

'Raspberry gelato!' sighed Tobias. His arms and head lolled over the edge of the fountain towards Vivi while the rest of his body floated in the water. He kicked his feet slowly up and down, and his grin grew wider and wider.

Finnegan ran a full lap of the pool, snapping at the water that tumbled down from the fountain.

Vivi threw back her head and laughed.

Freja shivered.

'You're cold, *bella*,' said Vivi. Taking a shawl from her shopping basket, Vivi wrapped it around Freja's shoulders, drew her close and rubbed her back. Freja leaned in, cherishing the warm, calming touch after the terrible fright.

'What are you doing here?' whispered Freja.

'Me? I'm on my way to Campo de' Fiori, to the market. My mamma and papà look after Café Vivi a few times a week so I can have a little free time — to walk, eat gelato, drink coffee with friends, shop at the markets.' Vivi paused and frowned at Tobias. 'I think the *greater* mystery is what are *you* doing here?'

Tobias shrugged and pulled himself out of the fountain. Water streamed from his clothes. His cardigan and trousers sagged more than ever, and his shoes squelched rudely with every step.

Finnegan leapt out of the pool and shook the water from his fur.

'I wish I could do that,' muttered Tobias.

Vivi pursed her raspberry-gelato lips and put her hands on her hips. '*Why* are you in the fountain, Signore Appleby?'

Tobias blushed. 'Well, technically, I'm not in the fountain any more.' He pulled the pencil from behind his ear, looked at it and tucked it back again. 'But of course! Of course! I *was* in the fountain … just moments ago … because of a spot of bother with a priest and a nun.'

'And some ink,' added Freja.

'Just a funny misunderstanding.' Tobias chuckled.

'And a little bit scary,' whispered Freja. 'I thought Tobias was going to get his nose broken.'

Vivi frowned, obviously confused, but asked no more.

Tobias peeled off his cardigan, wrung it out, then slung it over his shoulder. He pulled off his shoes, emptied them into the fountain and slipped them back on. Finally, he pulled his trouser pockets inside out and removed the pulpy wads of paper that had once been notes for his novel. 'Okay!' he cried, rolling the paper into a soggy ball. 'Market time. Let's go!'

'Campo de' Fiori means Field of Flowers,' explained Vivi as they walked the few blocks to the market. She was very kind and pretended there was nothing odd about the trail of water that Tobias left behind.

'Sounds beautiful,' sighed Freja, daring to squeeze Vivi's hand. 'I love fields and flowers. Larkspur, poppies, lupins ...'

But when they arrived, Freja realised that Campo de' Fiori was not a field at all, but another bustling city piazza. She dropped Vivi's hand and took a step backward. She stood as still as a granite rock, her eyes roving back and forth. There *were* flowers, but it must have been many centuries since they'd sprouted and bloomed right here on the floodplains of the Tiber River. Now the flowers were cut and sold in bunches at the market stalls. They sat alongside fruit, vegetables, fish, herbs, spices, clothing and souvenirs. And all around them, people bustled, jostled, shouted, poked and stared.

Freja's first instinct was to run. To find a secluded place where she could at least *imagine* herself alone in a field of poppies or lupins. But a small, quiet voice whispered in her head, 'Stop, listen, watch, smell, learn.' Clementine's voice! Her wise and gentle words.

Clementine was always in her thoughts.

Freja swallowed the lump in her throat. 'This is just like any other noisy gathering of animals,' she said to herself. 'A colony of penguins, a herd of reindeer, a flock of geese. Grunts, squawks, colour, energy, strange smells, artichokes.' She stopped and scratched her nose. 'Well, perhaps the artichokes are different ... but that's all right. Clementine would tell me to notice the differences. Learn something new from them.'

Freja wrapped her fingers around the felt hare in her pocket and whispered, 'Come on, little leveret. Let's be brave!' She stepped forward into the market.

Just metres away, a stout woman with a black apron and headscarf was arguing with a man selling chickens. Both were shouting, waving their arms, rolling their eyes and slapping the table. Just when Freja thought they might come to blows, they threw back their heads and laughed with as much passion as they had just argued. The woman bought *three* large chickens, kissed the man twice on each cheek and trotted off through the crowds.

Crazy, thought Freja. *They've just shouted their heads off at each other and they're still friends.*

A group of six nuns flocked to a stall that was selling cut-price footwear. Freja watched, open mouthed, as each and every one of the nuns pulled their skirt up around their knees, kicked off their black leather boots and slipped on a new pair of white sandshoes. Together, they bounced up and down on their toes, jogged on the spot and sprang from side to side, their pale blue habits flapping merrily about them. One of the nuns shouted, '*Attenzione!*' She bowed, held her old, worn boots aloft in the air, then tossed them into a rubbish crate. Her companions gasped, then cheered as the boots disappeared amidst soggy lettuce leaves, newspapers and fish heads. One by one, they followed her lead, tossing their own boots in the rubbish. Finally, they skipped away, laughing and clucking over their comfortable new shoes.

'That's sweet,' said Freja, feeling a slight ache in her chest. 'Look, Finnegan. Shared joy!'

But Finnegan wasn't listening. A small boy had come to a standstill right in front of them … and he was holding a big, fat cheese-and-salami *panino* in his hand.

'Woof! Boof!' said the dog, drooling.

'Finnegan,' snapped Freja. 'You *mustn't!*' But it was too late. The *panino* was gone and the dog was licking his chops.

The child howled and pointed, but his grandmother didn't understand. She swept the boy into her arms, showered his soft brown curls with kisses and whisked him away to a sweets stall. There, a white paper bag filled with *torrone*, soft Italian nougat, was pressed into the child's chubby hands. The tears stopped.

Freja laughed at a family of American tourists as they rushed from one souvenir stall to the next, buying plastic gladiator helmets, plates with pictures of the Pope and salad bowls shaped like the Colosseum. She watched, wide eyed, as a man stole a whole watermelon from a fruit stall and stuffed it up his jumper. And she gave a little squeak of delight as Giuseppe walked by, pushing his wagon with the beautiful pipe organ. Pazzo the monkey lounged across it, eating a bunch of grapes. On spying Freja, he leapt to his feet, danced up and down and blew her a kiss.

'*Buongiorno, bella!*' Giuseppe waved at her over his shoulder until the crowds swallowed them up.

'This really is rather fun,' said Freja. 'Market time at Campo de' Fiori is almost as entertaining as seeing bear cubs learning to catch salmon ... or Tobias acting out the next scene for his novel when he thinks nobody is watching. I'll describe it all in my next letter to Clementine.'

Finnegan grinned and dribbled on Freja's shoe.

'Ah, *bellissimo*!' cried Vivi, her voice ringing out above the babble. 'Freja, come here! Look at these tomatoes! Big and round and red. And still warm from sitting in the sun. And radishes, endives, onions, pink potatoes. Pink potatoes are much, much prettier than the white ones, don't you think?'

Vivi ran her fingers across the piles of produce like a musician fondling the keys of a piano. She nodded and murmured her delight. 'Uh-hum ... mmmm ... *sì, sì ... bella ...*' She squeezed and poked vegetables. She smiled. She spoke rapid, joyful Italian to the woman behind the table and her shopping basket started to fill.

Silently, Tobias took the basket from her arm. Vivi nodded her thanks, but neither of them spoke.

Freja stared and blushed. There was something here in the silent language of eyes and mouths, shoulders and hands, which she understood.

Vivi flitted to the next market stall, this time delighting in fruit. She smelt grapes, plums, peaches and oranges, her mouth pressed into a little pucker, her brow wrinkled with concentration.

Tobias grabbed a passionfruit and clutched it tightly in his hand. He tossed it into the air a few times. 'Do you think,' he asked, 'that a passionfruit could break a window? Or knock a grown man senseless? I mean, if one was feeling malicious and threw it *really* hard ...'

Vivi's eyebrows shot upward. She took the passionfruit from his hand and passed him a bunch of dark purple grapes instead. 'Smell these!' she demanded.

Tobias, eager to oblige, sniffed so hard that a small grape disappeared up his nostril. He gasped, coughed, dropped the shopping basket and staggered about. His wet shoes squelched and squeaked. His arms flapped and flailed, becoming entangled in strings of chillies and plaits of garlic. Finally, he snorted the grape from his nose and it rolled away across the cobblestones.

Freja giggled.

Finnegan chased after the grape and ate it.

'*Scusa, scusa!* So very sorry!' Vivi smiled and shrugged at everyone who'd been watching. She paid for the grapes, then whisked the girl, the dog and the writer away.

At the next stall, Vivi tasted berries, patted grapefruit, held oranges up to the sunlight and tore mandarins apart and inspected their flesh. And again, she sniffed everything. Deeply. Reverently.

'I'd rather *eat* the fruit,' Freja whispered to Finnegan. But just to see what all the fuss was about, she picked up a lemon and sniffed. 'Oooh!' A tingle of pleasure passed from her nose to her mouth, then spread across her entire body. 'It smells of sunshine! Sunshine ... steep hillsides ... and the sea sparkling on a bright blue summer's day!'

'Ah!' Vivi's eyes softened and she nodded to the man behind the stall. 'My little English friend has an Italian heart, I think!'

My little English friend. Was that how Vivi saw her? A friend?

Freja beamed.

Vivi took the lemon and lifted it up to her face. Closing her eyes, she sniffed, raised her eyebrows and exhaled. '*Delizioso!*' she sang, her eyes springing open. 'I will take a dozen of them and make a special lemon tart. And you, Freja, the English girl with the Italian heart, must come for lunch tomorrow and taste it. And you too, Signore Appleby.'

Vivi purchased the lemons and popped them in her basket. '*Ciao!*' she sang, and she was gone.

'Lunch tomorrow,' echoed Tobias. He grinned after her and leaned back against a crate of artichokes, toppling the lot.

'Tobby!' squealed Freja, and she chased after them. An elderly priest stopped to help and, together, they crawled around the cobblestones, laughing and rounding up the strange lumpy vegetables.

'Oh no!' cried Freja when they were done. 'Sorry, *padre*, all that crawling has worn a hole in the toe of your shoe!'

'No! No!' The priest chuckled. 'My shoes are always this way. To match my robe!' He pointed to several patches on his garment, then stuck his finger right through a hole in his sleeve.

Finnegan licked the finger where it poked through.

The priest smiled and nodded. '*Arrivederci*, my friend!' He trotted away, a long, thin thread trailing happily from the hem of his robe.

'Tatters and patches and holes in his holes,' whispered Freja. She giggled, then stopped.

Something poked at the back of her mind.

Something important.

Something confusing.

'Come along, old chap.' Tobias stood before her. 'Time to go. Lunch on the balcony today, I think. Sunshine. Fresh air. I have a spiffing loaf of bread here, as well as some tomatoes, cheese and prosciutto. Well, it's ham really, but it sounds much better when you call it prosciutto. And look! The crust on the bread is as tough as a crocodile's skin!' He knocked three times on the loaf and smiled as though it was the most remarkable thing he had ever seen.

'Woof!' said Finnegan, and he bounded after Tobias and the bread.

And Freja followed, leaving the confusing thoughts amidst the pink potatoes, the lemons and the artichokes.

CHAPTER 19

Jam ravioli

That evening, Freja stood at the kitchen table, a haze of flour dust hanging in the air. Her sleeves were pushed up around her elbows and a piece of eggshell dangled from one of her curls. The backs of all four chairs were draped with fine, long strips of fettuccine. The carved wooden seal sat amidst a pile of pasta scraps and the felt hare lay on top of a jam jar.

'We cook with our eyes and nose and mouth and these,' Freja said, wriggling her floury fingers. She giggled, satisfied that she had perfectly mimicked Nonna Rosa's croaky Italian accent. Cracking another egg, Freja used her fingertips to blend it with the mound of flour on the table. Then she worked the whole into a round of smooth, silky pasta dough.

She skipped to the kitchen door and stuck her head into the living room. 'I'm nearly finished the last batch of pasta. We can leave it out to dry overnight, then cook it tomorrow, if you like?'

'Uh-huh,' muttered Tobias, not really listening. He was standing in front of the desk, scratching his head with a nib pen. Red ink dripped from its point and ran down his forehead. He looked like he'd just received a nasty blow to the head.

'I hope it washes off,' whispered Freja, and she returned to her pasta-making.

Finnegan was working his way, slowly but surely, through the contents of the kitchen bin. So far, this evening, Freja had seen him eat a dry knob of bread, a fish head, two rejected pages of Tobias' manuscript, a tissue, a cockroach and three rotten figs. Now he was chewing a pork sausage covered in ants. The ants were obviously annoyed at the idea of being eaten and kept escaping his mouth and biting his lips. Finnegan thrashed around the kitchen, shaking his head, swiping his nose with his front paws and banging into the cupboard doors. A carton of milk toppled over on the bench and milk dribbled onto the floor, so once the dog had rid himself of the last pesky ant, he slurped that up too.

'Now, what to make next ...' Freja stared at her ball of pasta dough. 'I know! Arctic animal ravioli!' She rolled the pasta into a thin sheet, then used the tip of a knife to cut out a seal, a hare and a moose. She stepped back to survey the shapes.

'Hmmm,' she murmured, hands on hips. 'The seal

and the hare look just fine. But the moose looks blobby. I need a picture to copy.'

Finnegan licked some flour from behind her knee. Freja giggled and slipped into the living room.

'Tobias!' she gasped. '*What* are you doing?'

But the writer did not answer. He was standing on his desk, painting an elaborate diagram across the wall of the apartment. In black ink. Except for the bits where he had used red ink. The soft, powdery plaster of the wall absorbed the colour like a sponge soaking up water.

Freja muttered, 'That's not going to scrub off.' She stepped a little closer and realised that Tobias was drawing a kind of story map, including mountain ranges, climbing routes, caves and critical points where attacks, accidents and natural disasters might occur.

'I'm just getting a picture of a moose,' said Freja. Her scrapbook lay on the desk near Tobias' left foot. She reached across and grabbed it.

'Hmmm. Goodo,' murmured Tobias, without looking down. He dipped a fine brush into a pot of black ink and drew a long dotted line from the crest of a mountain right down to the valley below. He put the black ink down on his desk and picked up the pot of red ink. He dipped in a new brush and painted a fat red question mark where the dotted line ended. He tucked the brush behind his ear and stared at the ceiling.

Freja shrugged and returned to her pasta-making once more. She finished cutting out the animal shapes and filled them with jam.

Stepping back, arms folded, she surveyed her handiwork. 'Perfect,' she declared. 'Fettuccine for Tobias and me. Ravioli for Finnegan.'

Freja returned to the living room. 'I'm finished!' she announced. 'It's all ready for cooking tomorrow.'

Tobias wrote a final note on his wall diagram, screwed the lids back on his ink bottles and stuffed them into his pocket. He blinked down at the floury girl and slowly, vaguely, drifted back into the apartment and real life.

'Well done, old chap!' he cried at last. 'Making your own pasta with nothing more than flour and eggs and your wits is quite a feat! We'll make a chef of you yet ... or a magician! In fact, you are so jolly clever, you can probably be whatever you want to be!'

Freja smiled.

Finnegan sauntered into the living room, licking a plug of pasta out of his left nostril. One of his hind feet was stuck in a yoghurt container and made a light clicking noise on the floor tiles. He stopped at Freja's side for a pat, yawned, then stretched out beside the open fire.

Tobias half-leapt, half-slipped from the desk. A pile of journals toppled to the floor. He kicked them aside, flopped on the sofa and patted the seat beside him. 'Time to listen up, old chap!'

Freja sat down, tucking her knees underneath her oversized pinafore — which was really one of Tobias' knitted vests. She wrapped her arms around her legs and smiled, all teeth and sparkling eyes.

Tobias reflected her smile. 'The thing is,' he began, 'we must do something about your schooling.'

'Why?' asked Freja.

'Why?' repeated Tobias. 'Hmmm. Good question. A jolly important one to answer, I suppose. Well, let me see. First of all, there's your future to consider. Whether you want to be a chef or an astronaut —'

'Or a crime writer,' said Freja.

'Yes! Good choice! But then ... well ... Nonna Rosa and Vivi have both asked about your schooling ... and then there's your mother ...'

'But Clementine's not here,' Freja whispered. 'She's in Switzerland.' She could have added 'in the clinic', but she hated to think of such a place. Clementine should be outdoors, sitting on a mountain top watching fawns frolic, standing by the sea watching walruses wallow. And Freja should be with her.

'Hmmm,' agreed Tobias. 'Clementine might not be here with us, but I do think that she is expecting you to do a spot of schooling.'

'Oh, I don't think that matters,' said Freja.

'But education is of paramount importance!' cried Tobias.

'Oh, of course! *Education* is brilliant. I love it.' She frowned. 'It's *schooling* I don't like.'

Tobias ran a hand through his mop of hair and rubbed the back of his neck.

'School is scary,' whispered Freja. She picked at some loose wool at the elbow of Tobias' cardigan.

'I tried it once and I didn't fit in. The other children thought I was odd. I *was* odd. I didn't belong. And if you send me to school now, I still won't fit in.'

Tobias nodded as though he understood.

'I'm not normal,' she whispered.

'Good heavens!' cried Tobias, throwing his hands in the air. His face was filled with horror. 'Of *course* you're not normal! What a ghastly thing to contemplate. No, no, no, no, no! You, old chap, are a wonderfully unique child of great intelligence, astonishing creativity and marvellous appearance. I mean, just look at your hair today. It's like a haystack in a hurricane. Magnificent! Nobody else has anything quite like it.'

A blush spread across Freja's cheeks and the hint of a smile returned to her lips. But the nasty matter of school lingered in the air.

'So school is scary,' said Tobias.

Freja nodded. 'And it's *dull*. How can I possibly learn anything important from making papier-mâché crocodiles out of egg cartons … or growing an onion in a vase of water … or writing a story called "My Life as an Avocado"?'

'Oh dear! How indeed? Is that really what they subject you to in schools these days?'

Freja nodded again, her eyes wide and serious. 'I think it's always been that way.'

Tobias rubbed his chin. 'Hmmm, yes. I seem to recall a similar range of lessons. Although, in my day, we did crayon rubbings of bark, grew wheat in a saucer of damp cotton wool and wrote a story called "My Life as a Turnip". They were simpler times, I suppose — turnips instead of avocados and what not.'

'You see? School is a waste of time,' said Freja. 'There's just no point to it.'

'Well, it does seem that way. It's jolly awful!' Tobias frowned and tugged absent-mindedly at some eggy curls that stuck out from the top of Freja's head. 'But the thing is, old chap, you need an education.'

'But I'm getting one!' Freja replied. 'Why, just this week I have explored half a dozen historic sights, learnt about ancient Roman mythology, read a medical journal on lung failure at high altitudes, made pasta and bread, found my way around the city using a map, visited a bookstore, met a monkey, listened to music, tasted lots of new food and mastered the art of picking a lock with a bobby pin.'

Tobias rubbed his jaw, obviously impressed.

'And there's more,' said Freja. Dashing to the kitchen, she returned with her scrapbook and placed it on Tobias' lap. 'I have filled two whole pages with all the Italian words I now know. I'm afraid there might be a couple of rude ones, but Enzo and his friends don't always remember that I can hear them from Nonna Rosa's kitchen.'

Tobias ran his finger down the neatly written list.

'And then there's this.' Freja turned the page and unfolded a giant piece of paper that stretched from one side of the sofa to the other. A third of the page was covered in a finely drawn map that included buildings, food, people, fountains, parks, stairways and motor scooters.

'It's a map of Rome. I've been drawing it since we arrived. Every time we visit somewhere new, I memorise as many of the details as I can, then when I get home I add them to my map. I try to draw the churches and the fountains and the old Roman ruins just as they are. I've even included the people we've met and the special food we've eaten. Look! There's Nonna Rosa with a bowl of gnocchi. And there's the gelateria where we first tried raspberry gelato. It's like your story map on the wall, except mine's real. It's a type of diary, so Clementine will be able to see all the things I've done.'

Tobias stared at the map, open mouthed. 'It's brilliant, old chap. So much colour and detail and joy! A true work of art. I've never seen anything quite like it!'

'I'm sure there are many more things I've learnt,' said Freja, folding the map back into the scrapbook, 'but I'm too tired to recall them all right now. I *have* just made four chairsful of fettuccine and twelve pieces of jam ravioli in the shape of Arctic animals.'

'Jam ravioli?' asked Tobias.

'Jam ravioli *in the shape of Arctic animals*!' Freja emphasised.

'Impressive!' cried Tobias. 'They won't teach you that at school.'

Freja stared up at him, holding her breath.

'Well, that's sorted then,' Tobias declared.

Freja let out a sigh of relief. Then, quite unexpectedly — for both girl *and* writer — she threw herself at him, wrapping her arms around his neck and planting a kiss on his cheek. 'Thank you,' she whispered. 'Thank you! Thank you! Thank you!'

'Oh, it's nothing, nothing, absolutely nothing,' Tobias babbled, pleased and confused at the same time. 'Now why don't you run along and take a bath? Wash the flour and egg from your face ... and your hair ... and well, frankly, from the rest of you. I'll clean up the kitchen, pull the yoghurt pot from Finnegan's foot and wipe the jam from his ears. Then, when you're done, I'll tuck you into bed and read you a lovely bedtime story.' Tobias dropped to the floor and started rustling around beneath his desk. 'I'll see if I can find that old KGB journal from the Soviet Union. It's all about disguises — how to use them, how to see through them. There's a fascinating story about an American spy. He pretended to be a clown in the Moscow Circus, but made one tragic mistake. The plastic flower that he wore pinned to his braces squirted water three metres further than the Soviet-made water-squirting flowers. Only the Americans made such efficient squirting mechanisms at the time, so it gave him away. He was arrested and thrown into a prison where he had to use a bucket for a toilet and was fed nothing but black bread and water for twenty-seven years. Fascinating stuff. Just the sort of thing I like to read at bedtime.'

'Me too!' agreed Freja, and she skipped away, thinking that Tobias really did have all areas of her education sorted.

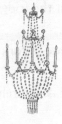

CHAPTER 20

A prayer for Clementine

'*Buongiorno!*' Tobias sang in his merriest Italian accent as Freja walked into the kitchen the next morning.

'Woof! Boof!' said Finnegan from his chair at the head of the table.

'*Buongiorno*, Tobias. *Buongiorno*, Finnegan.' Freja blew a stray curl from her face and sat down beside the dog.

Tobias plonked a bowl of steaming pasta in front of her. '*Buon appetito!*'

Freja leaned forward and inhaled. 'Yum! What is it?'

'Your magnificent fettuccine, of course, with my brilliantly complicated sauce of garlic, parsley and olive oil. As the Italians would say, *fettuccine aglio e olio!*' He flung his arms wide, forgetting that he still held the wooden spoon in one hand. Olive oil and garlic splattered against the fridge, then dribbled down to the floor.

Freja giggled and ate a forkful of fettuccine. 'It's good!'

'Good?' cried Tobias. 'Surely, old chap, it's more than that!'

Freja slurped another mouthful of pasta, chewed slowly and swallowed. 'Mmmm,' she sighed. 'It's delicious. The best *fettuccine aglio e olio* I've ever eaten for breakfast.'

Tobias narrowed his eyes.

'Woof!' Finnegan's large, hairy nose moved closer and closer towards Freja's bowl.

'Yes, yes. Here it comes, young pup!' Tobias clattered around between the stove and sink, then placed a loaded plate before the dog. 'Jam ravioli — *in the shape of Arctic animals* — served with burnt toast!'

'Boof!' said Finnegan.

'You're welcome,' replied Tobias. '*Buon appetito*, hungry houndo!'

Freja said, 'Do you think I should take some fettuccine down to Nonna Rosa and Enzo?'

'Spiffing idea!' cried Tobias. 'And I'll just do a spot of work on my novel while you're there. Maybe add to my story map on the wall. Perhaps read a little about how to stitch up one's own wounds after a nasty fall down a rock face.' He stared at the ceiling for a moment, tossed a saucepan into the sink, then disappeared into the living room. Within minutes, Freja could hear the typewriter clacking away and the writer mumbling to himself about blood, gashes, lesions, protruding flesh and the antiseptic properties of urine.

'Urine!' moaned Freja, pushing her bowl aside. 'I think I've had enough breakfast for now.'

'Woof!' replied Finnegan, and he gobbled her pasta before she could change her mind.

***

Freja crept into Trattoria Famiglia. '*Buongiorno*,' she whispered.

Enzo must have just told a very funny story because the old men at the bar were roaring with laughter, their shoulders shaking, their heads bobbing up and down. Edmondo slapped Xaviero's back so hard that his glasses fell off. This sent the old men into a fresh spasm of laughter, and Freja and Finnegan were able to slip by, unnoticed, into Nonna Rosa's kitchen.

'Freja!' cried Nonna Rosa. She waved a floury hand over the mound of dough she was kneading. 'Little angel! How beautiful it is to see you.'

'Woof!' said Finnegan.

'*Sì! Sì!*' Nonna Rosa rolled her eyes. 'It is good to see you too, you big, hairy lump!'

Freja held forth her bowl of *fettuccine aglio e olio*. 'For you, Nonna Rosa. I made the pasta just like you said. I asked my fingers to listen to the eggs and the flour, and they really did seem to get along just fine!'

Nonna Rosa wiped her hands on her apron. She took the bowl and gazed at it, nodding slowly. She grabbed a fork from the drawer, dug it deep down into the bowl and twisted it around and around until it held an impossibly large swirl of fettuccine. Opening her mouth wide, she shoved it all in at once.

'Mmm-mmm-mmm-*mmm*!' Nonna Rosa closed her eyes as she chewed. She swallowed with a noisy, theatrical gulp, then slammed the bowl onto the bench. Grabbing Freja's face in her hands, she kissed both cheeks with gusto. '*Mwah! Mwah!*' She smiled, then kissed each cheek once more!

'Clever *bambina*!' she cooed. 'It makes Nonna Rosa's tired old heart sing to taste such perfect pasta. You have learnt so quickly. I think you have Italian fingers, an Italian heart, an Italian soul!'

Freja blushed and smiled.

'Now, you must eat a little bit of Nonna Rosa's tiramisù while I finish making my bread and soup. And the dog might like a sausage, no?'

'Woof! Boof!' Finnegan jumped up so that his front paws rested on Nonna Rosa's shoulders and his big, wet nose pressed against hers.

'*Sì! Sì!*' Nonna Rosa grumbled as she pushed him away and waddled across to the fridge. '*Two* sausages for the dog.'

When the soup of the day — *ribollita* — was bubbling steadily along on the stove, Nonna Rosa pulled off her apron and announced, 'I'm going to the Church of Santa Maria in Aracoeli to light a candle for my sister.'

'Why?' asked Freja.

'I light a candle as a prayer to God,' explained Nonna Rosa, her voice suddenly soft and gentle. 'My sister, Carlotta, is very sick and I am asking God to give her peace.'

'Why don't you go to the Church of Trinità dei Monti?' asked Freja. 'It's just at the top of the Spanish Steps and it's ever so grand. The ceiling is higher than Paddington Station's in London! Tobias and I went in the other day, although we couldn't stay for long because Finnegan sat at the entrance and howled. He doesn't like being left out, you see.'

Nonna Rosa glanced through the door to where Finnegan was now standing with his front paws on the bar, licking up a spilt drink. '*Sì! Sì!* I have noticed that about the dog!' She smiled at Freja. 'You are right. Trinità dei Monti is a beautiful place in which to pray and, truly, God hears me everywhere, I am sure. Even in my kitchen. Even when Enzo is grumbling and wailing at the top of his voice. But I go to Santa Maria in Aracoeli because it is the place where my sister was baptised and she has asked me to light the candle there. I do it for her.'

Freja sighed. 'That's lovely.'

Nonna Rosa squeezed into a black coat and grabbed her handbag from a hook on the wall.

'My mother is sick,' whispered Freja. 'Clementine.'

Nonna Rosa did not make a fuss. She did not ask prying questions. She simply placed her soft, plump hand on Freja's shoulder and said, 'Clementine is a beautiful name for a beautiful woman, I think.'

Freja nodded and a little tear slipped down her cheek.

Nonna Rosa opened her handbag and drew out a white lace handkerchief. She wiped the tear away with a rough swipe, then pressed the handkerchief into Freja's hand. 'You might need this again, *piccola*. Come along.'

'Where?' asked Freja.

'To the church,' said Nonna Rosa, waddling to the front door. 'You can light a candle for your mother.'

Turning to the old men at the bar, she said something in Italian. The men argued amongst themselves for a moment, then Roberto, the oldest and frailest of them all, pulled on his hat and slipped off his chair. He followed Nonna Rosa and Freja outside and pointed at a tiny green three-wheeled truck. It looked like an overgrown tricycle. It looked familiar.

Freja turned to Roberto. 'You ...'

Roberto winked.

'How? Why?' Freja whispered, wide eyed.

'My son is a builder. I was visiting him yesterday at an apartment he was working on in Piazza Navona. I saw your crazy writer being chased, so I decided I must do something.'

'But *why* did you help?' asked Freja.

'He is your friend.' Roberto rested a gnarled hand on Freja's head. 'And *you* are Nonna Rosa and Enzo's friend … and *my* friend. So that makes the crazy writer my friend too.' He dropped his hand to his side and chuckled at the thought. 'See?'

Freja felt an unexpected flutter in her chest. Yes, she did see.

Friends. All of them. So quickly. And without even trying.

'*Grazie*, Roberto,' she whispered.

The old man flicked his hand as though it was nothing.

But it was, in fact, everything.

Freja squeezed into the truck's cabin, between Nonna Rosa and Roberto. Finnegan leapt up into the tray at the back.

Roberto turned the key, revved the engine and puttered away. He drove slowly, but straight down the middle of the narrow cobbled street, so that pedestrians, cyclists and mothers with prams had to jump out of his way. Nobody seemed to mind. Roberto waved his wrinkled hand out the window and sang, '*Buongiorno! Buongiorno!*' In return, they shook their heads and smiled. Some even waved and greeted him by name. Nonna Rosa barely seemed to notice the danger and chattered on to Roberto in her melodic Italian. It was all very friendly and calm.

But then the little green truck turned out of the alleyway and onto a busy two-lane road that soon became an even busier four-lane road. With one toot of a horn, Roberto was transformed from a sweet old grandpa into a madman. He sped up, careened in and out of the motorcycles and cars, honked the horn, shook his fist in the air and shouted to one and all, '*Buffone! Buffone! Buffone!*'

Freja giggled. She committed the new word to memory so she could record it later in her scrapbook. '*Buffone. Buffone. Buffone*,' she whispered.

They hurtled towards a traffic policeman who stood on a platform in the middle of a busy intersection. The policeman held his white-gloved hand towards them in a stop sign. Roberto ignored him, pressed down on the accelerator, swerved to miss a red Ferrari, zoomed around the corner and screeched to a halt.

Finnegan's large, hairy body slammed against the window at the back of the cabin. 'Woof!'

'*Grazie! Grazie*, Roberto!' cried Nonna Rosa as she almost fell out the truck door.

Freja followed and took the old woman's hand. Turning to Finnegan, she said, 'Stay here with Roberto. We'll be back soon.'

Finnegan lay down in the tray and whined.

Freja stared up at the Church of Santa Maria in Aracoeli. 'Urgh.' Her shoulders slumped. This did not look like the kind of place to offer a prayer of hope. It looked like a factory or a warehouse, flat faced and stark. 'What a grim building,' she whispered. 'Not at all pretty like the other churches I've seen in Rome.'

Nonna Rosa squeezed Freja's hand and, together, they climbed the stone staircase. It was long and steep, as though built to discourage people from visiting the church. Nonna Rosa huffed and puffed like a steam engine. On reaching the top, they were met with a grey timber door so large and heavy that it took their combined weight to force it open.

Not very welcoming, thought Freja, but she took a deep breath and stepped inside.

'Oh, Nonna Rosa!' she cried, dazzled by the sunlight streaming through the high windows. A smile spread across her face and she clasped her hands to her cheeks.

Nonna Rosa chuckled. 'It is not what you were expecting?'

'No,' said Freja. 'It's ... it's *magical*.' She spun slowly around, her eyes wide as she took in all the details — marble pillars, grand arches, soaring ceilings, half-hidden nooks, pastel paintings, golden altars and, amazingly, crystal chandeliers.

'Chandeliers!' Freja beamed at Nonna Rosa. 'They're *real* chandeliers. Dozens and dozens of them. Like they have in ballrooms in Vienna or châteaux in the French countryside.'

'They are a surprise,' agreed Nonna Rosa, 'but they look so very pleasing, no?'

Freja nodded. 'It looks like Heaven.' She closed her eyes and whispered, '*Feels* like Heaven.'

Face tilted upward, Freja drifted across the marble floor, delighting in the way the light danced and played with the crystals on the chandeliers.

At the far end of the church, a golden altar was framed by two giant arches. Each arch was adorned with fifteen chandeliers — exotic giant raindrops hanging from the ceiling of a cave. At the first arch, Freja stopped and stared.

'Look, Nonna Rosa!' she cried. '*That* chandelier, the one at the top of the arch, is special. It shines more brightly than the rest. I can see rainbows, bolts of lightning, tongues of fire, twinkling stars. There's a whole world caught in every crystal!'

'*Sì! Sì!*' said Nonna Rosa. '*Bellissimo!* It has been polished just now, perhaps after some repairs. If you look at the others, you can see dust and cobwebs. They are not easy to clean — too high and too many fiddly bits — but still they do their job and dance with the light. But you are right, this one is a little different. Maybe because it is the most important. It is right in the middle, above the sanctuary.'

'I'm going to make that one Clementine's chandelier,' Freja decided. 'If a candle helps a prayer make its way to God, then a chandelier will do an even better job. Especially one as splendid as this.'

Nonna Rosa chuckled, patted Freja's mop of curls, then stood reverently by, her handbag clutched to her body.

Freja shuffled about, making sure to position

herself right beneath the chandelier. She closed her eyes and pressed her hands together.

After a moment's pause, she opened one eye and whispered, 'Psst! Nonna Rosa. I've never prayed before. I'm not sure what to say.'

'It is God you are talking to, *bambina*,' said the old woman. 'Just say what is in your heart.'

Freja nodded and closed her eyes once more. 'Dear God,' she began, but then remembered that she was in Rome and wondered if, perhaps, God was actually Italian. He certainly had a lot of churches here! Even the Vatican. She cleared her throat and started afresh. '*Buongiorno*, God. *Ciao*.'

She opened one eye again and peeped at Nonna Rosa. Was the old woman shaking? And why was her mouth twitching at the corners?

Freja closed her eyes for a third time. '*Ciao*, God. Clementine is sick and that makes me sad ... and sometimes rather scared. Amen.'

'Amen,' echoed Nonna Rosa. 'That was a good prayer, *bella*.'

They walked over to the side of the church, where they each lit a candle. Nonna Rosa eased her plump body down into a pew and prayed for her sister, Carlotta.

Freja wondered how she should use her second prayer. 'Maybe a blessing for Tobias, or Nonna Rosa and Enzo,' she murmured. 'Or perhaps I should ask for God's help on the journey home. Roberto is *not* a good driver — worse than Tobias even — and he really could use all the help he can get. Yes, that's it!' Pressing her hands together, she closed her eyes and was just about to pray a special Three-Wheeled Truck Driving Prayer when she was rudely interrupted.

Finnegan had forced his way through the front door amidst a crowd of visiting nuns. Now he galloped across the church and leapt at Freja with a flap of tongue, a wag of tail and a whimper of joy that described his relief at finding her. He had, after all, been left outside, so far away, for such a long and trying time.

CHAPTER 21
Lemon tart with extra first aid

Vivi's lemon tart was delicious — sweet and sour, sharp and soft, all at the same time. It sat lightly in Freja's tummy and spread a warm, tangy buzz through the rest of her body.

Finnegan seemed to have mixed feelings about the tart. Each and every bite made him wince and cringe. He might have rejected the tart altogether, except that the sour lemon bits were tangled up with so many marvellous things — sugar, butter, almonds, eggs. What was a poor dog to do but soldier on and hope for a nice fortifying lump of cheese or salami at the end of it all?

Tobias, of course, was enraptured. He ate *three* slices of lemon tart, then licked the spoon until Freja thought he might dissolve the silver.

'That was delectable!' he declared. 'Best lemon tart in the world!' He threw his arms wide and slapped the bottom of a passing woman. Accidentally, of course, but the woman was not to know that.

Freja gasped. Finnegan grinned and dribbled on the tablecloth.

The woman swung around and glared at Tobias, but he barely noticed. He had eyes only for Vivi, who was, at that very moment, dashing by on the other side of their table, holding a large pizza above her head. As she passed, Tobias reached out absent-mindedly and grabbed the tie at the back of her pink-and-white polka-dot apron. Vivi was jerked to a halt, but the pizza kept moving, flying off the tray and onto the floor. Finnegan leapt from his chair and pounced. Within thirty seconds, all that remained was a little pile of dribble and a dozen black olives.

'Finnegan!' gasped Freja. She slipped from her chair, plucked the olives from the floor and stuffed them into her pocket.

'I don't know what happened,' cried Vivi, her eyes two round pools of chocolate surprise. '*Un momento* I was walking along with a perfect pizza for my customers and the next I came to a halt. *POOT!* Just like that! The pizza is gone!'

Finnegan trotted away, tail in the air. He leapt up onto the pink velvet lounge, stretched along its full length, yawned and fell asleep.

'*Strano!* Strange!' cried Vivi, shaking her head at the empty tray in her hands. 'I must be going crazy! *Pazzo* Vivi!' She sighed, apologised to the diners who were waiting for their pizza, then returned to the kitchen to make another.

'Tobias,' hissed Freja, slipping back into her chair. 'That was dreadful! I know you didn't mean to, but … poor Vivi.'

Tobias looked up at Freja and blinked. Just like Finnegan did when caught chewing on the curtains.

'Shall we go for a walk and buy raspberry gelato?' murmured Tobias.

'But you've just eaten *three* slices of lemon tart,' said Freja.

'Have I?' He tugged at his ear and chuckled. He sipped the last of his espresso and grinned stupidly. 'I say! Doesn't the sauce on that fellow's pasta look remarkably like blood?'

Freja giggled. 'I suppose so, but I wouldn't say it too loudly, or —'

Too late! Tobias was already making his way to the table where the man was eating fettuccine Napoli.

'Looks a little bit like the medical journals I was studying this morning!' said Tobias. 'Blood everywhere, I'm afraid.'

The man dropped his fork and gaped at the writer. 'Huh?'

'Look!' cried Tobias, jabbing his finger into the man's pasta. 'The contents of your bowl could be a nasty wound to the leg. The fettuccine might be bits of ligament and tendon. The sauce, obviously, is the large amount of blood that would be oozing out all over.'

The man stared at Tobias' finger where it poked and swirled around in his lunch.

'Tobby,' whispered Freja, now at his side and tugging at his cardigan.

But Tobias had already slipped away from the real world, into his writer's mind. He pulled out the pale yellow chair beside the man and made himself comfortable. 'Let's just say, my good fellow, that you have fallen off a cliff of some height and landed rather awkwardly on some jagged rocks.' He grabbed the man's foot, lifted it onto the table and pushed the leg of his jeans up to his knee. 'And let's imagine that this pasta sauce is your horrific wound.' Grabbing a spoon, he scooped out some of the rich red Napoli sauce and drizzled it along the man's shin.

The man stared, open mouthed, too stunned to protest.

By now, three other diners — a Chinese couple and an Italian woman — had gathered by the table to see what was happening.

'This poor fellow has fallen from a cliff,' explained Tobias. 'Well, he was *pushed* actually, but we won't go into the details just now. We really should tend to his wounds. He has a nasty gash, maybe even some mangled tendons.' Tobias draped two short strands of fettuccine along the line of sauce. 'These are the tendons, of course.'

'Ah yes! Of course,' said the Chinese man, rubbing his chin.

His wife clutched her hands to her chest.

Freja sighed and shook her head, making nervous sideways glances towards the kitchen. She hoped Vivi couldn't see what was happening in the middle of her pretty café.

'You are quite right to be concerned,' said Tobias, nodding encouragingly to the Chinese man. 'For this poor fellow is still halfway up a mountain and miles from any sort of medical help.'

'*Mamma mia!*' shouted the Italian woman. She leaned forward and wrapped her arm around the victim's shoulders.

'But,' Tobias continued, 'he is a resourceful man and decides that, if he is to survive, he must perform his own first aid.'

'*Incredibile!*' cried an Italian man who had now joined them.

'Yes,' agreed Tobias, 'incredible, and absolutely critical. First, he cleanses the wound with water from his canteen.' He tipped the man's glass of white wine over his leg, and most of the sauce and fettuccine washed away. Tobias dabbed it dry, ever so gently, with a serviette. 'Then he stitches up the wound the best he can using a blunt needle and nylon thread designed to mend his sleeping bag.' Taking a nib pen and a pot of red ink from his cardigan pocket, he drew a jagged line of stitch marks along the man's shin. 'And now he must bandage the wound to keep it clean and secure.' Tobias scanned Café Vivi for a suitable object.

'Quickly!' cried the Italian woman. She pulled the silk scarf from around her neck. 'Please, take this! *Prego!*'

'Very kind!' The Chinese woman smiled and bowed to the Italian woman. The Italian woman blushed.

Freja looked from one face to the next. The onlookers were completely spellbound by Tobias' drama. Except for the victim. His face had grown quite pale and small beads of sweat were breaking out across his forehead.

Tobias wound the scarf firmly around the man's calf. 'And now,' he explained, 'our brave friend is able to make his way down the mountain — slowly and painfully, I might add — to find proper medical help … Unless his enemy finds him first and shoves him off another cliff!'

Tobias leaned back in his chair, clasped his hands behind his head and smiled.

The audience, relieved that all was well, clapped and cheered.

The man with the bandaged leg fainted.

'What has happened here?' asked Vivi, pushing her way through to the table.

The Chinese man stepped forward. He placed his hand on Tobias' shoulder and announced, 'This genius has just saved this other man's life!'

CHAPTER 22

Flitting feet and dizzy heads

'*Mamma mia!* Did you see the pasta Signora Bandoni served her family last night?'

'Urk! That overcooked mess could be used to stick bricks together!'

'That's *exactly* what her husband said — so she smacked him over the head with the pasta pot!'

Freja laughed so hard that a piece of salami came out her nose.

Tobias bit into his focaccia and the pigeon gossip paused while he chewed.

The girl, the dog and the writer were picnicking by the lake in the Borghese Gardens. Finnegan lay on the grass gnawing on a bone — a gift from Nonna Rosa. Freja and Tobias sat on a park bench, nibbling their way through focaccia, salami, walnuts, figs and Vivi's pastel-coloured macarons. They'd barely unwrapped the focaccia when the flock of pigeons had arrived. Now the green-and-grey birds dithered back and forth on the ground at their feet, pecking, cooing, fluffing up their chest feathers. They were obviously gossiping and, of course, Tobias was there to interpret.

'Have you seen Signorina Moretti's new hairdo?' Tobias boomed in a deep Italian accent.

'Disastrous!' he replied in a high-pitched voice. 'Who dyes their hair that colour? Blue! Bright blue! As blue as the Tyrrhenian Sea!'

'Signore Rizzo has sold his house and run away to Spain.' Now a croaky, old voice.

'You know why, don't you?'

'*Everyone* knows why! He had to leave Rome before the law caught up with him. *Ten million euros* he stole from the bank where he worked!'

'I heard it was ten million *pillows* he stole from the *factory* where he worked.'

'Pah! Euros! Pillows! Ten million is still a lot. I hope they catch him.'

A pigeon landed on Tobias' head. He swiped it away, but it flapped lethargically about in the air and settled on his head once more. Freja giggled. Tobias pretended not to notice. He whistled and pulled an elephant-shaped teapot out of his backpack.

'A teapot?' gasped Freja. 'Why on earth did you bring a teapot on our picnic?'

'To make tea, of course,' said Tobias. 'One *cannot*

have a proper picnic without a nice cup of tea. It's simply not possible.'

Sitting the teapot on the bench between them, he continued to fossick in his backpack, pulling out a caddy of tea leaves, a teaspoon, a jar of sugar, a small bottle of milk, a Thermos of hot water and two cups and saucers.

'Oh poo!' Tobias examined one cup after the other. 'It would appear the handles have snapped off. Perhaps I should have wrapped the cups in tissue paper or a cloth.'

Freja bit into a strawberry macaron.

'Never mind! Never mind!' Tobias muttered. 'Nothing that can't be mended with a bit of glue or a good length of sticky tape.'

He carried on with the tea-making ritual, spooning tea leaves into the elephant pot, pouring over the hot water, popping on the lid, spinning the teapot three times, then leaning back against the bench to wait. The pigeon, still on Tobias' head, fluffed up its chest feathers and cooed.

Freja laughed.

'What?' asked Tobias.

'There's a pigeon on your head. I think it's planning to stay. Maybe forever.'

'Well, that's hardly anything to cackle about,' said Tobias. 'There's a *monkey* on your *shoulder.*'

And a split second later, there truly was!

'Pazzo!' cried Freja.

'Oooow,' whined Finnegan, a little scared, a little confused.

'*Ciao! Ciao!*' sang Giuseppe, pushing his pretty wagon around to the front of the bench. 'It's the golden princess and the dog that grows too big!'

Pazzo twitched about on Freja's shoulder, then quickly, shyly, planted a kiss on the top of her head.

'Aaah!' sighed Giuseppe. 'It's *amore*! Love! Pazzo might be a very naughty monkey, but he knows a beautiful girl when he sees one.'

Freja smiled.

Pazzo blew a raspberry at Giuseppe. Then, sitting down on the back of the bench at Freja's shoulder, he played with her hair. He pulled one of the golden curls as far as it would stretch, then watched, fascinated, as it bounced back against her head. He monkey-muttered and clapped his hands, then did it all over again.

Tobias leapt up. '*Ciao!* Hello, my good fellow.' He thrust his hand towards Giuseppe. 'My name's Tobias Appleby and this spiffing lass is my ... my ... my delight and joy, Freja Peachtree.'

The two men smiled and shook hands.

'Tea?' offered Tobias.

'*Grazie!*' sang Giuseppe, and he joined them on the bench.

Within moments, the girl, the writer, the organ grinder and the monkey were chatting, laughing and nibbling on macarons.

Finnegan did not join in. Still confused by the monkey, he commando-crawled beneath the bench. There he lay, his head between his front paws, whimpering and staring up between the slats.

'Aaah,' sighed Giuseppe, sipping tea and closing his eyes. 'Nobody makes a cup of tea like the English.'

'The secret's in the pot,' explained Tobias. 'It always tastes better when you use a truly marvellous teapot. Not expensive, mind you. Just one that tickles your fancy.'

'It is the same with any drink, any meal,' agreed Giuseppe. 'It is good to have fine crystal, beautiful china, even for a glass of water and a humble wedge of cheese. But the most important thing is to share it with good friends.' He lifted his teacup and smiled at the writer then the girl.

'Good friends,' whispered Freja, and she felt a glow spread across her cheeks. She passed the pink-and-white cardboard box of macarons around once more and they sat in companionable silence — the warm winter sun on their shoulders, pigeons fluffing and twittering at their feet, pistachio and strawberry sweet treats dancing across their tastebuds.

Freja rubbed her cheek against Pazzo's and whispered, 'Bliss.'

'EEEEEEE!' Pazzo squealed and sprang across to the top of the organ.

Freja jumped, knocking the box of macarons to the ground. The pigeons flocked all over them.

Finnegan let out a deep, menacing growl.

A hand rested on the back of the bench where Pazzo had just been. Freja's gaze ran from the long, well-manicured fingers, up the black sleeve, to the familiar white collar of a priest. She closed her eyes for a moment, swallowed hard and forced herself to look into the priest's face.

'Huh!' she said, surprised. For this was *not* Padre Paolo, who had chased Tobias from the bookstore four days ago. This priest was younger, thinner, taller. His black hair was oiled and combed so that it swept upward and backward. His face was adorned with a thin moustache and a second tiny clump of hair in the middle of his chin. And his mouth, although turned up at the edges, was not showing a jot of kindness or joy.

Freja thought, *His smile is all wrong. He looks like an Arctic fox creeping around a leveret nest.*

And then she realised, *He's smirking, not smiling.*

And then she wondered, *Are priests even* allowed *to smirk?*

'Hello there!' sang Tobias. '*Ciao ciao!*' He lolled over the back of the bench, a smile on his face. A real smile, which put wrinkles around the edges of his eyes.

The priest did not respond.

'We're having a tea party!' Tobias continued. 'Care to join us, *padre*? We always have room for one more. We can bunch up.'

The priest's smirk turned down at the sides. He growled, 'You are the English writer, no?'

Tobias flinched and the pigeon flew from his head, taking cover amidst the flock at their feet.

Tobias leaned forward and set his teacup on the ground. He sat back and tugged at his ear. He looked into Freja's wide and worried eyes. 'Me?' he cried. 'A writer? Oh, I don't *think* so. You've made some sort of mistake, my good fellow.'

The priest moved his hand to Tobias' shoulder. 'I, Padre Flavio, do not have time for filthy liars. You *are* the English writer. I know that is who you are.' Slowly, the hand squeezed through Tobias' cardigan, digging into flesh and bone.

Tobias winced.

Freja gasped.

'Oo-oo-oo!' squealed Pazzo.

The pigeons flapped into the air and whooshed away. A cloud of feathers and macaron crumbs settled in their wake.

Finnegan scrambled out from beneath the bench and lurched at the priest. A shiny black shoe met his shaggy grey chest with a *thud*. The dog leapt backward, more surprised than hurt. He had never been struck before.

Freja dropped to the ground and wrapped her arms around Finnegan's neck, but he shook her off. He stared at the priest, tail and ears aloft, paws planted wide apart on the grass.

'I say!' cried Tobias, trying to keep his voice light and untroubled. 'You seem to have made a dreadful mistake. I'm not a writer any more than you are a teapot.'

'Ho-ho-ho-ho!' chuckled Giuseppe, slapping his thigh. 'A teapot. That is very funny.'

But the priest was not amused. He snarled.

'Boof!' snapped Finnegan.

Padre Flavio loosened his grip on Tobias, but persisted. 'We both know, Signore Appleby, what it is that you are doing.'

'Pah!' grumbled Giuseppe. He heaved himself up from the bench and turned to face the priest. 'That is enough! Who is this Signore Appleby?' He shrugged, looking truly confused. 'He is nobody we know. *This* man is my assistant, Leonardo. He is *far* too stupid to be a writer. Stupid as a donkey with no brains.'

'It's true!' Freja chimed in, jumping to her feet. 'He's *so* stupid that he can barely write his own name! That's why we call him Leonardo Stupido.' She blushed a little as the words came out — partly from shame, for she did not like to call anyone stupid, but also from pride, because she thought the name had a charming ring to it.

Tobias stumbled to his feet. He swung his arms back and forth and grinned.

The priest flared his nostrils.

'So very, *very* stupid,' sighed Giuseppe. He slapped his forehead in despair. 'The only job he is fit for is to wind the handle on my pipe organ while I sing and my monkey dances.'

Pazzo bared his teeth.

The priest's eyes narrowed and he glanced sideways at Freja.

'The little girl is Leonardo Stupido's niece,' said Giuseppe. 'But she is smart. *Very* smart! Not like her uncle. Ah, look! Here comes an audience now. A busload of Russian tourists has wandered into the park. I'm sure they would love to hear us perform! Excuse us, Padre Flavio. It is time for us to work.'

Giuseppe grabbed Freja by the hand and swept away to greet the crowd. '*Ciao! Ciao*, my tourist friends!' he sang. 'Welcome to Rome, my city, my home, the place of sunshine and music and love! So beautiful, I must sing about it right away!'

Tobias ran forward, grabbed the mother-of-pearl handle on the organ and began to crank it around and around. The organ puffed once, wheezed twice, then sprang to life. Merry pipe music danced through the air, where it was soon joined by the high, sweet tones of Giuseppe's voice.

At the end of the first line of his song, Giuseppe lifted Freja's hand in the air, twirled her around, then swept her along in a light and pretty dance. The Russian tourists sighed and cooed with delight. Freja was confused by a rush of feelings — pride, embarrassment, happiness, fear.

Pazzo swayed back and forth on top of the pipe organ, his hands by his sides, his eyes cast heavenward in an angelic gaze. But as the second verse began, he pulled his lips back from his teeth, grimaced and started to kick Tobias in the side of the head with every turn of the handle. The crowd chuckled. Tobias cringed, but carried on.

Padre Flavio frowned. He ran his long, manicured nails through his slick hair. He pulled a pair of sunglasses from his breast pocket and slid them onto his face. He took one last long stare at Tobias, shook his head and stomped away.

Finnegan followed, slinking from tree to tree. Silently and with ninja speed, he lurched forward, nipped Padre Flavio on the bottom and retreated. The priest waved his fist in the air — perhaps at Finnegan, perhaps at Tobias — then disappeared through the park gates.

Freja hadn't realised she'd been holding her breath. But now it flooded out in a loud sigh of relief. She beamed up into Giuseppe's wide, friendly face and whispered, 'Grazie. Grazie. A million trillion grazie.'

Giuseppe nodded and smiled so that his cheeks plumped and his moustache stretched from ear to ear. Lifting the volume of his voice, he whirled the girl around and around to the piped music. Her feet felt as light as blossom petals caught in a spring breeze.

Around and around they danced, weaving in and out of the crowd. And before Freja knew what was happening, Giuseppe had passed her on to a new partner, a large, square Russian man. One by one, the people in the audience paired off and soon they were all spinning on the gravel paths, tottering at the edge of the lake, twirling over the grass, until the park was alive with melody, laughter, flitting feet and dizzy heads.

And the nastiness of the priest was almost forgotten.

CHAPTER 23

Little ears

That evening, Trattoria Famiglia was crowded and noisy. The regular customers had been joined by the Russian tour group from the Borghese Gardens. All thirty-six of them! The organ music, Giuseppe's singing and the wonderful dancing had thrilled and delighted them. Rome had truly come alive! They *insisted* on buying dinner for the performers.

Freja, Tobias, Finnegan, Giuseppe and a Russian couple called Boris and Nadia sat at the table closest to the kitchen and the enormous painting of the Pope. They watched, half-scared, half-laughing, as Nonna Rosa blustered back and forth. She charged from table to table, slamming bowls of pasta in front of her customers. She groaned and clutched her aching back. She shouted and threw her hands in the air. Then she started all over again. The old woman loved to see business booming. She also loved to complain. Here, now, she had both and was glowing with happiness. Not even her scowling and cursing could hide the fact that she was having the time of her life.

'*Mangia, mangia!* Eat, eat!' Nonna Rosa bellowed. She barrelled towards their table, a large pot of pasta resting on her hip. She spooned orecchiette with tomato sauce from the pot, filling everyone's bowls to the brim for the *third* time that evening. 'Eat more pasta! Drink more wine! Dip your bread in more olive oil! Eat, eat! Before these loud, greedy Russians suck my kitchen dry!'

Nonna Rosa smiled and pointed her serving spoon at Boris and Nadia. 'Not you,' she explained. 'Any friend of Freja's is a friend of Nonna Rosa's.'

'But *all* the Russians are our friends,' whispered Freja. 'You see, Tobias cranked the organ and Giuseppe sang and we danced and then we got the Russians dancing and we all had so much fun. I danced with *three* different people, Nonna Rosa, and I wasn't even scared. Well, maybe a little at first, but then not so badly. It was lovely! The Russians liked me and they all said I danced like an angel.'

Nonna Rosa stepped back from the table and stared. 'So many words, Freja!' She smiled, her eyes soft and warm. 'So many friends too. You are being a brave child, no? Like a true Roman girl — laughing, talking, dancing and enjoying yourself. You even look different today. What is that you are wearing in your hair? A wreath of tiny pine cones and twigs, no? Dashing and daring. *Bravo!* No more hiding behind the bushes or beneath the tables, you hear?'

'Phooey!' cried Enzo, squeezing in front of Nonna Rosa. He slid a tray full of drinks onto the table. 'Move aside, you silly old woman, and stop boss-bossing the boots off the poor child.' Enzo winked at Freja. He was enjoying the crowds and the arguing as much as Nonna Rosa. 'Here, my friends — Italians, Russians, Englishes. Drink more meatballs! Eat more serviettes! Dip your sleeves in more olive oil!'

Nonna Rosa slapped the back of Enzo's head. 'Are you mocking me, old man?'

'No! No!' shouted Enzo. He waved his tray, now empty, in the air. 'I am just trying to help these poor people out. Please. Everyone! Drink up before this grumpy old woman nags you to death!'

Enzo trudged back to the bar, where Pazzo the monkey was tormenting his friends. Nonna Rosa was right on his heels, badgering and bossing. Enzo looked back at Freja, rolled his eyes and used his hand to mimic Nonna Rosa's mouth: 'Blah! Blah! Blah! Blah!'

Freja giggled uncontrollably.

'Wonderful!' boomed Boris. 'The girl, she laughs like a hen who is celebrating a golden egg.'

'Exactly!' cheered Tobias. He slammed his hand down on the table, toppling a glass of wine. 'Hearing Freja's laughter is a real treat! It makes you feel marvellous! Like popcorn popping in your heart ... Like goldfish nibbling at your toes ... Like jelly beans raining down on your head.'

'What is this jelly beans?' asked Nadia.

'An English sweet,' Tobias explained. 'Brightly coloured sugar beans that taste as good as Freja's laughter sounds.'

'Aaaaah,' said Nadia, nodding and frowning. 'They sound spectacular! I must try these sometime, Boris. Maybe we go to England on our next holiday.'

'Maybe we do, Nadia,' said Boris, nodding and frowning at his wife.

Freja giggled once more. Not because of the jelly beans, but because Boris and Nadia looked like twins. They were both large and square, with brown eyes and short, cropped hair. They wore the same plain and practical clothing — grey zip-up jackets, black pants and hiking boots. When Boris threw back his head and laughed, Nadia threw back her head and laughed. When Nadia frowned, Boris frowned. When Boris took a mouthful of pasta and made murmurs of approval, Nadia took a mouthful of pasta and made similar murmurs of delight. The only real difference was that Nadia wore bright red lipstick and dangly earrings in the shape of fish. Boris did not.

Tobias lifted a forkful of pasta into the air. He stared at it from above, below and side-on. 'Fascinating shape,' he murmured.

'Orecchiette!' boomed Giuseppe. 'It means little ears. Each piece of pasta is shaped like a small ear, so it holds a drop of the delicious sauce.'

'Yes, I can see that,' said Tobias. He took one little ear in his fingers and squeezed it. 'Mmmm ... squishy ... slimy.'

He pushed a pile of little ears back and forth across the tablecloth.

He ran his finger around inside one of his own large ears.

'Uh-oh,' moaned Freja, and she sank low in her chair.

'A bowl of little ears,' murmured Tobias. 'My word! If you look at it the right way, it's quite dreadful! A bowl *full* of severed ears! Someone might have done a very bad thing! Of course, the ears are too little to be human. Perhaps they belonged to a rat or a monkey ...'

Giuseppe dropped his fork. His face turned as white as his shirt.

Tobias continued, oblivious to the discomfort of those around him. 'Or perhaps they are human ears that have been dehydrated. That would certainly make them smaller than usual ... although if they spent long enough in the pasta sauce, they might rehydrate and swell up to their original size ...'

Nadia and Boris stared at each other and pushed their bowls away.

Freja shrugged. She passed the rejected meals along the table to Finnegan and continued to eat her own orecchiette with tomato sauce.

'Now, my friend,' Giuseppe said, leaning across the table to Tobias. 'It is time. You must tell me about this priest, Padre Flavio. How do you know him? Why is he so angry?'

Tobias slouched back in his chair and sighed. He pulled a pencil from his shirt pocket and used it to scratch his head. 'The truth is, I've never seen him before.'

'But *he* knows *you*,' said Giuseppe.

Freja stopped eating and looked up at Tobias.

'Yes,' said the writer. 'I think he might be a friend of *another* priest who is angry with me. A chap called Padre Paolo.'

Boris thumped his fist on the table. 'That is very bad!' he boomed. 'A priest should be kind, not cross.'

Nadia thumped her fist on the table. 'Boris is right!' she boomed. 'A priest should love, not hate!'

'There was a mishap,' Freja explained. 'Tobias spilt ink all over Mother Superior Evangelista. Padre Paolo — the *first* priest — was cross. Perhaps he was Mother Superior's friend. He knew Tobias was the one who did it because Tobias had ink all over his fingers ... and his face ... and his clothes.'

'But you have no ink today,' Giuseppe pointed out.

Tobias wriggled his fingers in the air. They were clean and white, except for a bit of pasta sauce, which Finnegan licked off right there and then.

'This nun with the ink,' said Boris. 'Did it happen yesterday?'

'Oh no!' cried Tobias. 'Over a week ago. It's quite old hat.'

'Old hat?' asked Nadia.

'Old news,' explained Freja. 'Lots of stuff has happened between then and now. Padre Paolo tried to punch Tobias at the Trevi Fountain, then he chased Tobias from the bookstore, and now it looks like he's sent another priest, Padre Flavio, to catch him.'

'But this is nonsense!' cried Giuseppe. 'A little bit of ink is not so bad!'

'It did make a mess of Mother Superior's nice cream habit,' whispered Freja.

'No! No! No!' said Nadia. 'Giuseppe is right. It makes no sense. I think there is something more. Something you are not remembering.'

Tobias stared at the ceiling.

'Tobias did call Mother Superior "Mamma Spaghettiosa"!' said Freja.

Boris, Nadia and Giuseppe threw back their heads and laughed.

Giuseppe slapped his leg and wiped tears from his eyes. 'Mamma Spaghettiosa!' he bellowed. 'That is very funny. You should be writing comedies for the theatre, Signore Appleby, not crime novels!'

At that moment, their laughter was drowned out by an uproar at the bar. Pazzo had grown weary and fallen asleep in a bowl of walnuts. When Roberto had tried to take another nut, the monkey had grabbed his little finger, popped it into his mouth and sucked it like a baby. He would not let go.

The old men were now rocking back and forth, howling with glee. They called Roberto 'mamma' and shrieked even louder. Sebastiano and Edmondo collapsed into each other's arms, laughing so hard that Edmondo dribbled on Sebastiano's shoulder.

'I think,' said Giuseppe, 'it is time for me to go home. Pazzo will be too tired to perform in the morning if I do not tuck him into his bed.' He heaved himself out of his chair, then bustled around Trattoria Famiglia, singing, '*Arrivederci*, my Russian friends. Good evening! Good evening! Come and see me again before you leave my beautiful city. I will sing for you. You will dance for me!'

Freja squeezed out from the table and crept up beside him. She tugged at his sleeve and whispered, 'Thank you, Giuseppe. *Grazie.*'

'What for, *bella*?'

'For helping us trick the priest,' she whispered. 'And for being kind … and for teaching me to dance … and …' She barely dared say the words. Her voice grew even quieter. 'And for being my friend.'

'Aaah, but that is so easy,' he said, his voice softer than usual. '*Grazie* for being *my* friend. I think we have the same heart, Freja — soft and full of things we cannot always say. I have learnt to pour these things from my heart into my music. You will find your own special way to pour the beautiful things from your heart.' He leaned forward and kissed Freja on the top of her head.

'Goodnight, Giuseppe,' she whispered.

The organ grinder smiled. He scooped Pazzo out of the nut bowl and into the crook of his arm, then disappeared into the street.

When the Russians had left, the girl, the dog and the writer sat alone at their table, eating tiramisù, enjoying a moment's quiet reflection.

Finnegan was obviously reflecting on how rapidly his dessert had disappeared and how much of Freja's remained. He stared and dribbled and moved closer and closer to Freja's bowl.

Tobias patted his tiramisù with the back of his spoon while reflecting on orecchiette. 'It might be fun,' he murmured, 'to include a severed ear or two in my current novel ... It could easily happen if someone plummeted from a cliff and caught their ear on a sharp rock on the way down ... Or if my villain became particularly enraged and ran amok with a knife ...' He whipped his pencil from his pocket and began to scribble notes on one of Nonna Rosa's menus.

Freja was reflecting on the day's astonishing run of events, but was continually drawn back to one detail in particular.

'Tobias,' she said, her spoon freezing halfway to her mouth.

'What is it, old chap?'

'Giuseppe said I'm your niece. Why do you suppose he did that?'

'It was a trick, of course. Part of the lie we told to coax Padre Flavio away from the truth — the fact that I really *am* Tobias Appleby, the English writer he was hoping to find.' Tobias ran his hand through his hair. His mop of curly, feral hair.

Freja recalled the two women in the library at Little Coddling. 'And that hair,' the husky-voiced woman had hissed. 'Feral and curly! Just like ... well, *you know* ...'

Freja now stared at Tobias' hair. She patted her own hair, mouth open, eyes wide. She plucked at the end of one of her curls, pulled it out and let it spring back against her forehead. 'We *could* be uncle and niece,' she whispered. 'We have the same sort of hair.'

'Yes, I suppose we do, old chap.' Tobias smiled and tapped his pencil on the table.

'And we *are* very fond of one another.'

'Absolutely! Not a doubt about it!'

Freja poked at her dessert for a moment, then pushed the bowl towards Finnegan. The dog slurped the leftovers into his mouth, licked his lips and blinked with satisfaction.

'Tobias?' Freja's voice was a mere breath. '*Are* you my uncle?'

The pencil dropped from Tobias' hand and rolled across the floor. 'No. No, old chap.' He blushed and tugged at his ear. 'No. Well, no. No, no, no, no! It's a little more complicated than that. What I mean is, would you like another glass of lemonade?'

'No, thanks. What do you mean "a little more complicated"?'

'Oh, nothing. Just babble. Well, you know, Clementine is my chum and she asked me to look after you and of course I said yes and it has been an absolute joy and delight to have you here with me, not at all a chore, and we are having a jolly spiffing time, don't you agree? So I suppose it is not really complicated at all but a great deal of fun and excitement, and I am not your uncle but I'm still the one who must see that you are safe and sound, and it's getting rather late and I think I might say goodnight to Enzo and Nonna Rosa before Nonna Rosa tries to feed us another mouthful, or we will surely burst, and I dare say it's way past your bedtime.'

He scraped back his chair, stumbled, then dashed to the bar. He patted Enzo on the back until the old man coughed and gasped for air. He kissed Nonna Rosa — twice on each cheek, then once on the nose. He knocked over three stools, then set them upright. He shouted, 'Come along, Finnegan! Come along, Freja! Goodnight, Enzo! *Buonanotte*, Nonna Rosa! *Ciao! Ciao*, orecchiette! *Arrivederci*, fettuccine!' and tumbled out into the cool night air.

CHAPTER 24

A busy night

Freja slept fitfully. Her dreams were filled with strange and disturbing images. Pigeons flocked into Café Vivi and gobbled up all the macarons. Giuseppe was chased by the police for stealing ten million pillows. Tobias and a priest were having a swimming race across the Trevi Fountain.

'The winner gets to be Freja's uncle!' the priest said, smirking. But the fountain was so wide that the race never ended. It went on and on until Freja feared that Tobias might drown.

'Help!' he cried. 'Throw me a macaron!'

Freja didn't want to waste the delicious macarons, so instead she threw the little treasure chest and it hit him on the head. 'Oh no!' she cried. 'Tobias is sinking and the priest will win the race and be my uncle and I don't even like him!'

Freja woke, her face wet with tears. Wiping her eyes on the sheet, she opened them as wide as possible to make sure she was truly awake.

A beam of moonlight streamed through the window, lighting up the dressing table and the battered little chest. 'Rotten treasure chest,' she grumbled. But at least it was here and not sinking to the bottom of the Trevi Fountain. That proved the nightmare was not real.

Freja stared at the treasure chest for several minutes, then narrowed her eyes. 'Secrets,' she muttered. 'Secrets locked away.'

She rolled over and bumped into Finnegan. The hairy grey hound was stretched along the full length of her bed, sleeping. He sneezed, licked his nose, then grew still again. Freja wrapped her arms around his neck, pressed her face against his and fell back to sleep.

Next time she woke, it was to the sound of footsteps. Pazzo was tiptoeing through her bedroom door!

'Cheeky monkey!' she cried. 'What are *you* doing here?'

Pazzo waved a small black key in the air.

Freja sat up.

The monkey danced across the room and sprang onto the dressing table. He leaned over the treasure chest and slipped the key into the lock.

'Wait!' shouted Freja. 'I want to open it myself.'

But Pazzo ignored her. He turned the key and flipped open the lid.

'Oo-oo-oo!' he sang, jumping up and down.

Freja leapt out of bed and ran across the room. She leaned over the treasure chest and gasped. 'Walnuts! There's nothing inside but *walnuts*!'

Pazzo pulled on a tiny white sleeping cap and climbed into the treasure chest. He wriggled around on the pile of walnuts until he was comfortable. He smiled, closed his eyes and fell asleep.

'Ridiculous!' scoffed Freja.

Pazzo began to snore. It was a deep, rumbling sound, far louder than she expected from a small monkey. It went on and on and on. Finally, she became so irritated that she shouted, 'STOP!'

Freja woke with a start. Now she really *was* awake, her heart racing, her hands clutching the quilt to her chest. Finnegan was still snoring, making a deep, rumbling sound like the monkey in her dream.

She looked over to the dressing table. The treasure chest was locked. Of *course* it was locked! And it was *not* full of walnuts. She could only imagine the secrets hidden inside. Tobias' and Clementine's secrets.

All I really know, thought Freja, *is that Clementine is my mother ... and Tobias is not my uncle.*

She tossed and turned, fluffed up her pillow and settled once more.

'I am *not* Tobias' niece,' she whispered.

She twisted handfuls of quilt.

'I am *not* Tobias' niece,' she whispered to the moonlit room. She whispered it over and over again until the tears dribbled down the sides of her face and dampened the pillow.

Because the truth was she *longed* to be his niece.

Tobias was strange, certainly, but he was also funny, clever and terribly kind. She'd be proud to call him her uncle.

Then, just to see how it felt, she said, 'Hello, my name is Freja Peachtree and I'm Tobias Appleby's niece.'

She sniffed and said, 'Hello, my name is Freja Peachtree and I'm Leonardo Stupido's niece.'

She wiped her eyes on the edge of the quilt and sighed. 'Hello, my name is Freja Peachtree and I am *nobody's* niece ... but I *am* Clementine Peachtree's daughter.'

Clementine.

'Mummy Darling Heart,' she whispered.

The homesickness that had been circling the room for the last ten minutes now swooped in. Grabbing at Freja's throat, it squeezed its talons shut until she could barely breathe.

'Clementine,' she sobbed. 'Come back soon.'

Getting to the Church of Santa Maria in Aracoeli was easy in the early hours of the morning. The streets of Rome were dark and empty. Except for a few three-wheeled trucks making deliveries. And the cats. The cats were everywhere — scavenging in rubbish bins, prowling along the tops of walls, slinking down alleyways. Rome at night belonged to the cats.

Getting to the church was easy. Getting *inside* the church was not so simple.

Freja climbed up the long flight of stairs and pushed against the heavy wooden door. It wouldn't budge.

She tried again. Nothing gave. Which was not surprising, really. Last time she was here it had taken her and Nonna Rosa's combined strength to open the door.

This time, Freja tightened her scarf, pulled her beanie down low on her brow, took a run-up and threw her shoulder into the door. It didn't make a scrap of difference. Except that a few splinters of dry timber fell to the ground. And now her shoulder ached.

'Of course!' Freja moaned. 'The door's locked! I suppose it should be at this time of night!' She slumped against the wall and sighed.

Something soft and warm brushed against her leg. She looked down and saw a cat, a tabby with a white chest and paws.

'Hello, puss,' Freja whispered. But when she bent down to pat it, the cat trotted away. Freja watched as it padded along the front of the church. Coming to a second, smaller door at the end of the wall, it disappeared through a crack.

'It's open!' cried Freja. And before she wondered why the door might be ajar, or whether she really should be going inside, she had dashed along the terrace, pushed the door a little wider and crept into the church.

'Urgh!' Freja froze. The vast space was cold, grey and lifeless. The chandeliers no longer danced and sparkled. Robbed of all light, they looked dark and heavy, like giant bats hanging from the ceiling of a cave. Freja shuddered and realised there might be some sense in discouraging children from wandering out alone at night.

'Nevertheless,' she told herself, 'I've made it this far. I might as well do what I came here for.'

Slipping from one marble pillar to the next, she made her way silently to the front of the church. The pale moonlight did not reach this far and all Freja could see was a gaping black space in front of her. She opened her eyes wide, willing them to adjust to the dark. She looked up to where the special chandelier hung. The one that had shone most brightly. The one she had chosen as Clementine's chandelier.

'There it is!' Freja whispered as the silhouette came into view. She walked forward until she was standing right beneath it. Closing her eyes, she clasped her hands together and prayed. '*Ciao*, God. It's me again. Freja.'

Something thudded to the floor!

Something in the darkness, behind the altar!

'Oh!' Freja cried out in surprise. Her head prickled all over.

She dashed behind the nearest marble pillar and pressed herself hard against it. Her tummy clenched in fear.

'God?' she whimpered. 'Is that you?'

She waited.

Her mouth turned as dry as sand.

'Probably not God,' she whispered. 'God wouldn't knock something over in his own church. Surely he'd know where everything was.'

She began to shake. Her hands and feet felt suddenly cold.

But then she remembered the cat.

Of course! The tabby cat had entered the church before her. Perhaps it had jumped off the altar, knocking a candle or a prayer book to the floor.

'Puss?' she hissed. 'Is that you, kitty?'

She waited, then raised her voice a little. 'Here, puss, puss, puss.'

'Meow.' The soft, warm body pressed against her leg.

Freja collapsed to the floor. She swept the cat into her arms and stroked its fur over and over again, until the jelly in her legs turned back into bone.

Silly, she told herself. *Scared by a sweet little cat.*

Then, closing her eyes, she did what she had come here to do. She prayed. Quietly. Earnestly. '*Ciao*, God. I hope I haven't interrupted your sleep. But it's important. Clementine is sick. Really sick. There's no use pretending she's not. She hasn't written or sent me her beautiful drawings for weeks. I miss her. I want her to get better and come back to me forever.'

'Mew!' The cat wriggled from her arms and headed towards the door.

'Puss! Come back!' begged Freja. 'Please don't leave me.'

But the cat had vanished.

And now the church seemed too dark. Too quiet. Too far from Finnegan and Tobias.

Freja leapt to her feet and ran. Her footsteps echoed across the empty church, sounding like another pair of footsteps behind her. Or maybe there *was* another set of footsteps behind her! She ran and ran. Not daring to look back. Not stopping. Not even when her cherry-red beanie fell off. She ran straight for the faint crack of light in the wall. Grabbing the edge of the door, she pulled it open and stumbled out into the chilly morning air.

'Oooh!' Freja shivered with relief and cold and lingering fear.

Turning back to the door, she yanked it shut. The latch caught with a *clunk*.

Freja breathed deeply, three times, then strode across the terrace to where the tabby cat was waiting. She looked up into the sky. The dark purple of night was fading to pink. In less than an hour, the sun would pop its head above the crumbling columns, the marble arches and the terracotta roofs of Rome.

'I'd better dash,' Freja said to the cat. 'I have to get home before Tobias and Finnegan realise I'm gone.' She tightened her scarf and trotted down the stairs. But on reaching the bottom, she remembered one last thing. Turning back to face the church, she closed her eyes, pressed her hands together and whispered, 'Amen!'

She breathed deeply, allowing herself to feel the pleasure of a job well done.

And then she opened her eyes.

Just in time to see a door closing at the front of the church.

The same little door that she herself had closed just minutes before.

CHAPTER 25

Cheese wheels
and little sacks of chocolate

'CHEESE!'

'Woof,' said Finnegan. He leapt off the bed and barrelled out of the room.

'Cheese?' whispered Freja. She sat up in bed and blinked at the bright daylight. Her coat and scarf were tangled and twisted around her body. She was still wearing her boots. 'I must have fallen asleep the moment I got home from the church.'

Freja stumbled into the living room. She leaned against the doorjamb, yawned and straightened her coat.

'I'm a giant cheese wheel!' cried Tobias from the kitchen.

Something smashed, Finnegan barked and Tobias somersaulted through the door. He tumbled, head-over-bottom-over-heels-over-head, across the room, arms and legs flapping and flailing, until he collided with the desk. *Thud!*

Finnegan galloped around his master. He dribbled and drooled. He licked and grinned. He barked and snapped until his fang got caught in the end of Tobias' scarf.

'Grrrr!' Finnegan growled and tried to pull free. But as he tugged backward, the scarf yanked Tobias' head against the leg of the desk. *Thud! Thud! Thud!*

Freja slapped her hand across her mouth. Her shoulders shook, her face turned red and the laughter burst out between her fingers.

Finally, after a dozen thuds, the loop of yarn snapped and Finnegan was free. He dropped to the floor and licked Tobias' face.

'Yes, yes. Apology accepted, puppy.' Tobias rubbed his head and stared up at Freja. 'Good morning!'

'Hello,' said Freja, and she giggled some more.

Tobias sat up and squinted. 'Just look at you!'

Freja blushed. Was it obvious that she had slept in her clothes? That she had been out on her own at night?

Tobias sprang to his feet. He pulled her into the middle of the room. He walked around her, nodding and mumbling. 'Yes ... uh-hmmm ... perhaps ...' Finally, he announced, 'You're *just* the right size!'

'The right size for what?' asked Freja.

'Why, to be my cheese wheel, of course!'

Finnegan grinned and licked Tobias' shoe.

'I ... I don't really know how to be a cheese wheel,' Freja confessed.

'Of course you do!' cried Tobias. 'A spiffingly clever lass like you. You just roll up in a ball and tumble along the floor as fast as you can!'

'But *why*?' asked Freja.

'Research!' declared Tobias. 'For my novel.'

Freja looked blankly into his face.

'I need to feel the power, the momentum, the ugly threat of a cheese wheel!' Tobias tumbled his hands over one another. 'If I sent a giant cheese wheel rolling down the hillside through a Swiss village, it would gain great speed. Within minutes, it would have become a dangerous object capable of squashing cats, toppling butter churns, breaking through doors and — most important of all — cracking a grown man's skull!'

'Oh, I see,' said Freja.

Tobias smiled. 'Fascinating idea for a murder scene, don't you think? A seemingly innocent cheese wheel turned into a deadly weapon.'

Freja nodded. She walked into the kitchen, curled herself into a ball and somersaulted out into the living room, where she collided with Tobias' legs. She stared up at him from the floor.

Tobias rubbed his chin. 'Yes, that was jolly good. You make a marvellous cheese wheel, old chap. I'd even go so far as to say a *splendid* cheese wheel. It's just that ... well, you're not quite heavy enough to send a grown man flying.'

'I *was* on flat ground,' said Freja. She sat up. 'Perhaps if I had a hill ...'

'Yes! Yes! We need a hill. A steep hill.' Tobias paced back and forth across the room, tugging at his ears and chewing his lips. He stopped, grabbed his little brush and a pot of ink from the desk and began to paint numbers on the wall. 'Weight,' he muttered. 'Gradient ... speed ... momentum ...'

'Woof!' said Finnegan, and he flopped down in front of the fire.

'Aha!' cried Tobias, spinning around to face the room. 'What we need is twofold: a steep slope, as suggested by my clever colleague.' He pointed his paintbrush at Freja. 'And a large breakfast.' Tobias grabbed his coat and wallet. 'Come along, old chap.'

Freja jumped up and ran after him. 'What's the large breakfast got to do with it?'

'Well, first of all,' Tobias explained, 'I'm hungry. But second of all, you're too light. I calculate that my cheese wheel needs to be more than forty-two kilograms to crack a man's skull. You don't look nearly that heavy. But if I fill you up with breakfast, and perhaps a gelato or two, then take you to a steep hill, you can at least be a better cheese wheel than you are at the moment.'

Freja giggled. 'I'd like to be a *great* cheese wheel.'

'That's the spirit!' cried Tobias. 'Come along, Finnegan.'

And together, the girl, the dog and the writer trotted downstairs, across the courtyard and into the sunshine, in search of a hearty Roman breakfast.

'This one looks good!' cried Tobias. He dashed down an alleyway towards a tiny but crowded café. 'It smells delicious and it's busy. Full of fascinating people. People *begging* to be written into a novel. Just look at that man standing by the window. His fingers are so fat he can't even hold his coffee cup by the handle; he has to cradle it in the palm of his hand. If I had to guess, I'd say he has butcher's hands. Fingers like sausages. Enormous pork sausages. Hmmm ... I might put a butcher in my next novel. Knives ... chopping ... blood ... bones ...'

Freja grabbed the corner of Tobias' coat and dragged him through the front door. There was standing room only, for the café was bustling with men and women grabbing a quick breakfast on their way to work. Shouted greetings, hurried orders and noisy kisses mingled with the bitter smell of coffee. The air was fuggy with chaos, hunger and happiness.

Finnegan, invisible amidst the crush of bodies, slunk about, nibbling the corner off a pastry here, the ham from a *panino* there. An entire *zeppola* tumbled to the floor and rolled right up to his front paws, a gift from the Roman god of doughnuts. He gobbled it up and continued hunting and gathering.

Tobias stood in the middle of the crowd, smiling stupidly. 'Ears!' he sang. 'I am surrounded by ears. Glorious ears.' He stared. He pointed. He chuckled. He committed the details to memory and, in doing so, spoke rather loudly. 'Ears as large as saucers! Great flapping plates of flesh ... Delicate pink seashells ... Hairy earholes ... Pointy elfin ears ... Mangled ears that look like they've been caught in a car door ... Hairy *earlobes*! My word! You don't see that every d—'

'Tobias!' cried Freja. 'What about our breakfast?'

'What? Breakfast?' The writer scratched his head. He frowned at Freja. 'I say, old chap, why don't you scurry along to the counter and order us something delicious while I finish up here?'

'On my own?' asked Freja. 'In front of all the other customers?'

'Well, of course!' cried Tobias. 'Just look at you with your brilliant blue eyes, your garden-gnome scarf and that tangle of golden hair that drifts and bounces about your head like a halo. *Everyone* will notice you!'

Freja's eyes widened in horror.

'That's a *good* thing!' explained Tobias. 'You'll be served at once. We can gobble our breakfast and be in search of gelato and a good steep hill down which to tumble before you can say "scary hairy earlobes" three times!' Tobias smiled and carried on with his too-loud observations.

Freja sighed. 'The sooner I bring Tobias his breakfast,' she muttered, 'the sooner he will stop talking about that poor man's ears.' She shoved her way between handbags and elbows until she found herself at the counter.

'*Ciao, bella!*' The man behind the bar smiled.

'*Ciao, signore*,' whispered Freja, her cheeks turning pink. 'I'd like two of those big, fat croissants, please.'

'*Cornetti*,' said the man. 'Croissants are what the French call them. If you want to be a true Roman, call them *cornetti*.'

'I'd like two of those big, fat *cornetti*, please.' Freja bit her lip. 'No! Four *cornetti*! I'm terribly hungry and I want to be really, really heavy by the time I leave this café.'

The man threw back his head and laughed like an opera singer, the notes dancing over the heads of his customers. He reached forward and held Freja's small chin in his big, olive-skinned hand. 'So you are a very hungry angel! I will give you four *cornetti* and two of my favourite pastries.' He snapped a pair of tongs in the air, then lifted a flaky golden roll from its basket. 'This is a little sack of chocolate! *Saccottino al cioccolato!* It sounds good, no? It is delicious! It will make your heart sing and your mouth water for more!'

'*Saccottino al cioccolato*,' echoed Freja. She smiled.

'Excuse me!' cried Tobias. 'Coming through. Mind your bottom there, *signore* ... although it can't be easy when it's so large. Excuse me. Whoopsy-daisy! Ever so sorry, *signora*, but your elbows really were flapping about like the wings of a crazed turkey.'

Freja turned around and gaped. Tobias was pressing towards the counter, leaving a trail of disaster in his wake — spilt coffee, stomped toes, bruised kidneys, laddered stockings. He stumbled, his face ending up in the middle of a greeting between two women, where he stole *all* of the kisses! Accidentally, of course, but now his cheeks were smeared with pink and red lipstick. He arrived at the counter looking more dishevelled than usual.

After they'd each eaten their first *cornetto*, Tobias said, 'Have you noticed that this café is a bit like a layer cake?' He sipped his cappuccino and continued. 'Puckered lips, perfumed necks and hairy earholes at the top. Silk ties, pearls and cappuccino cups in the middle. Shiny shoes and squashed pastries at the bottom.'

Freja giggled. 'The squashed pastries are *your* fault, I think.'

Tobias grimaced.

Freja said, 'I find this café busy-bustling, but in a happy way.'

'Yes!' Tobias nodded. 'What can you hear?'

Freja closed her eyes and tilted her head to one side. 'Happiness humming ... Kisses squishing ... Coffee cups clattering ...' Her brow wrinkled in concentration. 'Crumbs mumbling!'

Tobias chuckled. 'I do like that last one, old chap. "Crumbs mumbling." Absolutely spot-on. And what about the smells?'

Freja opened her eyes and looked up to the ceiling. Her nose twitched. She sniffed slowly and deeply. 'Toasty almonds and icing sugar snowing through a fog of jasmine, roses and ...' She stared at Tobias. '*Hair oil!*'

Tobias tilted his head towards the young man at his side. He was dark and lean, with his hair slicked sideways over his head. He'd used enough oil on his hair to fry two-dozen *zeppole*.

Freja giggled and whispered, 'Slippery-slimy oil-slick hair!'

'Brilliant!' cried Tobias.

Freja smiled and looked down.

The young man's shoes caught her eye. Made of fine leather, they were delicate, black and shiny. Expensive. Freja had seen a similar pair in the window of a shop just two days ago. They cost more than all the breakfasts in the café combined. Perhaps more than Roberto's little three-wheeled truck.

'Shiny shoes,' she whispered, and something poked at the back of her mind once more.

Something important.

Something confusing.

Something a little bit worrying.

CHAPTER 26

Two uses for glue

'I say, old chap! There's a window *full* of teapots! I might buy a new one — to replace the one I smashed this morning!' Without looking to the left or the right, Tobias drifted across the road. A small cream Fiat swerved to miss him, skittled a rubbish bin and drove on. Tobias didn't flinch. He hadn't noticed a thing.

Freja and Finnegan waited until the road was clear, then crossed over.

'Look!' shouted Tobias. 'I LOVE that pink teapot. The one with white polka dots.'

Freja giggled.

'Yes, yes, I know,' said Tobias. 'I do normally like a teapot to be shaped like something fun — a turkey, a telephone, a caravan. But this one, well, I find it strangely appealing. Soothing. Shall we go in and buy it?' And without waiting for Freja's answer, he ducked inside the little shop.

While Tobias clattered amongst the teapots, Finnegan trotted about, licking a rolling pin here, a mixing bowl there, until his tongue got caught in a whisk.

'Ooow!' He threw back his head to howl, which made the whisk pinch even harder. 'Ow-ow-ow-ooooow!'

Freja dashed to his aid. She pulled the whisk free and hugged the hound until he stopped shaking. When she looked up, Vivi was standing by her side.

'*Ciao! Ciao!*' Vivi leaned forward and kissed the girl on each cheek. 'How good it is to see you! But where is Signore Appleby?'

'Over there,' said Freja, pointing towards the window display. 'He's getting a teapot.'

Vivi nodded.

'A *pink* one,' said Freja, slowly and deliberately, '*with white polka dots.*'

'Aaah,' said Vivi, a smile twitching around the corners of her eyes and mouth. She shifted her shopping basket from one hand to the other. It was overflowing with small pink bowls and pale green glasses.

'Your shopping matches your clothes!' said Freja.

Vivi curtseyed, then danced in a little circle to show off her outfit — her pink mohair sweater, her pale green skirt and her pink high-heeled shoes.

'You look wonderful,' whispered Freja. 'Like fairy floss and spearmint.'

'Like cherry blossoms and green tea,' sighed Tobias, his head poking through a shelf full of pots and pans.

Freja looked from Vivi to Tobias and back again.

Vivi gasped. 'Signore Appleby! You have pink lipstick on your cheek!' She frowned. 'And you have red lipstick on your other cheek!'

Tobias blushed. 'It's not what it looks like!'

'It looks like you were caught in the middle of a greeting between two friends,' said Vivi.

'Oh!' cried Tobias. 'Then it *is* what it looks like!' He leaned against the shelf and three saucepans clattered to the floor.

Vivi smiled, her raspberry-gelato lips stretching the full width of her face. Her chocolate eyes were soft and warm like ganache, and her liquorice-thick lashes seemed to flutter a little faster than usual.

Tobias stepped out from behind the shelving. He cradled a teapot in both hands, like a child protecting a precious kitten.

'That is a very pretty teapot,' said Vivi.

'Yes,' sighed Tobias. 'It's delightful! Pink with white polka dots. I simply *must* have it ... although I don't know why ...'

'Really?' asked Freja. 'You *really* don't know why?'

Tobias shrugged.

Finnegan flopped to the floor and rested his chin on his paws.

Vivi threw back her head and laughed.

After an awkward pause, during which there was a great deal of sighing (Tobias), eyelash fluttering (Vivi) and loud, lusty yawning (Finnegan), Freja suggested they pay for their goods and carry on searching for the perfect hill.

'You need a hill?' asked Vivi as they stepped back out into the street. 'The Spanish Steps are not so far away.'

'Oh no!' cried Freja. 'If we tumbled down there, we'd hurt ourselves dreadfully.'

Vivi frowned. 'But why are you tumbling?'

'Cheese wheels,' said Tobias, as if that explained everything.

'I do not know this game called Cheese Wheels,' said Vivi. 'You need somewhere soft? With grass?'

Freja and Tobias nodded.

Vivi stopped walking and pointed back behind them. 'Gianicolo! The English call it Janiculum Hill. It's on the other side of the Tiber River, not so far from the Vatican. There's a steep slope covered in thick green grass. No prickles. No rocks. Just clumps of trees and bushes here and there.'

'Brilliant!' cheered Tobias. 'We'll take the motorcycle for a spin.'

'Come with us, Vivi!' suggested Freja.

Tobias blushed. He tugged at his left ear. He shuffled his feet. 'Jolly good idea. Come along. We'll make an outing of it. We can pack a picnic, bring my new teapot.'

'I would like that very much,' said Vivi, 'but, sadly, I must work today. My café awaits, and my mamma and papà cannot be left to do everything on their own. I am not free until Friday.'

'Friday it is then!' cried Tobias. 'Couldn't have picked a better day myself.' He grinned and leaned back against a Vespa. It was the first of a long row of motor scooters parked at the edge of the street.

'Tobias!' gasped Freja, but it was too late. The Vespa toppled sideways against the next scooter, which then toppled against the next, going on and on until all twenty-seven motor scooters were lying on their sides.

Vivi's eyebrows shot to the top of her forehead.

'Friday then,' sang Tobias. He waved up at her from where he lay strewn over a Vespa, his new teapot now scattered in little pieces at his side.

'Friday,' Vivi replied, her voice high and shaky. She bit her lip, turned on her heel and disappeared down the nearest alley. Her laughter, however, lingered in the air long after she was gone.

On returning to their apartment, Tobias settled down at the kitchen table. He pulled the spout and the handle of the teapot out of one pocket, then a dozen shards of pink-and-white china from the other. Placing them all on the table, he began to sort them and glue them back together. Finnegan sat in the chair beside him, eating a jar of jam.

Freja wandered into the living room and picked up one of the postcards she'd bought yesterday. It was a photo of the Spanish Steps and bore the words 'Greetings from Rome'.

'Greetings from Rome,' muttered Freja. 'I've sent so *many* greetings from Rome and haven't had a word in reply. Oh, Clementine! What's happening?'

Freja grabbed a pencil and forced herself to write another short but cheerful message on the back of the postcard to her mother. She stuck on a stamp, propped the card on the windowsill and looked about for a distraction. Something to shoo away the tears that were loitering in the corners of her eyes.

Freja flicked through the papers on Tobias' desk. She realised that she had, in fact, read all of his current research. Even the book on cheese-making at high altitudes and the pamphlet on training goats. She swelled with pride as she realised how much she had learnt in the last few weeks — about frostbite, thermal underwear, altitude sickness, broken bones, knots, bandages, Swiss chocolate, eagle eyries ... The list went on and on. She'd even learnt how to use a pair of bootlaces as a weapon!

But then her eyes fell on something she had not yet read — *Rome's Reward*, the book that had brought them to Rome in the first place! She snuggled down on the sofa, pressed back the cover and began to read.

By the end of the first chapter, she was hooked. All thoughts of Clementine were pushed aside and she read greedily onward. She was fascinated to learn that many of the buildings in Rome were connected by underground passageways. Some of the tunnels were subterranean quarries from which the early Romans had dug stone to build their city. Others were the remains of ancient streets and buildings that had crumbled and been built over as the centuries passed. Tunnels connected churches, mansions, dungeons, wine cellars and secret treasure troves. Many had collapsed or been closed in. Others had been forgotten altogether.

Freja wondered if she might find a tunnel beneath their courtyard. She giggled. 'I could sneak underground to Trattoria Famiglia! Imagine Enzo's surprise when I popped up, unannounced, from his wine cellar!'

She read on, gasping in delight when twin sisters Bianca and Antonia Silvestro discovered a tunnel connecting their parents' home to the bowels of the Vatican Museums. Her eyes grew wide as she read of the daring haul of giant rubies, sapphires, emeralds and diamonds that they stole. And she laughed with glee at the sheer simplicity — but the incredible brilliance — of their plan to conceal the jewels when every policeman in Rome was trying to recover them.

'Tobias! Tobias!' She ran into the kitchen, waving the novel in the air. 'Best book ever! I love it. How terribly clever. I'm up to the part where Bianca and Antonia have glued the jewels to the saddles and reins of the wooden horses on the merry-go-round. It's ingenious! Everyone will think they're bits of coloured glass, won't they? Nobody will *dream* that the jewels are real. The merry-go-round is right in the middle of Rome! The police will be walking by all day long. Mammas and nonnas will be staring at the horses. Children will be riding them and touching the jewels! *Actually touching the jewels!* And yet nobody will suspect a thing. Oh, I do want to read on and find out what happens next, but the story is so delicious, I don't want to finish it too soon. It's like trying to make your raspberry gelato last a little bit longer!'

Tobias looked up from his reassembled teapot. 'Did you say "raspberry gelato", old chap? Good idea!' He flung his arms wide with excitement and swept the teapot to the floor.

Crash!

He pushed back his chair and shrugged. 'Oh well. No use crying over spilt milk. Or broken china. I dare say raspberry gelato will make us all feel a lot better.'

And he charged out of the apartment at such speed that Freja and Finnegan had to run to catch up.

CHAPTER 27

What nobody knew about the Trevi Fountain

'Signore Appleby!' A priest stepped out from the shadows, into the street in front of them.

The girl and the writer stopped licking their gelato and stared. Partly because they were astonished to meet yet *another* priest who knew Tobias' name. But also because he looked so very odd. He was short, fat and bald, with a nose that looked like a blob of Nonna Rosa's bread dough. His black robe stretched tightly across his belly and his trousers were too long, bunching up at the top of his crocodile-skin shoes. In one of his plump, hairy hands, he held a half-eaten slice of pizza.

Freja stared at the crocodile-skin shoes. How very strange! Even more strange than the doughy nose and the ill-fitting garments.

The priest looked at his pizza as though deciding whether to eat or talk. He took one last bite and tossed the rest to Finnegan. Finnegan gobbled it up.

Wiping his greasy hands on his robe, the priest snarled, 'Signore Appleby!' He stepped closer, both hands now balled into fists.

Finnegan licked his lips and pricked his ears. He seemed confused as to whether the stranger was a friend or an enemy. Freja knew that the pizza in his belly would be telling him 'friend', but the tension in the air would be whispering 'enemy'.

'You,' snapped the priest, 'are Tobias Appleby, the English crime writer.'

Freja dropped her gelato. She slipped her hand into Tobias'.

'What a lark!' shouted Tobias. 'As if I could be a writer!' He smiled down at Freja and squeezed her hand — a secret signal.

Freja tried to smile back. She bared her teeth and wondered if she looked like Pazzo the monkey when he was in a bad mood.

'I, Padre Nico, am no fool. You *are* Tobias Appleby!' The priest moved even closer.

'No, no, no,' Tobias muddled on. 'My name is Donald Dawkings and I'm a tour guide.'

'Donald Dawkings!' echoed Freja. 'And I'm his niece, Daisy Dawkings.'

Tobias squeezed her hand once more and she knew that he was pleased with her quick thinking.

'Yes!' cried Tobias. 'Donald Dawkings, tour guide, at your service! Except I can't really be at your service, because I'm due at the Trevi Fountain this very minute. I have a talk starting soon. Very soon! Must dash!'

'But the Trevi Fountain is this way!' said the priest, pointing in the opposite direction to which they had been walking.

'Yes, of course! Of course!' babbled Tobias. 'But we're doing a lap of the block so we enter the piazza from the *other* side. It's my favourite view, you know. The other side ...'

'You don't want to be late.' Padre Nico smirked. 'Here, let me walk with you, show you the shortest way.' And taking Freja's free hand, roughly, tightly, he guided them along the cobbled streets to the Trevi Fountain. Finnegan trotted along behind, still confused.

'Here we are!' said Padre Nico. He held fast to Freja's hand. 'Where is your tour group?'

Tobias made a great show of peering around the piazza, towards the fountain, stretching up on tippy-toes and squinting.

'He doesn't have a tour group,' said Freja. 'He just rounds people up and then, when he has an audience, he gives his talk.'

'Yes! Great idea!' cried Tobias. 'I mean, that's *exactly* what I do!'

Pushing a little further into the piazza, Tobias clapped his hands. 'I say! Listen up, everyone. I have a jolly good tale to tell about the Trevi Fountain ... Anyone want to hear a story? ... Hello? Helloooo?'

But the crowds bustled on by, laughing, talking, snapping photos. They ignored the muttering man waving a melting raspberry gelato in the air.

Padre Nico squeezed Freja's hand until it hurt.

She frowned up at him. 'Let go of me! I have to help my uncle, Donald Dawkings.'

Padre Nico sneered. 'Donald Dawkings. Ha! We know who he is and what he is trying to do. And it won't work. We have ways and means of persuading him to stop.'

Freja longed to shout, 'Stop *what*?' But that would be admitting Tobias' true identity. And that didn't seem like a wise thing to do right now.

She felt confused, scared and angry all at once. She wanted to cry. She wanted to throw back her head and howl like a wolf. She wanted to run away and hide like a leveret in a mossy green nest. But she knew that this was one of those times when she needed to be brave.

Really brave.

Braver than she ever thought might be possible.

Taking a deep breath, Freja shouted, 'LET! ME! GO!' She kicked the priest in the shin, yanked her hand free and ran. She heard barking and the sound of fabric tearing, but she didn't look back. She pushed through the crowds, further and further into the piazza, until she reached the front of the wide blue pool. There, she flitted along the steps at the edge of the water until she reached the towering wall of the fountain. Hoisting herself up onto the rough rocks, she hopped from one outcrop to the next, towards the great marble statues of Oceanus and his Tritons.

Her foot slipped. She stopped to regain her balance. Oceanus, giant spirit of the sea, frowned down at her from his shell chariot. The short, fat priest glared up at her from the edge of the rocks. Tourists were starting to point and laugh at her from all over the piazza.

Freja reached into her pocket and touched the little felt hare. She whispered, 'Bravery is forging ahead, even when you're scared.' And before she had time to think about what she was really doing, she climbed up onto one of the marble seahorses and stood between its wings. She took a deep breath and shouted above the gushing water. 'Hello! Greetings! *Ciao!*'

Padre Nico dropped to all fours and clambered down off the rocks — a fat black crab scuttling for shelter. There was a flash of red — his underpants. The seat of his trousers was missing!

'Finnegan!' Freja gasped in delight. 'What a clever puppy!'

She felt suddenly happy. Strong. Bold. Brave.

Truly brave!

Her spirits soared and mingled with the mist that rose above the cascading waters. She, Freja Peachtree, was standing in the middle of the Trevi Fountain, on the back of a marble seahorse, beneath a bright blue Italian sky, in front of an enormous crowd, and her knees weren't even knocking!

Thrusting her arms into the air, she flashed her most dazzling smile and shouted even louder. '*Ciao*, beautiful people!'

Tourists all over the piazza turned to look up at her. Coffee cups froze, halfway to mouths. Women slid their sunglasses down their noses and peered over the top. Men took off their hats and stared. Tour guides lost their places mid-story.

Tobias pushed his way to the front of the pool and smiled up at her. His face was filled with pride.

'*Ciao ciao*, beautiful people!' sang Freja. 'Welcome to Rome!'

The crowd began to clap.

'In a moment,' Freja shouted, 'I, Daisy Dawkings, will be down there ...' She pointed to where Tobias stood on the steps at the front of the fountain. 'Down there with Donald Dawkings, the handsome man with the tattered brown cardigan and hair that looks like a mop!'

People chuckled and craned their necks to see.

'Down there with my lovely uncle,' Freja announced, 'who will tell you the secrets of the Trevi Fountain!'

Dazzling them with another smile, she waved and scrambled down from the seahorse's back. She flitted the rest of the way across the fountain to the side opposite Padre Nico. By the time she reached the steps, a small crowd had gathered. They clapped and laughed as she arrived.

Tobias bent down and whispered in her ear, 'Brilliant, old chap. Quick thinking and ever so brave. Clementine would burst a boiler if she could see you now.'

Freja planted a quick kiss on his cheek. 'You'd better start talking, Donald Dawkings. The priest is just over there and we need to keep pretending.'

Tobias nodded. He turned to his audience and sang out, 'Welcome! Welcome! *Ciao! Ciao! Ciao!*' He flung his arms wide and slapped a backpacker across the nose. The audience roared with laughter. Except for the backpacker. He sneezed and took a few steps to the right.

Tobias blushed and stuffed his hands into his pockets. 'Welcome to Rome and the Trevi Fountain!' he cried. 'It's a corker, an absolute gem! This fountain might be old and it might be full of rude nude statues ...' The crowd tittered. 'But it is also a place of real magic.'

'Magic!' An elderly woman sighed and held her hands to her face.

Tobias leaned in and lowered his voice. 'The Trevi Fountain holds the power to draw you back to Rome, time and time again.'

'Oooh! Oooh! I know about this!' yelled a large lady at the front of the crowd. She was American and wore a purple tracksuit with the name 'Samantha' embroidered on the jacket.

'Audience participation!' cheered Tobias. 'We like a bit of that.'

'It's the coins!' Samantha drawled. 'Throwing coins in the fountain will bring you back!'

At the edge of the crowd, Padre Nico was scratching his head.

Tobias continued. 'Legend says that if you throw a coin in the Trevi Fountain, you are sure to return to Rome one day. But it has to be done in *just* the right manner.'

'Show us! Show us!' cried a woman at the back of the crowd.

'Yes, show us how it is done,' said a familiar voice. It was deep and booming, with a Russian accent.

Freja looked up and found herself staring into Boris' face. He pressed a coin into her hand and winked to show that he was in on the trick.

Freja returned the wink, lightning-quick so that no-one else would see. She walked down the steps to the edge of the water. Facing the crowd, she curtseyed, then tossed the coin high into the air, over her left shoulder. It soared upward, spinning and twirling, then tumbled down into the middle of the fountain.

Plop!

The crowd rippled with excitement. Women giggled and clutched their chests. Children begged their parents for a coin to toss. Fathers reached into their pockets. Padre Nico pushed forward, his smirk returning.

'Tobias!' hissed Freja, tugging at his cardigan. 'If the crowd starts tossing coins, they'll drift away and there'll be no-one to shield us from the priest.'

'WAIT!' roared Tobias. 'There's more!'

The crowd fell silent. Padre Nico rolled his eyes.

'Tossing a coin is just the *beginning* of the magic,' said Tobias. 'Ladies! Toss a tube of lipstick into the fountain and you will meet your true love before leaving Rome!'

The women twittered and clucked. Samantha blushed like a tomato and unzipped her bumbag. She rustled about, dropping bus tickets, sweets and tissues until, finally, she pulled out a silver lipstick tube. Her cheeks dimpled.

'What about the men?' yelled the backpacker. 'Don't give the ladies all the fun!'

'Yes. A story for us lads!' cried another.

'Of course!' agreed Tobias. 'Something for the men.' He looked up into the sky and rubbed his chin.

'Socks!' shouted Freja. 'Toss a sock into the Trevi Fountain and a pretty girl will kiss you on the cheek.'

The backpacker chuckled and nudged his friend.

'How do I get a kiss on the *lips*?' asked one bold fellow.

'Toss *two* socks!' cried Tobias. 'One over each shoulder!'

Everyone roared with laughter.

'Toss in a chocolate gelato and you will win at your next game of cards!' sang Tobias.

'Toss in a hat and you will never go bald!' Freja promised.

The girl and the writer were on a roll, and the audience loved it. The sillier they became, the more the audience laughed and clapped.

All except for Padre Nico. He looked confused.

'Toss in a cat and you will live for many, many years!' Tobias shouted. 'The cat's nine lives will become yours!'

'Toss in a roll of toilet paper,' cried Freja, 'and you will *never* get diarrhoea again.'

'Toss in a gold watch,' roared Tobias, 'and you will become a *millionaire!*'

The crowd went wild. They whistled. They cheered. They hugged one another and shouted in delight.

'Brilliant!'

'Marvellous!'

'Wonderful!'

'*Fantastico!*'

'Woof! Boof!'

Boris and Nadia pressed forward and hauled Tobias up onto their shoulders.

'The girl!' Nadia yelled. 'Lift the little girl too!'

The backpacker and his friends hoisted Freja into the air.

The crowd closed in and, as one giant, excited mass, they paraded the girl and the writer around the piazza — between café tables, through the middle of a British tour group, past Padre Nico (who was now biting his fingernails) and back to the steps. They set Freja and Tobias down. One by one, they pressed money into Freja's hands and drifted off, chuckling and shaking their heads, until all who remained were Boris and Nadia. Padre Nico loitered by the edge of the pool a few metres away.

Boris slapped Tobias on the back. 'Donald Dawkings!' he shouted. 'You are the best tour guide we have met in Rome! Come! Let us buy you a drink!' Wrapping his thick, short arm around Tobias, Boris led him away.

And as Boris walked away, he just happened to pass the priest.

And as he passed the priest, he just happened to stumble.

And as he stumbled, he just happened to push the priest into the pool. Head first.

Boris and Tobias walked on as though nothing had happened.

Freja stared, open mouthed, as Padre Nico floundered about in the shallow water, trying to stand.

Nadia shrugged and roared, 'Voopsy-daisy!' She took Freja by the hand and, together with Finnegan, they followed Tobias and Boris out of the piazza, along the street and away to safety.

CHAPTER 28

Chocolate gelato at last!

Side by side, they sat on the Spanish Steps, eating chocolate gelato — Tobias, Freja, Nadia and Boris. Finnegan frolicked in the pretty fountain nearby, a piece of black fabric clenched in his teeth. Every now and then, he stopped and shook it violently to make sure it was dead.

Freja was grateful that Boris had chosen the gelato. Firstly, because chocolate was her favourite, but Tobias seemed unable to buy any flavour other than raspberry. Secondly, because Tobias could eat a chocolate gelato like a normal person. If he had a raspberry gelato, he'd be sighing, puckering his lips and daydreaming about Vivi. They wouldn't get a jot of sense from him.

'Thank you, Boris and Nadia,' said Freja. 'And not just for the chocolate gelato. You rescued us.'

'Ha!' roared Nadia. 'You were doing just fine on your own. You are a brave girl, Freja.'

'And smart!' roared Boris. 'I think you might be a hero!'

Nadia scowled and pointed her gelato at her husband. 'We don't *think* she is a hero, Boris. We *know* she is a hero!'

Tobias leaned in and nudged Freja with his elbow. 'Brave as a bear, old chap.'

The girl smiled at them, all teeth and chocolate-gelato lips.

'Still,' said Tobias, 'it was jolly good to have your assistance, Boris and Nadia. Lucky you happened by. But how did you know we needed help?'

'Nadia saw the priest chasing Freja up onto the fountain,' Boris explained.

Nadia nodded. 'I said to myself, "Aha! There is the bad priest! The same one, I am sure, who was bothering my friends in the Borghese Gardens just yesterday."'

'But that's the mystery of it all,' said Tobias. 'It *wasn't* the same priest!'

'No,' whispered Freja. 'It was a brand-new priest. One we've never seen before.'

'No-o-o-o!' barked Nadia. '*Another* one?'

'Poo!' barked Boris. 'That makes Boris cranky. *Three* bad priests? There is no room in the world for even *one* bad priest!'

'But why do they chase you?' asked Nadia. She glared at Tobias. 'And do not tell us about the ink and the nun. A priest does not chase an angel like Freja, because a silly writer has spilt his ink!'

Tobias scratched his head with the point of his gelato cone.

'Think!' snapped Boris. 'You are the crime novelist. You must know all about bad men and why it is they do horrible things to harmless writers!'

'Woof!' Finnegan bounded across the piazza, dripping wet. Stopping in front of Tobias, he shook the water from his fur, then flopped to the ground. There, he gnawed at the strip of fabric from the priest's pants.

Boris laughed. His gelato fell from its cone onto his boot.

Finnegan crawled forward, swallowed the gelato in two great gulps, then licked the boot clean.

'Look how shiny Finnegan has made your shoe!' Freja giggled, then stopped. She squealed and slapped her hand across her mouth. For the thing that had poked and prodded at the back of her mind for days had now marched boldly forth to the sound of a trumpeted fanfare.

'I say, old chap.' Tobias frowned. 'Are you all right?'

'Shoes!' gasped Freja. 'The clue is in the shoes!'

Boris and Nadia looked at one another, each raising a single eyebrow.

Freja turned to Tobias. 'Remember the journal we read for our bedtime story — the one about disguises?'

'Absolutely!' said Tobias. 'That poor American spy slipped up on one little detail with his disguise.'

'Yes!' shouted Freja. 'The plastic water-spurting flower was all wrong.'

Tobias held out his hands in a silent question.

'But *this* time,' Freja explained, 'it's not about plastic flowers. The mistake is with the shoes. It's all about the shoes!' She grabbed Tobias' knee. 'Don't you see, Tobby? THE PRIESTS HAVE BEEN WEARING THE WRONG SHOES!'

'Aaaaah!' said Boris, nodding. 'The wrong shoes.'

'Yes!' cried Freja. 'I was thinking of all the nuns and priests I've seen in Rome — Mother Superior with her scuffed boots; the cycling nuns wearing sandals and socks; the kind priest with the hole in his shoe; the sisters in Campo de' Fiori who tossed their old boots in the bin and bought cheap sandshoes for five euros; and even now, *look*!' She pointed at three priests who were clomping across Piazza di Spagna in long brown robes and khaki gumboots.

'Farm priests,' said Nadia. 'They are from the countryside. Perhaps their gumboots are the only shoes they own.'

'Exactly!' shouted Freja. 'Nuns and priests are poor. They don't have money for fancy shoes. Sometimes they don't have any money at all. But Padre Paolo — the priest who came into the bookstore — had shiny black shoes that looked like something a movie star would wear. I got all excited because I thought he was a rich man who would buy lots of Tobias' books. But he wasn't … and he didn't …' Her eyes boggled.

'Padre Flavio, the priest in the Borghese Gardens, kicked Finnegan, so I noticed his shoe. It was pointy and shiny, made of fine leather. It was similar to the shoes worn by the man in the café this morning. You remember him, Tobby — the one who used too much hair oil. Those were expensive shoes. I've seen them in a shop window. Eight hundred euros!' Freja jumped to her feet. 'And now Padre Nico, the silly fat priest at the Trevi Fountain ... well, he had shoes made of crocodile skin. *Real crocodile skin!*'

'Aaah!' said Nadia, nodding so that her fish earrings dangled back and forth. 'Crocodile skin is *very* expensive, I think.'

'Yes, yes,' agreed Boris. 'Shoes made of crocodile skin cost a lot of money. Hundreds and hundreds of euros a pair, I think.'

Tobias leapt to his feet. 'By gum, you're right, old chap!' He tottered at the edge of the step, tugging at his ears. 'Shoes. Yes, shoes,' he muttered. 'Priests who care too much about shoes ...'

He fell silent.

The girl and the writer stared at each other.

'I suspect,' said Freja, talking slowly and precisely, 'that the three nasty priests are not really priests at all.'

That evening, back in their apartment, Freja and Tobias sat on the sofa, sipping milk and nibbling on biscotti.

Finnegan dozed by the fire, his nose wedged into an empty biscuit box.

'The million-dollar question is this,' said Tobias. 'Why are the priests — who are not really priests at all — pretending to be priests? And why are they chasing after me?'

'That's two questions,' said Freja.

'So it is!' cried Tobias. 'Well then, I might as well throw in a third: How do they know what I am trying to do, when I don't even know what it is myself?'

Freja scrunched her nose. Tobias scrunched *his* nose. They both bit down on their biscotti and stared at the ceiling.

Finally, Tobias said, 'The thing is, old chap, you had better not go out alone any more.'

'But it's *you* they're after. Not me.'

'Yes ... but now they've seen you and me together. They know you're an important part of my life.'

Freja's heart leapt at his words. An important part of Tobias' life! How good it felt.

'I'll be okay,' said Freja. 'Finnegan will take care of me.'

They looked over at the dog, who was now chewing on the biscuit box in his sleep.

Freja smiled. 'He's probably dreaming about pizza.'

'Well, that's just the problem,' said Tobias. 'Finnegan is a marvellous dog and a faithful friend and would do anything in the world to keep you safe and sound ... unless something edible gets in the way. Actually, it may even be a problem if something *inedible* gets in the way. Just look at the meal he made of the seat of that priest's pants today! No, no, no. He's just a puppy and can't be depended upon.'

Freja slumped into the cushions.

'You can still visit Nonna Rosa,' explained Tobias, 'as long as I walk you there and Nonna Rosa walks you home. And we'll still have lots of outings. I thought we might go to the Vatican someday soon. Light a candle. Climb the stairs to the top of the dome. Say hello to the Pope.'

'I'd like that,' said Freja.

Tobias babbled, 'We'll just play it safe until we work out what's what and who's who and which way is up and why blue and green should never be seen unless a colour is in between!'

Freja giggled and spilt her milk in her lap.

'That's better now!' cried Tobias. 'A cackle and a swim in a puddle of milk and everything seems much brighter.'

But as he took their empty glasses to the kitchen, Freja noticed that he stopped to peer out the window.

And on his way back, he closed the shutters on both the window and the French doors.

And as Freja got ready for bed, he checked twice that the apartment door was locked and that the ancient bolt, which they had never used before, was pushed firmly into place.

CHAPTER 29

A tingling neck and jelly knees

The next morning, Tobias walked Freja and Finnegan to Trattoria Famiglia.

'Here you go then, old chap.' He squeezed Freja's shoulder. 'You'll be as safe as houses here in Nonna Rosa's kitchen, frolicking amongst the pots of pasta. No outings! I'll be back to fetch you when I've done a spot of writing.'

Freja pushed open the door and crept inside.

'*Buongiorno*, Freja!' Enzo slammed a bottle down on the bar and beamed at her. His cheeks were round and rosy, and his eyes danced with delight. 'Welcome! Welcome! So good to see you, my little friend. And look how beautiful you are. Like a building that is overgrown with ivy.'

Freja had worn green clothes today and decorated her hair with tendrils of ivy. She'd clipped them from the courtyard wall just that morning, so they were fresh and shiny and sprang about merrily amidst the curls of her hair.

The four old men turned around from the bar, stared for a moment, then broke into raucous greetings.

'It's the little golden-haired angel!' cried Xaviero. '*Buongiorno!*'

'*Ciao, bella!*' sang Roberto. He blew a kiss from his knobbly hand to her cheek.

'Hello and good morning, Freja. You are looking very green today.'

'*Ciao! Ciao!*'

Freja clenched her fists, took a deep breath and waited for the panic to rise up inside.

But it didn't.

Her cheeks burned a little, but before she knew what was happening, she found herself smiling and whispering, '*Ciao ciao.*' She even blew a kiss back to Roberto. The old man caught it in his hand, pressed it to his cheek, closed his eyes and sighed.

Nonna Rosa crashed through the kitchen door, a lump of bread dough in her hand. 'You noisy old goats!' she yelled. 'How can I plan my day's menu when —'

Her eyes fell upon Freja and she stopped, her mouth still open for the next angry word. She squeezed the dough so it bulged between her fingers. 'Ah, my beautiful girl. It does my heart good to see you standing up to these ugly old men and not letting them scare you away beneath the tables. I hope you are scolding them for their silly stories and lazy ways.'

Freja giggled.

'Pah!' scoffed Enzo. 'She is an angel and would never say a cross word to anyone.'

'You old fool!' cried Nonna Rosa, slapping the lump of dough down on the bar. 'Even an angel would be driven insane if she had to listen to you and your stupid old friends, day in, day out!'

Enzo swallowed a chuckle and pasted a mock frown on his face.

Nonna Rosa rolled her eyes, grabbed her dough and retreated to the kitchen. Freja followed, but Finnegan stayed with the old men. They had been drinking grappa and nibbling on bread. There were puddles to be slurped, crumbs to be licked.

Nonna Rosa and Freja worked together in companionable silence, kneading bread dough and shaping it into long, thin loaves. They were just beginning to roll large sheets of pasta for lasagne when Finnegan slunk into the kitchen and cowered under the bench.

'Finnegan,' soothed Freja. 'What's wrong?'

The dog whimpered and hid his head beneath Nonna Rosa's apron. Nonna Rosa shrugged and continued to work her rolling pin back and forth.

Freja peered into the restaurant. 'It's Pazzo!' she cried. 'Giuseppe and Pazzo are here!'

Nonna Rosa threw her hands in the air. 'Mamma mia! That is just what Nonna Rosa needs!' She sighed.

'Another silly old man at the bar to tell stories and a naughty monkey to eat all my walnuts and figs! Freja, be a dear. Go out and keep an eye on them.'

Freja nodded and slipped from the kitchen.

Pazzo was wearing a bread basket on his head and juggling walnuts. The old men rocked back and forth, laughing themselves stupid.

Freja crept closer. 'Hello, Giuseppe.'

'Ah, my dancing partner!' Giuseppe wobbled forward on his stool and kissed her once on each cheek. A tendril of ivy dangled from Freja's hair and tickled his nose. He sneezed loudly, wetly, three times.

Pazzo screeched in fright and dropped his walnuts. Seeing Freja, he scuttled along the bar, stood before her and patted her curls. 'Oo-oo-oo,' he murmured.

Giuseppe smiled. He tossed down the last of his drink, grabbed his hat and stood up. 'Off to work I go. It is a slow day for organ grinders at this end of the city. Pazzo and I will drag our weary feet to the Colosseum and see if we can find some tourists with hearts full of love and pockets full of coins.'

'Wait! Wait!' cried Roberto, stumbling off his stool. 'I will drive you in my truck. I must go and help my son who is working near the Colosseum.'

'*Grazie! Grazie!*' Giuseppe clicked his fingers. 'Pazzo! Come!'

Pazzo screeched and leapt onto Freja's shoulder.

'Pazzo!' grumbled Giuseppe. 'It is love, I know. And Freja is a true beauty. But it is time to go. Come!'

Pazzo wrapped his arms around Freja's head and buried his face in her wild curls and tendrils of ivy.

Giuseppe slumped his shoulders and sighed. 'I am too old and too tired to be arguing with a monkey today!'

'Perhaps,' said Freja, 'I could come too. I haven't seen the Colosseum yet.' To go would mean ignoring Tobias' instructions to stay with Nonna Rosa. But she'd hardly be alone. Finnegan, Giuseppe and Pazzo would be right by her side. In fact, Pazzo might stay stuck to her head!

Giuseppe smiled and nodded. 'You are always welcome, my friend! And Pazzo will be happy.'

The organ and its wagon were loaded onto the back of the tiny green three-wheeled truck. Freja and Pazzo followed. Finnegan squeezed into the cabin with Roberto and Giuseppe, casting anxious glances back at the monkey from time to time.

As Roberto's truck chugged into the middle of the street, a red three-wheeled truck pulled out from an alley just half a block behind them. Freja watched as the red truck wobbled and bobbed along the rough cobblestone surface. It was a wonder that it stayed upright. She laughed and closed her eyes. The fresh winter air felt delicious blustering through her hair.

When Freja opened her eyes once more, the red truck was still following them. Roberto turned onto the main road and the red truck turned after them. Roberto sped up and zipped in and out of the traffic, and the red truck did the same.

Freja felt her throat tighten, her breath catch. 'I'm just scared because of Roberto's driving,' she told herself as they flew around a corner at breakneck speed. 'I'd forgotten how bad it is.' But as the red three-wheeled truck flew around the same corner, her breath caught again.

They zoomed past bustling piazzas, monstrous monuments, marble arches and ancient Roman ruins and, still, the red truck followed.

'Why didn't I listen to Tobias?' Freja scolded herself. But at that moment, the Colosseum loomed into sight, Roberto slammed his foot on the brakes and the red truck zoomed on by. Within moments, it had disappeared around a bend in the road.

'Phew!' Freja flopped forward, resting her forehead on the pipe organ. 'Silly me. I'm as dotty as an otter, muddling real life with one of Tobias' novels.'

While Giuseppe and Pazzo charmed the crowds and filled their money pouch with coins, the girl and the dog explored the Colosseum. They wandered around inside the soaring walls, peering down into the space that would once have been alive with gladiators, chariots, lions, tigers and elephants. Sometimes the Romans had even filled it with water and real ships to re-enact famous battles. Freja tried to feel the wonder that a child would have felt two thousand years ago at seeing such a spectacle. But she couldn't. All she felt was a prickling at the back of her neck, as though she was being watched. She tried to imagine herself surrounded by thousands of spectators, cheering, clapping, stamping, but she continued to feel very small … very alone … very exposed.

'Come on, Finnegan.' Freja rested her hand on the dog's neck. 'Let's go down.'

But downstairs, the nasty feelings remained. And even though she tried to follow the main passageways that were flooded with sunlight, a sudden wrong turn found them all alone in a cold, dim corridor.

A noise echoed in the dark behind them. Footsteps, perhaps.

Again, her neck prickled, as though she was being watched.

'Hello?' said Freja, but the word came out as a mere whisper.

Finnegan stiffened at her side.

'Is anyone there?' she squeaked.

Three pigeons flapped out from the darkness, swooping so close that Freja felt wings brush her cheek. She turned on her heel and ran. She ran like a lion being chased by a gladiator until she stumbled upon the exit and burst out into sunshine, fresh air and crowds of people. Happy, harmless people.

A group of schoolchildren walked by in pairs, their teacher speaking rapid Italian as he pointed up at the stone arches. An acting troupe, dressed in togas, strolled along, laughing and licking pistachio gelato. Finnegan ate a slice of salami that someone had dropped on the ground. And the high, sweet notes of Giuseppe's voice drifted through the air and mingled with the distant sound of traffic.

'Silly,' muttered Freja. 'I'm such a scaredy-cat.' She wiped her eyes and laughed. She grabbed a handful of Finnegan's fur and, together, they pushed through the crowd and headed towards the music, the monkey and the organ grinder.

'Boof!' Finnegan stopped. He spun around so that he faced the Colosseum once more.

Freja tugged at his fur. 'Come on, puppy.'

But he refused to budge. 'Woof! Boof!'

Freja followed his gaze. 'My beanie!' she cried. 'You're right, Finnegan. It's the beanie that Clementine made for my birthday. The one I lost in the church in the middle of the night. I'd recognise it anywhere!'

The girl and the dog watched as the cherry-red pompom bobbed above the sea of heads, getting closer and closer.

Hackles rose on Finnegan's neck and shoulders. A thunderous rumble welled up inside his chest.

Freja held her breath.

The person wearing the cherry-red beanie broke from the crowd, strode forward and glared down at them.

Freja's blood ran cold.

For the person wearing the beanie was also wearing the robes of a priest. He scowled, the scar on his face puckering and wrinkling in a familiar and terrifying manner.

Freja's mind screamed, 'Run! Run!' but her legs had turned to marble. She might just as well tell Oceanus to run from the Trevi Fountain.

Padre Paolo leaned forward so that his nose almost touched Freja's. His breath blew hot and garlicky on her face. 'You tell Tobias Appleby to do his *own* dirty work from now on,' he warned. 'Only a coward sends a little girl to spy on his enemy.'

Finnegan snarled, his sharp white teeth glistening with spit.

Padre Paolo stood upright. He pulled the cherry-red beanie from his head and threw it at Freja's feet.

Freja's mouth opened and closed, but no sound came out.

The priest touched two fingers to his face below his eyes, then stabbed them at Freja. 'I'll be watching you,' he hissed. He stepped back and disappeared into the crowd.

Freja bit her lower lip to stop it from wobbling. She bent down and grabbed her beanie. She brushed some dirt off the pompom, whispering, 'I'm all right. I'm all right. Everything's all right.'

But even Finnegan seemed rattled. He continued to stare in the direction the priest had gone and showed not a jot of interest in the giant cherry-red pompom on Freja's beanie.

'Everything's all right,' the girl whispered once more.

But as she walked back to Giuseppe, her heart slammed against her ribcage over and over again, declaring that she was a liar and everything was far from all right.

CHAPTER 30

Lies, lies, despicable lies

An hour later, Finnegan and Freja were back at Trattoria Famiglia, sitting at the table by the kitchen door. Finnegan had already wolfed down two enormous servings of Nonna Rosa's spaghetti Alfredo and was now licking the bowl as though he hoped to wear a hole in it.

Freja poked and prodded her pasta with a fork, but couldn't eat a bite. She pushed her bowl towards Finnegan. He gobbled and guzzled, then slurped the final strand of spaghetti so quickly that the loose end flicked wildly from side to side. Creamy sauce splattered all over the tablecloth, the wall and Freja's shirt.

'Boof!' said the dog, perhaps in apology, then licked the sauce off Freja's sleeve, working his way from the cuff upward. When he reached the top, he swiped his tongue around her ear and dribbled on her shoulder, then trotted off to the bar for a glass of lemonade.

Freja looked down at the cherry-red beanie where it sat in her lap. She plucked at the pompom, frowning.

How did Padre Paolo get hold of her beanie? It had fallen off her head when she'd fled from the Church of Santa Maria in Aracoeli. She'd been so frightened that she hadn't dared stop to pick it up.

'Terrified,' she whispered, 'by the cat and the echo of my own footsteps.' But even as the words came out, she realised they were false. For she now remembered another detail, one that had been pushed to the back of her mind by everything else that had happened over the last two days.

'The door!' gasped Freja. 'I closed it when I left the church. I felt the latch click into place. But then ... when I looked back, it closed *again*. Someone was inside the church. They must have been there *the whole time*!' She shuddered. 'It was a person that made the bump near the altar, not the cat! It was another set of footsteps, not the echo of mine. And it was that same person who opened the church door and spied on me as I walked down the stairs.'

She closed her eyes tightly. She squeezed the pompom on the beanie.

'It was *him*!' she cried, her eyes flying open, her chair clattering backward as she sprang to her feet.

A man at the next table got such a fright that he stuck a forkful of veal into his cheek, missing his mouth completely. His wife made a *tut-tut* sound with her tongue. Although whether this was aimed at Freja or her husband was not completely clear.

Freja righted her chair and sat down again. 'It was *him*,' she whispered to the painting of the Pope on the wall. It helped to have someone listening. It made her think more clearly. 'Padre Paolo was in the church. He was already there when I went inside to pray for Clementine. And *that's* how he got my beanie.' Her stomach clenched. 'Padre Paolo saw me in the church and he thinks I *knew* that he was there. He thinks I went there to *spy* on him!' She leaned closer to the Pope and gasped. 'He thinks *Tobias* sent me to spy on him ... *that Tobias was sending me to do his dirty work!*'

Freja felt a spark of excitement. Surely this was another piece of the puzzle solved!

But what would the priest — who was not really a priest — be doing in the Church of Santa Maria in Aracoeli in the middle of the night? Not praying, that was for sure. If he was pretending to be a priest, he'd be *glad* to be caught in the middle of a prayer. Instead, he was furious! He must have been doing something wrong. Something illegal.

Something bad.

She must tell Tobias.

The Pope stared at her in disbelief.

Of course! The Pope was right. She couldn't tell Tobias. For then he would know that she had been wandering around Rome alone at night. And she would have to tell him that she had left Nonna Rosa's this morning too. Because how else could she explain her discovery?

Tobias would be disappointed in her. He might even be cross.

'What a mess!' she moaned.

She pulled the beanie onto her head, down over her eyes, and flopped forward. Her glass fell over. Water ran across the table and dribbled onto the floor.

'I say, old chap, you're looking a bit green around the gills.'

Freja lifted the beanie from one eye and peered up at Tobias. 'I'd like to go home now, please,' she whispered.

As they stepped out into the street, Freja froze. She glanced nervously from side to side, taking in every detail, until she was certain no-one was loitering in the shadows. She slipped her hand into Tobias' and willed her jelly legs to walk.

Tobias frowned down at her. 'Your fingers are like ice, old chap!'

Freja forced herself to smile up at him.

His frown deepened. 'I don't remember you wearing that hat when I walked you to Nonna Rosa's this morning. How terribly odd! I know that I'm dreadfully absent-minded and sometimes forget my own name. But that hat is a jolly marvel — not the sort one fails to notice.'

'I wasn't wearing it,' said Freja. 'I left it at Trattoria Famiglia the other day and Nonna Rosa gave it back to me this morning.'

Tobias nodded.

Freja burned with shame. The lie had slipped so easily from her lips.

Of course, they had both told many lies over the last few days — that Tobias was Leonardo Stupido; that Freja was his niece; that tossing a lipstick into the Trevi Fountain would bring you true love. But they'd lied for good reason, to fool the nasty priests who were not really priests at all. Here, now, she was deceiving Tobias, the sweetest, kindest person she had ever known. It felt rotten.

Back in the apartment, she slipped into her room and closed the door. She sat at her dressing table and stared at her reflection in the mirror. The cherry-red beanie glared at her, accusing her of telling lies and keeping secrets that should be shared. She swiped it off.

Dropping her chin, her eyes fell upon the battered little treasure chest. She reached out and flicked the rusty metal lock with the tip of her finger. 'More secrets,' she snorted. 'Secrets under lock and key.'

She frowned. She picked up the treasure chest and turned it over in her hands. The secrets inside rattled and clunked.

Freja shrugged and stuffed the little chest into her cherry-red beanie. She stood up, marched across the room, shoved the bulging beanie inside her satchel and buckled the flap. Dropping the satchel, she kicked it. Hard. It slid across the floor and disappeared beneath the bed.

'There!' She stepped back and dusted her hands together. 'All of the secrets are out of sight!'

'Ow-ow-ow-ooow!' Finnegan hollered from the other side of the door.

Freja let the giant hound in. He leapt up, placing his front feet on her shoulders, and swept his broad tongue back and forth across her face, whimpering all the while. He was relieved, excited and delighted to see her, as though they'd been separated for five weeks rather than five minutes.

Freja laughed, despite her bad mood, and kissed his enormous, wet nose.

Satisfied, the dog released her. Trotting to the bed, he jumped up onto the quilt, stretched out and settled in for a good chew on the corner of the pillow. Freja flopped down beside him and lost herself once more in the pages of *Rome's Reward*.

CHAPTER 31
Tumbling down Janiculum Hill

The girl, the writer and the pretty chef stood side by side on Janiculum Hill. The Tiber River wound its way along the bottom of the hill, slithering through the arches of one marble bridge after the next. Rome stretched out before them — domes, bell towers, ochre walls and endless terracotta rooftops. Ancient pine trees soared above their heads, a light breeze whispering through their branches.

'Beautiful,' whispered Freja. 'It's all so very beautiful.'

'Oh yes,' sighed Tobias. 'Beautiful.' But he wasn't looking at the view or the ancient pines or even the brilliant blue sky filled with powder-puff clouds. His gaze was directed at Vivi. Today, she was dressed all in white — crisp white shirt, white jeans, white sandshoes and white headband. The only touch of colour was a pale yellow scarf around her waist and the yellow-and-white striped box of macarons she held in her hands.

'Beautiful,' repeated Tobias. 'Like a meadow full of daisies on a warm summer's day.'

Vivi blushed.

Freja wrinkled her nose.

'Woof! Boof!' Finnegan bolted across a grassy clearing a little further down the hill. His ears flapped in the air and a black hat flapped from his mouth. Moments later, an elderly man tottered into view, shouting and waving his walking stick in a threatening manner.

'Finnegan's a bit skittish today,' said Freja. 'He stole a box of biscotti from the kitchen cupboard and gobbled them all up. And he'd already eaten five pieces of burnt toast with marmalade and his daily jar of raspberry jam. We think he's had too much sugar. It does make him rather silly.'

'He *is* just a puppy,' explained Tobias. 'We can't expect too much of the poor little thing.'

Vivi watched as the poor little thing ran back towards the elderly man, bowled him over and licked his bald head until it glistened in the sunlight. 'Woof! Boof!' the dog barked. The man sat up, shook his head and burst out laughing.

'Astonishing!' gasped Vivi.

'Yes,' sighed Tobias, still looking at Vivi.

Her eyes twinkled and she said, 'Shall we eat?'

Tobias grabbed the picnic hamper from the back of the motorcycle.

Vivi spread a yellow-and-white chequered rug on the grass and laid out a white linen serviette for each of them. She unpacked the hamper and the centre of the rug was soon filled with a delicious Italian picnic — a large, crusty loaf of bread, sun-dried tomatoes, marinated artichoke hearts, anchovy-stuffed olives, paper-thin slices of prosciutto and salami, small, soft balls of bocconcini, fresh tomatoes and large yellow pears.

Meanwhile, Tobias pulled a Thermos, a teapot shaped like a sheep and a canister of tea leaves from his backpack. 'Can't have a proper picnic without a pot of tea,' he murmured. 'My word, no. A picnic without tea would be a disaster ... as bad as trifle without jelly ... a book without words ...'

'The Trevi Fountain without water!' shouted Freja.

'Rome without ruins!' cried Vivi.

Tobias nodded. 'So we're agreed: A picnic without a cuppa would be an absolute disaster. It's a jolly good thing I remembered my teapot!'

They sat and nibbled and laughed and chatted. Freja told Vivi everything she knew about walruses, spending quite some time describing the way they used their whiskers to locate clams, mussels and bottom-dwelling organisms. 'Like using a metal detector to find gold,' explained Freja.

Tobias ate an artichoke heart and confessed that artichokes always made him think of a character in his second novel. 'His name was Artie,' said Tobias. 'The jolly thing is, he choked. *Artie choked!*'

Vivi stared at him.

Tobias tugged at his ear. 'Well, actually,' he muttered, 'someone else choked him ...'

Freja giggled and bit into a macaron, a yellow one because it matched Vivi's scarf and the picnic rug. Sugar danced across her tongue, chased by a lemony tang and a quick sour buzz. So much magic in one small bite.

'Vivi,' she said, 'is it hard being a chef?'

'Yes and no,' said Vivi, smiling. 'It's hard work, but it's a lot of fun. It brings me great joy to fill people's bellies with delicious food and their hearts with warm feelings.'

'Warm feelings,' echoed Tobias. His voice was dreamy, his grin wobbly.

'Here!' said Freja, thrusting the yellow-and-white striped box towards him. 'Have a macaron!'

Vivi smiled. 'My nonna used to own my little café. It was called Café Delizioso back then and I trained in the kitchen as her chef. My nonna worked in her café for fifty-five years. Then one day, a little over a year ago, she took off her apron and passed it to me.' The smile lingered on Vivi's raspberry-gelato lips, but tears welled up in her eyes. 'Nonna said, "Enough. I'm tired. Now it is your turn, Vivi." She went upstairs to bed and she didn't wake up the next morning.'

Vivi stared at an ant as it crawled slowly across her serviette. She sniffed.

Tobias reached across the bocconcini, the artichoke hearts and the cups of tea to place his hand gently on top of Vivi's.

Freja watched, open mouthed, as Vivi's olive-skinned hand turned upward and her petite fingers entwined with Tobias' long, ink-stained fingers. The breeze dropped, the pine trees ceased to whisper and Freja stared. Something magical was happening. Something that filled Freja with longing and loneliness and happiness and a sense of wholeness all at the same time. It was, she realised, love.

'Boof!' Finnegan bounded into their midst, breaking the spell and squashing the remaining macarons.

Vivi threw back her head and laughed. Finnegan gobbled the squashed macarons, then leapt at Tobias, bowling him over.

'So!' cried Vivi, jumping to her feet. 'Now we have full bellies and lots of energy. Perhaps it is time for you to teach me your special game. The one you call Cheese Wheels.'

CHAPTER 32

A thrilling game of Cheese Wheels

'Cheese Wheels in five easy steps!' Tobias stood at the top of the grassy slope, a frown on his brow, a slice of salami stuck to his knee.

The girl and the pretty chef stood to attention.

The pretty chef giggled.

Freja elbowed her. 'Shhhh! This is serious, Vivi.'

'*Scusa*,' whispered Vivi, then burst into a peal of laughter.

Tobias scratched his head. 'I say, Freja, old chap. Vivi's cackle is as bright as yours. Brilliant! Cheering, rousing, wild and melodic all at once! Like a bell tower in a windstorm! A brass band on a sugar high!'

Vivi hiccuped and brought herself under control.

'Thank you, *signorina*,' said Tobias. 'Now, where were we? Cheese Wheels in five easy steps. One:

Position yourself at the top of a steep, grassy slope, preferably one that does not end in a plummeting cliff. Two: Tuck yourself into a tight ball, wrapping your arms around your knees and pressing chin to chest. Three: Lean forward and —'

He was gone, tumbling down the hill like a giant cheese wheel. Tumbling, bumbling, roaring and rolling, until he crashed into a stand of bushes. A flock of birds flew into the sky and flapped away towards the Vatican: 'Ga-a-awk! Ga-a-awk! Ga-a-awk!'

'What about the other two and a half steps?' asked Vivi.

Freja shrugged.

Vivi tightened the scarf around her waist, moved forward, tucked herself into a ball and tumbled down the hillside.

'Excellent!' cried Tobias, helping her to her feet. 'You're a natural cheese wheel, Vivi!'

Hand in hand, they tramped back up to the top of the slope.

'Your turn, old chap.' Tobias patted Freja on the shoulder. 'Once down for practice, then I shall stand at the bottom of the slope and allow you to cheese-wheel smack-bang into me. It'll be fascinating to see the sort of damage you can do. Absolutely fascinating! A broken leg or two ... Concussion ... A cracked skull would be exciting!'

Freja stepped to the edge of the slope, tucked herself into a ball and tumbled forward. She rolled like a perfect cheese wheel, her path smooth and straight. She gained speed, tumbling faster and faster, until she could no longer tell which part of her body touched the grass and which flew through the air. Faster, ever faster, until she crashed into the bushes, snapping twigs, ripping off leaves. The dense branches scratched her arms and tugged at her curls, but still she tumbled on until, at last, she emerged from the other side and found herself sprawled out in the middle of a flowerbed.

Freja sat up and pulled a twig from her hair.

She rubbed her eyes.

She blinked and gasped.

For there, parked not five metres away, was a little red three-wheeled truck.

And leaning against its side were two priests.

One priest was tall and thin with slicked-back hair — Padre Flavio! A pair of binoculars hung from his neck. He held a mirror in one hand, a pair of scissors in the other, and was halfway through trimming his moustache.

The other priest was short and fat with a bald head and bushy black eyebrows — Padre Nico! He held an enormous calzone up to his mouth, but had stopped eating mid-bite.

The girl stared at the priests.

The priests stared at the girl.

'Spying,' whispered Freja. 'You're spying on us.'

Padre Flavio tossed his mirror and scissors to the ground.

Padre Nico took two slow chomps of his calzone.

Both kept their eyes glued to the girl.

Freja sat as still as a granite rock. She moved her eyes from side to side, taking in as much of her surroundings as possible. The door to the truck was open, but the keys were not in the ignition. The narrow road on which the truck was parked continued for at least a hundred metres before it made a hairpin bend and headed uphill to their own picnic spot. The bushes at her side now had a tunnel right through the middle thanks to her perfect impersonation of a cheese wheel. And the short, fat priest was still stuffing the calzone into his mouth.

Padre Flavio elbowed Padre Nico.

Padre Nico gulped and started to choke.

Now! thought Freja. She launched herself at the bushes, scuttled through the tunnel on her hands and knees, leapt to her feet and scrambled up the hillside.

'Tobby! Tobby! Tobby!' she shouted as she ran. 'The priests are here! They have binoculars and a truck, and they're coming to get us! The priests! The priests! The nasty priests!'

'Priests?' said Vivi.

'No time to explain,' said Tobias. 'Just follow me!'

Grabbing Freja's hand, he dragged her up the last part of the slope, swept her through the middle of their picnic and tossed her into the sidecar.

'Finnegan!' he yelled. 'Come!'

The dog came crashing out of a nearby stand of trees, an acorn clamped between his teeth, an angry squirrel at his heels. He galloped across the grass and leapt into the sidecar on top of Freja.

Tobias jumped onto the motorcycle. 'Get on behind me, Vivi. Hang on tight.'

Vivi climbed onto the motorcycle and wrapped her arms around Tobias' waist. She squeezed tightly and pressed her cheek into his back, ready for take-off, but the hasty escape came to a halt.

Tobias closed his eyes.

His hands fell off the handlebars and dropped to his knees.

His mouth flopped into a wobbly grin — and Freja could practically see love hearts drifting around his head. Big, fat pink love hearts. And if she didn't do something, they'd soon be joined by pretty bluebirds, lemon macarons and scoops of raspberry gelato. Tobias would be *completely* lost in Viviland.

'Tobby!' shouted Freja, slapping his leg. 'Wake up! I can hear the truck coming up the hill!'

Tobias jumped and blinked. He grabbed the handlebars, kick-started the motorcycle and revved the engine. At the same moment, the little red three-wheeled truck rounded the bend and zoomed towards them.

'Tobby! Tobby! Tobby!' cried Freja.

'Woof! Boof! Boofety! Woof!' barked Finnegan.

'Are we still playing the Cheese Wheel game?' asked Vivi.

'No,' said Tobias. 'This one we call Chasies.' He winked at Freja, and the motorcycle roared forward, screeched around the corner and jumped the gutter. They side-swiped a park bench, ripped through a wide garden bed, soared up and over a grassy knoll and rumbled out onto the main road.

'Hold on to your hats!' shouted Tobias as they hurtled down Janiculum Hill, back towards the centre of Rome.

'Well, that was fun!' gasped Vivi. She tried to smile, but her white knuckles betrayed her.

'It's not over yet!' cried Freja. 'Look!'

The little red truck flew over the rise, becoming fully airborne. It thudded back to earth and sped down the hill after them, wheels wobbling, engine screaming.

'Head for Trastevere!' shouted Vivi. 'Over there to our right. It's an old part of town. Dark and crumbly. Crooked and dishevelled. The buildings are squashed together. We can lose them if we wind back and forth along the alleyways.'

'Brilliant!' cheered Tobias. They screeched off the main road, along a cobbled street and into a small piazza with a fountain and a pretty church.

'That's the Church of Santa Maria in Trastevere!' cried Vivi. 'It is very lovely and —' But already they'd flashed past and were now zooming down a narrow street. Here, the cobblestones were rough and uneven, and their teeth rattled like dice in a cup. Tobias slowed down, but a moment later, unbelievably, the red truck barrelled down the narrow street after them.

Tobias accelerated, swerved around a cyclist and zipped down an even smaller street. This one was barely wide enough for two bicycles to pass.

'No! No! No!' A small, wrinkled woman stood at her door, waving her arms in the air. 'Stop! Stop!'

But it was too late. They rounded a bend and drove straight through a line of washing that had been hung between the buildings to dry. A wet white sheet caught on the handlebars, ripped from the line and fell on their heads. Now they were driving blind, a large, clumsy ghost bumping and bouncing along the cobblestones, toppling pot plants, swiping the edges of buildings.

Vivi pulled the sheet free and they surged onward, weaving back and forth along the tiny streets — past crumbling houses, stone churches, badly parked cars, sunbaking cats, shady cafés, pocket-sized gardens, artists' studios, fountains sprouting from walls. Finally, they shot out of the shadows, alone, and headed for the nearest bridge.

They flew across the Tiber River and drove along the wide, open streets until they arrived at the Colosseum. There, Tobias took the girl, the dog and the pretty chef on a victory lap.

'We're gladiators!' shouted Tobias, thrusting an ink-stained fist in the air. 'My motorcycle is our chariot! We are victorious! Our enemy is conquered! Hear the ancient crowd roar!'

Finnegan turned around, grinned and licked Freja's nose. Freja laughed and licked Finnegan's nose in return. Vivi wrapped her arms a little tighter around Tobias' middle and sighed.

'Tobias Appleby! Freja Peachtree!' Boris and Nadia called out and waved from the midst of a crowd that was shuffling its way through the entrance to the Colosseum.

Tobias slowed down and might have stopped to chat, but at that moment, a high-pitched whining sound cut through the air, followed by the appearance of the little red truck.

'Amazing!' gasped Vivi. 'They play the Chasies game well, no?'

'Yes!' cried Tobias. 'But not as well as us!'

He revved the engine and roared away with such a lurch that Finnegan and Freja cracked heads. By the time the stars cleared and Freja could see again, they had passed the ancient ruins of the Forum and were leading the priests on a game of cat-and-mouse through the busy streets of Rome. They zigzagged back and forth until they found themselves at the top of the Spanish Steps.

'Noooo, *signore!*' gasped Vivi.

'Boof!' said Finnegan.

'Yes!' shouted Freja. 'They wouldn't *dare* follow us!'

Tobias gave the engine full throttle. Dirt spun into the air, Finnegan howled, Vivi screamed and the motorcycle zoomed forward, plummeting straight down the Spanish Steps.

Freja tried to shout, 'Everyone get out of the way!' but her head bounced up and down like a rubber ball on a concrete path and what came out of her mouth sounded like a flight of stairs: 'Ev-ev-ev-every-one-get-et-et-out-of-the-way-ay-ay-ay-ay!'

There was a moment's relief as they reached the first terrace and the bouncing stopped. But the priests, either brave or stupid beyond compare, decided to follow. The little red truck plunked, rattled and rocked from side to side, threatening to topple with every step.

Tobias forged onward, down one flight of stairs after another, until they reached the bottom. The motorcycle tilted to the right, the sidecar lifting from the ground for a few startling seconds. They swerved to the left, tore around the marble fountain and chugged to a halt at the far side of Piazza di Spagna.

The girl, the dog, the writer and the pretty chef sat and watched, entranced, as the little red three-wheeled truck wobbled and lurched the rest of the way down the Spanish Steps. *Donkety-plonkety-thumpety-bump!* It plopped off the last step, hitting the flat ground with a *crunch*. One of the rear wheels flew off, bounced three times, then rolled across the piazza and into the nearest bar. The rest of the truck scraped forward, metal howling against stone, sparks spraying out like a fireworks display. Colliding with the edge of the fountain, it flipped over and landed with a *splash*, upside down in the crystal-clear pool.

Never before had Piazza di Spagna fallen so quiet. All that could be heard was the pitter-patter of water hitting the side of the battered red truck.

A crowd gathered around the fountain. They watched in silence as Padre Flavio kicked open the door, released his seatbelt and fell out into the pool of water. The truck wibbled and wobbled, then Padre Nico tumbled out the same door and flopped on top of Padre Flavio.

The crowd tittered.

Padre Flavio cursed and punched the water with his fists.

A siren sounded somewhere in the distance.

'Tobby,' whispered Freja. 'The police are on their way. Do you think we should slip away now?'

'Good idea, old chap,' said the writer, and slowly, quietly, he drove around the corner to Café Vivi.

Vivi climbed off the motorcycle and walked unsteadily to her doorstep. Holding the doorjamb, she stared at the girl, the dog and the writer.

Finnegan blinked back at her and yawned.

'Oh, I almost forgot!' cried Tobias. He pulled a book from behind Freja's seat in the sidecar. 'I'd like you to have a copy of my latest novel, *Rome's Reward.*'

'I've just read it,' said Freja. 'It's very exciting, but rather scary!'

Vivi accepted the book. '*Grazie,*' she whispered. But the width of her chocolatey eyes and the surprised

'O' formed by her raspberry-gelato lips seemed to be saying, 'What on earth could be more exciting or terrifying than an everyday picnic with Tobias Appleby?'

CHAPTER 33
Maps and stories and musings

The following day was sunny and warm, reminding everyone in Rome that spring was just around the corner. Tobias pushed the old oak desk out onto the balcony and settled down with paper and ink, typewriter and tea. Freja longed to be out and about, exploring the streets and piazzas, but Tobias was soon lost in the world of his story and even *she* could now see that venturing out alone was not wise. A morning with her scrapbook, pens and pencils would have to do.

Freja spread a quilt on the ground beside Tobias' desk and worked on her map of Rome. Finnegan lay at her feet, licking her toes and gnawing on her pencils.

Freja sketched the outline of Janiculum Hill, then filled it in with pathways, grass, bushes, ancient pine trees and a yellow picnic rug. The picnic rug was soon laden with artichokes, macarons, pears and salami. She chewed thoughtfully on the end of her pencil for a moment, then added a small pair of hands with the fingers entwined.

Tobias sprang to his feet. He peeled off his cardigan and vest and tossed them to the ground. He kicked off his shoes and socks, unbuttoned his collar and rolled up his sleeves. Returning to his chair, he leaned back and stretched. 'Aaah. There's nothing quite like the sunbeams in Rome!' He smiled down at Freja. 'I say, old chap, that map is looking absolutely spiffing! Better than anything I've seen in the shops.'

Freja smiled up at him, her blue eyes sparkling. 'I'm just about to draw Trastevere, the crumbly, old area with the washing line and the angry housewife,' she said.

'Well, that's jolly clever of you. After all, we spent so very little time there!' He grimaced.

'Yes.' Freja giggled. 'But we did see a lot, with all that zigzagging up and down the alleyways.'

Tobias nodded. He cracked his knuckles and returned to his work — typing, muttering, stopping every line or two to sip his tea.

Freja leaned over her map. She drew a tangled maze of narrow alleyways, then filled it in with crooked buildings, cats on rooftops, washing strung from one building to another, cafés, galleries and nuns. Finally, she squeezed in the Church of Santa Maria in Trastevere that Vivi had pointed out as they zoomed by. She took extra time drawing the church's arched portico, square bell tower and fine piazza with hexagonal fountain. It was, she recalled, a very pretty church. She would have to go back there one day when she had time to go inside and look around.

Finnegan stretched, yawned and began to eat Freja's green pencil. It was obviously time for a snack. Freja ducked inside and returned with a packet of biscuits. The moment she started to unwrap it, a flock of pigeons swooped down from the rooftop and landed on the desk. Tobias swept them away, but they simply flapped about in the air, shedding feathers and dust, then returned to the desk. A latecomer landed on the writer's head, another on his shoulder.

Tobias grimaced and pushed back his chair. 'Look! Look!' he sang in his best Italian pigeon accent. 'The *bella bambina* has brought us biscuits for our lunch.'

'Biscuits!' he screeched, now in a high-pitched Italian voice. 'I can't eat biscuits! Just look at how fat I am getting!'

Freja gasped in delight, for the pigeon on Tobias' shoulder now fluffed up her feathers and turned into a chubby, round ball.

'You think *that* is fat!' cried Tobias in a third voice. 'Have you seen how fat Signore Alfonzo has grown?'

'It's because of all the salami he eats. He *loves* salami. He loves salami like the rest of us love to breathe! Yesterday, he ate three whole salamis for breakfast and when his wife asked where they had all gone, he blamed it on the cat.'

'That is a fat cat the Alfonzos have. Perhaps he truly *did* eat the salamis.'

'No! No!' sobbed Tobias in a mournful voice. 'The Alfonzo cat is fat from eating pigeons. My poor cousin Fredo ...'

Freja giggled helplessly. Finnegan snatched the packet of biscuits from her hand and gobbled them up, paper and all.

'*Ciao!*' called a voice from down in the street.

Tobias stared at Freja. 'I say, old chap! You don't suppose there's a pigeon down there who's really talking?'

'*Ciao! Ciao!* It's me! Vivi!'

Freja ran to the edge of the balcony, leaned over the railing and waved. '*Ciao*, Vivi! You're looking very pretty today.'

Vivi smiled and curtseyed. She wore a white dress patterned with large pink cherry blossoms. Her feet looked delicious in macaron-pink shoes with bows on the toes. Pinned to her shoulder was an oversized brooch in the shape of a bluebird.

Tobias leaned over the railing beside Freja. The pigeons still clung to his head and shoulder.

Vivi slapped her hand across her mouth, but could not contain her laughter. It gurgled up inside, slipped through her raspberry-gelato lips, floated up into the air and danced around the balcony.

'Oooh,' sighed Tobias.

'Boof!' said Finnegan, and he nipped at the seat of his master's pants.

Vivi held up *Rome's Reward* and a pale blue-and-white striped box. 'May I come up?'

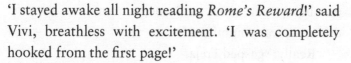

'I stayed awake all night reading *Rome's Reward*!' said Vivi, breathless with excitement. 'I was completely hooked from the first page!'

'Me too!' said Freja, licking macaron crumbs from her lips.

'This morning, I rang my mamma and begged her to look after Café Vivi so I could come and tell Signore Appleby how very much I like his work.'

'*Grazie*,' sighed Tobias. Although Freja was not sure whether he was thanking Vivi for the compliment, the lemon macaron he held in front of his mouth, or the fact that she had come to visit him in his apartment and was now sitting on his sofa looking like a cherry tree in full bloom.

'I *loved* your thieves!' crooned Vivi. 'Bianca and Antonia were so very smart: discovering the tunnel from the basement to the Vatican; sending their parents on a cruise to get them out of the house while they did their dirty work; collapsing the tunnel once they had committed the robbery; and hiding the jewels on the merry-go-round horses. Brilliant! *Fantastico!*'

'*Fantastico!*' Freja giggled as the Italian word rolled off her tongue.

'*Fantastico*,' sighed Tobias, gazing at Vivi's pretty face.

'Tobias' other books are wonderful,' said Freja, 'but *Rome's Reward* is the best. It feels so real. Like it truly could happen!'

'That is because it could!' cried Vivi. 'In fact, just before you came to Rome, a crime, not so very different, was committed.'

'Really?' gasped Freja.

'Really,' said Vivi. Her chocolatey eyes grew as wide as saucers. Her voice became low and secretive. 'Some diamonds, *very* large, *very* precious, were stolen from the vault of a bank right here in the city. The bank is in a building that, hundreds and hundreds of years ago, was the mansion of a cardinal. That cardinal looked after the Church of Santa Maria.'

'I just drew the Church of Santa Maria!' cried Freja. 'This morning. On my map of Rome.'

Vivi nodded. 'Yes, you know it, of course. It is beautiful and very unusual. Once, many centuries ago, there was a tunnel from the basement of the cardinal's mansion to the Church of Santa Maria. The cardinal liked to keep it in good repair so he could slip between his home and his church without going into the smelly, disease-ridden streets of Rome. Now the police suspect the diamond thieves discovered this old tunnel and used it to get to the basement of the bank without being seen.'

'Just like Bianca and Antonia used the tunnel in *Rome's Reward*!' Freja clasped her hands together and felt a tingle of excitement run up and down her spine.

Vivi nodded again. 'But when the police looked, the tunnel was collapsed — perhaps it had been that way for years, perhaps it had happened recently with the help of a little dynamite. There was too much damage, too much of the tunnel filled with rock and soil and the crumbs of ancient buildings to tell. Besides, the tunnel led only to the Church of Santa Maria and the priests at the church say *their* end of the tunnel has been blocked for many years. At least as long as they have been there.'

'So the real crime hasn't been solved?' asked Freja.

'No,' said Vivi. 'But the investigators do not think the thieves have left Rome with the diamonds. There have been too many eyes watching, waiting, hoping to catch them. They must have a very good hiding spot. For themselves. And for the diamonds.'

Freja slumped back into her chair. 'How thrilling,' she whispered.

'Wouldn't it be delicious,' said Vivi, 'if the diamonds were just like Bianca and Antonia's jewels on the merry-go-round? *Sitting right under our noses all the time.*'

Freja nodded. 'Right under our noses,' she echoed.

'Delicious,' sighed Tobias, and he stared directly into Vivi's wide, chocolatey eyes.

Tobias and Freja hung over the balcony and waved as Vivi walked away down the street, her pink shoes clip-clopping on the cobblestones, her cherry-blossom skirt swaying from side to side.

She turned back one last time and blew them both a kiss. '*Ciao! Ciao*, my beautiful friends!'

'Beautiful,' sighed Tobias, and he leaned further over the railing to keep Vivi in sight just a little longer.

As he leaned, a thin length of twine dangled forward from the open collar of his shirt.

At the end of the twine hung a key.

Freja stared.

It was not a normal, everyday key like one would use to open a cottage door or the lock on a suitcase. It was small and solid, its rusty head shaped like a heart, the other end shaped like an elaborate capital E.

It looked like the type of key that might open something special ...

Something old ...

Something like a little treasure chest ...

CHAPTER 34
Secrets revealed

Freja lay in bed, flat on her back, and waited.

All across Rome, hundreds of church bells chimed midnight. The last cars and three-wheeled trucks zoomed by in the street below. Two cats started a yowling competition on a nearby rooftop. Finnegan yawned, stretched across the bed and the girl and fell asleep.

When all had been quiet for some time, Freja squeezed out from beneath the hound, grabbed her scissors from her pencil case and crept from the room. She pressed her ear against Tobias' bedroom door and listened. All she could hear was a snoring sound, not so very different from the noise Finnegan was making in her own room.

Turning the handle, she pushed open the door and slipped inside. She tiptoed to the edge of the bed and stared down at the sleeping writer. His quilt and sheets lay in a tangled mess at his feet. His winter pyjamas, patched and frayed, were pushed up to his knees and elbows. And across his body, his pillow and the mattress was a scattering of books, journals and small scraps of paper. His pencil, of course, was still tucked behind his ear.

A breeze blew in through the open window, and something dangled back and forth from the bed lamp.

'The key,' whispered Freja. She relaxed a little; she would not be needing the scissors after all. 'Too easy.'

Smiling, Freja unhooked the twine from the lamp, slipped it around her neck and crept back to her own room.

There, she closed the shutters, placed her pillow against the crack at the bottom of the door and turned on the light. Crawling beneath the bed, she dragged out her satchel. From the satchel she took her cherry-red beanie and from the cherry-red beanie she took the battered little treasure chest.

Her breath caught.

This was a very important moment. She, Freja Peachtree, was about to release the secrets belonging to Clementine Peachtree and Tobias Appleby.

'All will be revealed,' she whispered. She smiled because the words sounded important. A little pompous even.

She carried the treasure chest from the bed to the dressing table — an archbishop bearing a crown towards a new queen. She took the key from around her neck and listened for some kind of fanfare.

'Boof!' said Finnegan. He sneezed, whimpered and started to snore again. It would have to do.

She pushed the key into the lock, turned it and opened the lid.

'It worked! It worked!' She clapped her hands, allowed herself a quiet, little squeal of delight, then delved into the secrets.

'Puffin poop!'

Freja peered into the treasure chest for the *third* time, squinting, frowning. Each and every object looked so terribly, terribly normal. Boring. Pathetic even.

Of course, these were not necessarily treasures. 'Secrets', Clementine had called them.

'Clementine,' whispered Freja. 'Clementine would tell me to look carefully. To look again. To search for new things no-one else would notice. To make up my own mind about what I'm seeing.'

Slowly and methodically, Freja pulled out each object, examined it and laid it on the dressing table. There was a tiny white seashell, an acorn grey with age, a smooth, round pebble, a small brown feather, another stone shaped roughly like a heart and a pressed flower. The flower had crumbled and lost most of its petals to the bottom of the treasure chest. Freja wondered if these were Clementine's secrets, dreams of a future spent amongst the beauty of nature.

Next, she pulled out the stub of a candle, a mint chocolate (the wrapper faded but still completely intact), a crystal like one might see on a chandelier and a short lock of hair that had been kept together by tying it into a knot.

Freja held the lock of hair in the palm of her hand and peered at it. 'Oh! There are *two* lots of hair,' she whispered. 'One golden and straight, the other brown and curly. Clementine's and Tobias' hair! But why is it knotted together?' She rubbed it softly against her cheek, then sat it next to the chocolate.

The crystal caught her eye once more. Holding it up to the ceiling, she turned it around and around in her fingertips. The light danced, sparkled and shattered into a thousand miniature rainbows. 'Beautiful,' she sighed.

Next, she took out a piece of paper, yellowed and covered with the large, crooked writing of a small child. Freja unfolded it and began to read:

Hero Boy and Reskew Girl
A really trew story by Grape Smith
PREPEAR TO BE ASTONISHED AND AMAZED
UNTIL YOUR EYEBALLS POP OUT AND EXPLODE
Once up on a time there was a bewtifool girl.
Her name was Anne.

Astonishingly, at the very same time there was a plane but powerfool boy called Grape. This was real lucky for Anne because she was in trubble.

'Help! Help!' she cried. 'I am in trubble. Dubble trubble some mite say.'

Grape was in trubble too. But as we alreddy no, he was very powerfool. His trubble was that

The story ended. Both sides of the paper were full.

'Grape Smith,' mused Freja. 'What a weird name. Maybe he was a friend of Tobias' and Clementine's ... And who's Anne? Someone real or someone pretend?' She felt a rush of excitement. This might be a proper secret — at last! After all, the story did say that it was 'really trew'. Then again, it might just be a scrap of paper that got messed up with Clementine's and Tobias' secrets. It might have nothing at all to do with their lives. Things like that did happen.

Freja read through the half-story again, then set it aside. She looked down into the treasure chest. All that was left was a small piece of card. Tucking her fingernails carefully under the edge, she pulled it out.

'Oh!' Her hand flew to her chest. It was a strip of three tiny black-and-white photos, the sort one took in a booth at a fair. Two children, a girl and boy, sat with their heads pressed together, their eyes twinkling. In the first photo, they were smiling, all teeth and gaps where the tooth fairy had been. In the second photo, they were screwing up their faces and poking out their tongues.

And in the last photo, they were laughing, their mouths wide, their eyes turned towards each other.

A tear slipped down Freja's cheek. For the photos were, of course, of Tobias and Clementine.

'*This* is a big, fat secret,' whispered Freja. 'Tobias and Clementine have known each other since they were children ... Maybe forever ... Maybe they're brother and sister!' Her breath caught. 'And that would make Tobias my uncle, no matter how many times he says he isn't!'

Secrets and lies. Lies and secrets. Tobias was so very good with both. But why would he and Clementine keep such a *wonderful* thing a secret?

'Perhaps,' said Freja, 'there is a complicated and mysterious reason why Tobias cannot tell me the truth. It happens in stories, so why not in real life?'

She smiled. The idea made her heart swell and her spirits soar. 'I am Tobias Appleby's *secret* niece. Tobias Appleby is my *secret* uncle. One day the world will know, but for now it has to remain a big, fat *secret*.'

Pressing the photo to her lips, she kissed girl Clementine and boy Tobias.

And then, although she knew it was wrong, she slipped the photo between the pages of her scrapbook.

One by one, Freja placed the other items back in the little treasure chest until all that remained was the crystal. She held it up to the light once more and watched the rainbows dance inside. Bigger rainbows danced across the ceiling and the walls.

'Magic,' she sighed. 'Like the crystal chandeliers in the Church of Santa Maria in Aracoeli.' She smiled. 'Like the diamonds that were stolen and carried away through the tunnel between the bank and the Church of Santa Maria in Trastevere.'

Freja moved the crystal towards the treasure chest and stopped. '*Two* Santa Marias!' She clasped the crystal in her hand until it bit into her flesh. 'There are *two* churches called Santa Maria and Vivi didn't say *which one* was connected to the bank by a tunnel. I thought ... I presumed it was Santa Maria in *Trastevere* because it was the church I had just drawn on my map. It was the church we had zoomed past on Tobias' motorcycle just the day before ... But perhaps ...' Her voice dropped to a mere hush. 'Perhaps I was wrong. Perhaps the church that was connected to the bank by a tunnel is actually the Church of Santa Maria in *Aracoeli* ... The church where Nonna Rosa and I went to pray ... The church with all the crystal chandeliers ... The church where *one* crystal chandelier shines brighter than all the rest ...'

She opened her shaking hand and stared at the crystal. 'Tobias,' she whispered, then raised her voice to a shout. 'Tobias!'

Tossing the crystal into the treasure chest, she ran from her bedroom, yelling at the top of her lungs, 'Tobby! Tobby! Tobby! We have to go to church!'

CHAPTER 35
Mystery solved!

'Are you sure about this, old chap?' Tobias tugged at his scarf and frowned as Finnegan chased three cats down an alleyway. 'Church? In the middle of the night?'

Freja nodded. She grabbed his hand and, together, they walked up the long, steep stairway that led to the Church of Santa Maria in Aracoeli. Tobias pushed against the large wooden door, but it would not budge.

'It's this way,' said Freja. Quietly, carefully, she tiptoed along the terrace, pushed open the smaller door and slipped inside. Tobias followed.

'Oooh.' Tobias shuddered. 'Gloomy.'

'Shhhh,' whispered Freja. 'It is gloomy at night, but in the daytime, it's the most beautiful place you've ever seen — bright and sparkling. Like Heaven.'

'Why are we whispering?' asked Tobias.

Freja took his hand once more and led him silently up the middle of the church.

A door banged, and the beam of a torch darted back and forth across the sanctuary. Freja ducked behind a marble pillar, dragging Tobias with her.

'Why are we hiding?' asked Tobias.

'You'll see,' whispered Freja.

The light was poor, but they could just make out three priests dragging a ladder across the marble floor. They stopped beneath the arch in front of the altar. Two held the base of the ladder while the third climbed up with the torch in his hand. As the beam of light fell upon the chandelier, it burst to life. A thousands bolts of lightning shot out across the walls and ceiling of the church.

'It's magnificent,' Tobias said in a hushed tone. 'I've never seen anything like it.'

'That,' whispered Freja, 'is because chandeliers are usually made of crystals. But this one is special ... This one is made of diamonds.'

Tobias did not make a sound.

Perhaps, thought Freja, *he didn't hear me*. She tugged at the edge of his cardigan and whispered, 'Tobias?'

'Diamonds?' he asked. 'Are you sure, old chap?'

'Yes.'

The torch shone for a moment on the face of the priest at the top of the ladder. He had thick, dark hair, a muscular jaw, hard eyes and a nasty scar running from the middle of his left cheek to his chin.

'Freja!' gasped Tobias. 'It's Padre Paolo! What? How? But ...'

'I know,' she replied. 'It's astonishing, isn't it? The three priests — who are not really priests at all — are the diamond thieves. The ones Vivi was telling us about. They're here because they used the tunnel that leads from *this* church to the basement of the bank.'

'But that was the Church of Santa Maria in Trastevere,' whispered Tobias. 'That's on the other side of the Tiber River.'

'No,' said Freja. 'Vivi didn't say that. I just *presumed* she was talking about the church in Trastevere. But there are *two* Santa Marias.'

'Two Santa Marias,' echoed Tobias, but still he didn't seem to understand. Of course he didn't. He hadn't been creeping around at night, like Freja had, losing his cherry-red beanie, gathering clues he could not share for fear of being scolded.

The chandelier rattled as Padre Paolo unhooked it and carefully lowered it down from the arch.

'I think,' said Freja, 'they might have blown up the tunnel between this church and the bank's vault once they had stolen the diamonds. And then they *hid* the diamonds. Somewhere safe. A place where no-one would look.'

'And what better place,' said Tobias, his voice slow and deliberate, 'than hanging from a chandelier in the middle of a church that is *full* of chandeliers?'

'Right beneath our noses,' whispered Freja.

'Astonishing!' gasped Tobias. 'What a brilliant plan!'

'No more brilliant than Bianca and Antonia's plan in *Rome's Reward*,' said Freja.

'Aaah,' sighed Tobias, his mind untangling the mystery of the three angry priests. '*They* think I've been taunting them. That I know exactly what they have done because my book tells the same sort of story. *And* I arrived in Rome just days after they committed the robbery and hid the diamonds. I suppose they think I planned to blackmail them. You know, "Give me some of the diamonds, or I'll turn you in to the police!"' Tobias slapped his forehead so hard that the sound echoed through the marble arches.

'Huh?' Padre Paolo grunted. He shone the torch back and forth across the church, muttering. From what Freja understood, he was blaming the noise on the smelly cats that roamed about at night and slipped, uninvited, in and out of the church.

'Golly,' said Tobias. The whites of his eyes showed in the dark.

'I don't know how they got to be in charge of this church,' said Freja. 'Maybe they sent the real priest away on a cruise, like Bianca and Antonia did with their parents in *Rome's Reward*. Or maybe they did something worse ...'

'I say, old chap. You're right! This is all pretty serious. We could be in terrible danger.'

'We can't leave now,' Freja pointed out. 'They might see us.'

Tobias nodded.

Padre Paolo climbed to the bottom of the ladder and, together, the three thieves slid the chandelier into a large canvas bag. Padre Paolo grabbed his biretta from the altar and placed it at a jaunty angle on his head. He chuckled. Padre Nico and Padre Flavio smirked along with him and exchanged fist bumps.

Padre Paolo lifted the canvas bag into his muscular arms and the three thieves swaggered down the centre of the church.

'Boof!' A large, dark beast flew from the shadows and flung itself at Padre Paolo. Priest, beast and canvas bag crashed to the floor. The sound of growling, snapping, snarling, yelling and ripping cut through the air.

'It's Finnegan,' hissed Freja. 'Finnegan is attacking the priest's biretta.'

Freeing the prized pompom, Finnegan shook it from side to side, then bolted from the church.

'Hooray!' cheered Freja, then clasped her hand across her mouth.

The torchlight, which had waved about so wildly during the attack, now homed in on Freja's face. She froze, blinded by the beam. Moments later, a hand grabbed her painfully by the arm and she was dragged into the middle of the church.

Padre Paolo heaved himself up from the floor. His left sleeve was in tatters and his hair stuck out at strange angles. Anger twisted his face and puckered his scar.

Padre Nico squeezed Freja's arm. She yelped.

'Hang on there!' cried Tobias.

Padre Flavio pinned Tobias' arms behind his back.

Padre Paolo smirked. 'This little girl has been nothing but trouble. I think it is time we teach her a lesson.'

'No!' shouted Tobias. 'Let her go. Don't hurt her! She's precious! She's my —'

The writer slumped to the floor.

'Tobby?' whimpered Freja. Then, turning to Padre Flavio, she cried, 'What did you do to him?'

Padre Flavio smacked the solid barrel of the torch into the palm of his hand. 'It's not as fancy as using a golden candlestick, but it does the job just as well.'

'You beast! You're nothing but a bully!' shouted Freja.

'Lock her in the cupboard!' ordered Padre Paolo.

Freja kicked and wriggled like a reindeer caught in a blackberry bush, but she was no match for fat Padre Nico. He dragged her across the church, shoved her into a cupboard full of musty, old robes and locked the door.

She heard a shuffling sound, like a body being hauled across the floor. 'Tobby,' she whispered. 'What are they doing to you?'

Freja stood amongst the robes, paralysed by fear. Not for herself, but for Tobias. It was bad enough that Clementine had been taken rudely from her life for now. But at least she had gained Tobias. Beautiful, kind Tobias, who loved her exactly as she was. Tobias, who had done everything in his power to heal her lonely heart and make her happy once more — even bringing her to Rome. Tobias, who had told her how brilliant and spectacular she was, every single day, until she had started to believe it herself. What would she do if he, too, was ripped from her life? The hole in her heart would be far too big to fill.

'Oh, Tobby,' she whimpered. 'I'm sorry.' For it was completely and utterly her fault that they were here in the Church of Santa Maria in Aracoeli in the middle of this terrible mess.

A deep sob shook her entire body and she slumped against the cupboard door.

'Ouch!' Something sharp stuck into her head.

Freja ran her fingers across the door, but there was nothing there. She leaned forward and the sharp object jabbed her head once more.

'A bobby pin!' she gasped. 'I must have left one in when I went to bed!'

There was no time to lose. She reached up beneath her beanie and pulled out the bobby pin. 'Thank you, Natasha Andronikov!' she whispered, bending the wire into shape. She felt around for the keyhole, poked in the bobby pin, twiddled until it caught on the locking mechanism, then turned it to the side. The hours of practice on the apartment door had paid off! The lock clicked.

Freja kicked open the door and tumbled out of the cupboard. She raced to the spot where Tobias had been, but he was gone! She dashed to the little door at the front of the church, flung it open and ran straight into Padre Nico's fat, hairy arms.

CHAPTER 36

Friends and foes

'*Bambina terribile!*' Padre Paolo stamped his foot. He glared at Freja over his sack of diamonds. 'Enough is enough! You have made more mischief than a school full of naughty children.' Turning to Padre Nico, he said, 'It is time we were going. She will have to come with us.'

Padre Nico grabbed Freja by the scruff of her coat and her feet lifted from the ground. She felt like a puppet dangling from a string. So very helpless. So dreadfully alone. Tears that she thought had run dry now dribbled down her cheeks.

Freja reached into the pocket of her duffel coat for her little felt hare. Instead, her fingers closed around a piece of crumpled card. She took it out and stared at the thick pencil letters she had written on a tag many weeks ago: 'THIS CHILD BITES.'

She sniffed and was about to put the card back into

her pocket when she changed her mind. She held it out so that Padre Nico could see it.

'What is this?' With his free hand, he reached for the card. 'This child bi—'

Freja sank her teeth into the hairy hand.

Padre Nico squealed like a baby and released her coat. He staggered backward, away from the church, until the ground beneath his heels disappeared. Freja watched, open mouthed, as he tottered on the edge of the terrace, fat hands grabbing at thin air, then toppled down the long, steep staircase in front of the church, all the way to the bottom.

THUD!

His body lay as still as a lump of lard.

'*Imbecille!*' snarled Padre Paolo. 'I will deal with the girl myself!'

He tossed the canvas sack to Padre Flavio, but it was too heavy for the tall, thin man and he fell flat on his back. The chandelier landed on his stomach and knocked the wind from him. He lay on the terrace, gasping like a fish out of water.

Padre Paolo waved his fists in the air and bellowed across the rooftops of Rome, '*MAMMA MIA!*'

A flock of pigeons awoke and flapped out from the eaves.

Freja whimpered.

Padre Paolo stepped forward, his nostrils flaring, his hands shaking with rage. 'I will see that you cause me no more troubles, you stinking little sewer rat.'

'I don't think so!' roared a deep Russian voice.

'No, I don't think so either!' roared a second deep Russian voice.

The priest froze.

Freja beamed, her teeth flashing, her eyes sparkling in the lamplight.

For strutting around the corner of the church were Boris and Nadia. And right behind them was a small crowd: Nonna Rosa and Enzo, Giuseppe and Pazzo with their pipe organ, and all of Enzo's silly old friends from the bar — Roberto, Sebastiano, Edmondo and Xaviero. Edmondo and Xaviero were wearing their dressing gowns and slippers.

Freja ran to Boris and threw herself into his big, friendly arms. Boris passed her to Nadia and stepped towards Padre Paolo. Nadia passed her to Nonna Rosa and stepped forward to join Boris.

'Nobody harms one of Boris Sokolov's friends and gets away with it!' roared Boris.

'And nobody harms one of *Nadia* Sokolov's friends and gets away with it!' roared Nadia.

Boris folded his arms, looked at Nadia and nodded. 'I suppose that means that this so-called priest is in *double* trouble.'

Nadia folded her arms, looked at Boris and nodded. 'Double *Russian* trouble, Boris. The worst kind of trouble you can get!'

Padre Paolo's left eye began to twitch above his

scar. His gaze wandered to the canvas sack on Padre Flavio's stomach, then back to Boris and Nadia. He snorted, dashed across the terrace, seized the canvas bag and started down the steep stairway.

At the same time, Tobias staggered out of the little door at the front of the church. He frowned and rubbed the back of his head.

His eyes fell upon Freja, safe in Nonna Rosa's arms, and his hand flew to his heart.

His gaze darted to Padre Paolo running down the stairs with the diamonds. He blinked and stumbled to the edge of the steps.

'I think,' Tobias muttered, 'it's time for a game of Cheese Wheels.'

And without further thought, he squatted down, wrapped his arms around his legs, tucked his chin into his chest and rocked forward. Freja winced as Tobias' hips, shoulders and head smacked against the hard edge of one step after another. But there was no denying it — he made a wonderful cheese wheel. His path was straight and true, and he quickly gathered speed. By the time the priest was two-thirds of the way down the staircase, he was bowled off his feet. He took the rest of the journey tangled and toppling with a tall, gangly, slightly concussed writer.

THUD!

THUD!

KERPLUMP!

Freja broke free from Nonna Rosa and ran down the stairs. She threw herself on Tobias and sobbed, 'Oh, Tobby, Tobby, Tobby!'

Tobias propped himself up on his elbows and gave her a weak and wobbly smile. 'I was right, old chap. A cheese wheel of a great enough size really *can* do a spot of damage to a grown man. I think I might have broken that fellow's leg before we landed. The Cheese Wheel of Destruction is going *straight* into my novel.'

Boris and Nadia marched down the stairs. Boris stood, hands on hips, one foot resting on Padre Nico's fat belly. Nadia stood, hands on hips, one foot resting on Padre Paolo's belly. They nodded at each other and allowed themselves small smiles of satisfaction.

Giuseppe yawned loudly, operatically, and pushed his little wagon across the terrace at the front of the church. He parked it over Padre Flavio's body so the wheels on either side pinned his robe to the ground. Pazzo sat by Padre Flavio's head and poked his finger up the thief's nostrils, making happy little 'oo-oo-oo' sounds.

Nonna Rosa and Enzo hobbled slowly down the stairs, leaning on one another for support. Nonna Rosa bent over and stroked Freja's cheek. '*Bella bambina. I am glad that you are safe.*'

Roberto, Sebastiano, Edmondo and Xaviero doddered down from the terrace. Together with Enzo, they sat in a row along the bottom step. Roberto rested his feet on the bag containing the diamond chandelier.

It clanked and clunked as the broken pieces shifted beneath his heels. Xaviero pulled a bottle of grappa from his dressing-gown pocket, took a sip and passed it along. Edmondo said something in rapid, melodic Italian. The old men nodded, cried, '*Sì! Sì! Splendido! Magnifico!*' and slapped each other on the back.

'Look at those *stupid* old men, Freja!' cried Nonna Rosa. 'They think they are heroes and they have done nothing, *nothing* to help!'

'Pah!' snorted Enzo. 'Don't listen to the cranky old bat. We are all here, aren't we? We came to protect our precious Freja.'

'You almost made us *too late* to protect our precious Freja!' snapped Nonna Rosa.

'But how did you even know we were here and that we needed help?' asked Freja.

'Boris and Nadia!' said Nonna Rosa.

Boris nodded. 'Nadia and I ... Ha! How can I say it? ... We are a little bit suspicious. It is our training. We used to be spies, you know.'

Nadia nodded. 'Russian spies! Good spies! Very thorough!'

'Spies!' gasped Freja. 'Tobby, did you hear that?'

Tobias rubbed the back of his head and grinned.

Boris continued. 'We have been keeping a little eye on you, Freja, since the night at Nonna Rosa's trattoria, when you told us the strange story of the grumpy priests. We say to ourselves, "Aha. This sounds fishy."'

'Fishy,' agreed Nadia. 'Like my earrings.'

'And then,' explained Boris, 'we see the priests chasing you past the Colosseum two days ago. We think things might be getting a little bit dark, a little bit dangerous. We think it is time to get serious.'

'Serious?' asked Freja.

'Boris and Nadia have been keeping watch over you and Tobias for the last two nights,' said Nonna Rosa, 'and the day in between.'

'We had good help.' Nadia pointed to the top of the stairs. 'Giuseppe and Pazzo have shared the duties. And Nonna Rosa and Enzo have sent their friends out with food so we could stay at our post.'

Boris turned to Nonna Rosa, rubbing his tummy. 'Nonna Rosa's pizza capricciosa is the best thing I have ever tasted!'

Nadia continued. 'When you and Tobias went out for a walk at two o'clock this morning, we followed. Just to make sure you stayed safe. Giuseppe was arriving to relieve us for a few hours' sleep, so he and the monkey came too.'

'I could not sleep,' said Nonna Rosa. 'I was down in the trattoria making bread and saw you all pass by. I woke Enzo and *we* followed.'

'When we passed Roberto's house, I threw a rock at his window,' said Enzo. 'He jumped into his little green truck, picked us all up and we followed at a distance.'

Roberto nodded. 'And when we saw you go into the church, I said, "Aha! Now they are safe in God's house for a moment, we can zip around and pick up our old friends."'

'But they were *not* safe!' shouted Nonna Rosa, waving her hands in the air. 'By the time we had picked up Sebastiano, Edmondo and Xaviero and squashed them all into the back of that ridiculous little truck, *anything* might have happened.'

'It *did* happen!' cried Sebastiano. 'Edmondo and I fell off and had to use our skinny, old legs to run along behind you!'

The old men chuckled. Edmondo showed everyone the holes in the knees of his pyjama pants as proof of the disaster, and they laughed even harder, clutching at one another's arms and knees.

'I don't care about *you*, you stupid old men!' snapped Nonna Rosa. 'I meant the girl and the writer!'

'Pah!' cried Enzo. 'Nag! Nag! Nag! It has all worked out. The writer has a bruise or two. Perhaps his brain is battered. But Freja is as beautiful as ever and we have all had a little bit of adventure.'

Edmondo said something in rapid Italian, and the silly old men laughed as though their faces would crack and their sides would split.

'What did he say?' asked Freja.

Nonna Rosa sighed heavily and frowned. 'He's a stupid old man like the rest of them! He left his apartment in such a rush to join us that he grabbed his *wife's* false teeth instead of his own.'

'Teeth?' whimpered Padre Nico. He lifted his fat head, looked at the teeth marks on his hand, then passed out once more.

The old men threw back their heads and howled. They rocked back and forth, stamping their feet, clutching their bellies, laughing, laughing, laughing, until the tears ran down their faces and Nonna Rosa, Boris, Nadia, Tobias and Freja all joined in.

CHAPTER 37
Plenty

It was still dark when Roberto drove the girl and the writer home in his little green three-wheeled truck. Finnegan was waiting by the door to the courtyard, grinning and dribbling on the cobblestones. There was a piece of melted cheese stuck to his eyebrow, a sun-dried tomato wedged in his ear and small bits of cooked spaghetti tangled everywhere in his shaggy grey fur. He had, it seemed, had a wonderful time raiding Rome's rubbish bins.

Freja wrapped her arms around Finnegan's grubby neck and closed her eyes. She leaned more and more heavily against his body.

'Come along, old chap!' Tobias hoisted Freja into his arms and carried her through the courtyard, up the stairs and into the apartment. He peeled off her coat, boots and beanie and helped her into bed. Finnegan stretched out at her side, licked her cheek and nuzzled his nose deep into her wild golden curls.

Tobias plucked the sun-dried tomato from Finnegan's ear. He pushed a stray curl from Freja's face and hummed a little tune until her eyes closed and her breathing became slow and heavy. He leaned forward, kissed her softly on the forehead and whispered, 'Precious little Freja. I love you.'

Freja kept her eyes closed, but as Tobias walked from the room and shut the door, she whispered, 'I love you too.' She pulled the quilt up over her head and murmured into the fuggy darkness, 'Uncle Tobby.'

When Freja awoke, it was late afternoon. The dog was gone, but a few pieces of spaghetti remained on the pillow.

The little treasure chest was gone too. Sitting on the dressing table in its place was some sort of note. Freja felt a stab of panic as she wondered what it might say: 'I have removed the treasure chest and you are never to speak of the things you have seen.' Or simply: 'Shame on you!' She had, after all, stolen a key and poked her nose into Clementine's and Tobias' secrets. She had betrayed their trust.

She crept towards the dressing table feeling small and ashamed. But when she picked up the note, the nasty feelings melted away.

In large, loopy letters, written in cheerful red ink, it said: 'You're awake! Have a bath. Dress yourself in something truly special. There's a party brewing and you are the guest of honour!'

'My dear Freja! You look simply spiffing.' Tobias stopped at the front door of Trattoria Famiglia and gazed down at her with real admiration. 'That brown knitted vest of mine really does look rather good as a dress. Especially teamed with that pink shirt and those pink tights. And I do like the way you have decorated your head! Correct me if I'm wrong, but that magnificent wreath in your hair is made completely from fruit and nuts!'

Freja nodded. 'Strawberries, cumquats, walnuts, chestnuts and figs.'

'Woof!' said Finnegan.

'That's right!' Freja giggled. 'There were going to be grapes too, but Finnegan ate them.'

The dog dribbled on Freja's shoe.

'Well, it looks sensational,' cried the writer. 'Colourful, delicious, nutritious, slightly feral and *totally* unique. You are an exceptional child, Freja Peachtree, and I would be honoured if you would escort me in to dinner.' Bending his knees to make himself a little shorter, he offered Freja the crook of his arm.

Freja smiled and hooked her arm through his. Then, together with the giant Irish wolfhound, they stepped into Trattoria Famiglia to the cheers of the waiting party.

'*Urrà! Urrà! Urrà!*'

'It's Rome's beloved heroes!'

'*Buonasera!* Good evening and welcome!'

'Freja! Tobias! Come here! Come join us! Come tell us everything once more!'

'Three cheers for the *bella bambina* who conquered the villains. *Urrà! Urrà! Urrà!*'

Freja gasped. So many faces and all turned towards her!

Her cheeks warmed a little, but her tummy did *not* turn to sludge. Her eyes didn't dart about the room in search of a place to hide. She didn't even clench her teeth. For once, she did not feel afraid.

Because I'm with friends, she thought. *Precious, beloved friends.* And she realised that the tingles running up and down her spine were of the happy sort.

Freja relaxed and gazed at the marvellous scene before her. A number of tables had been pushed together to make one great, long banquet table. There were red-and-white chequered tablecloths, red serviettes and dozens and dozens of large white candles. The flickering flames reflected off glasses, water jugs, wine bottles and sparkling eyes so that the room danced with a thousand gleaming lights. Along both sides of the table sat all of their friends: Vivi, wearing a pink dress that looked like it had been spun from silk and fairy floss; Boris and Nadia, wearing dinner suits; the four old men from the bar — Roberto, Sebastiano, Edmondo and Xaviero; Giuseppe and Pazzo; and, strangely, Samantha, the plump American tourist from the Trevi Fountain, accompanied by a rather handsome Italian man.

Samantha waved. 'Hi there!' She pointed to her date and smiled, all teeth and gums. 'This is Uberto. We met yesterday!'

Freja and Tobias waved back at her. Samantha giggled like a little girl.

'Sit! Sit!' cried Nonna Rosa, waddling towards them. 'We have saved two seats at the head of the table for our distinguished guests.'

'Boof!' said Finnegan. He jumped up so that his front paws rested on Nonna Rosa's shoulders and his big, wet nose poked her cheek.

The old woman rolled her eyes and pushed him away. '*Sì! Sì!* Everybody this side of the table move down one place so the dog can sit with the girl and the writer. It would seem that there are *three* distinguished guests, not two!' She threw her hands in the air, then waddled away to the kitchen, grumbling and shaking her head.

Enzo led Freja to her chair as though she was a queen. 'Don't worry about Nonna Rosa,' he whispered. 'She loves that big, hairy dog almost as much as she loves you.'

At the far end of the table, Pazzo jumped up and down on Giuseppe's shoulder. He screeched and tugged and bit Giuseppe's ear, but the organ grinder held fast to his tail. 'Calm down, you naughty monkey. You are scaring the big grey dog. Tonight, you behave.'

Freja blew the monkey a kiss and he settled a little. His eyes, however, did not leave the wreath on Freja's head.

Nonna Rosa returned and slammed a basket of bread, a bowl of olives and a plate of pastrami in front of them. '*Mangia, mangia!* Eat, eat! You English are too skinny. Tear off some bread, pop some olives into your mouth, sink your teeth into a slice of pastrami. It will do you good.' She leaned forward and grabbed Freja's face in her soft, old hands. 'It will make your pretty cheeks grow plump and rosy like Nonna Rosa's.'

Enzo set down two glasses of lemonade before Freja and Finnegan. 'Pah!' he cried. 'Leave the poor child alone! She does not want to look like you. She is beautiful! A golden angel with fruit in her hair. Whereas you, Nonna Rosa, are an ugly old bat.'

The trattoria fell silent.

'Me?' roared Nonna Rosa, trying to make herself tall, but not succeeding. '*Me?* Ugly? Have you looked in the mirror lately, old man? *You* have a face like the rear end of Xaviero's donkey!'

The old men all burst out laughing and slapped the table with their wrinkled hands.

Enzo grabbed Nonna Rosa by the shoulders and stared at her, frowning. Then, suddenly, he pulled her towards him and planted a big, sloppy kiss on her lips.

Nonna Rosa beat her hands against his shoulders until he let her go. 'You stupid old man. Nobody wants to kiss a face like a donkey's bottom!'

'I know!' cried Enzo. 'But I did it anyway!'

The entire gathering exploded into roars of delight. Enzo smiled and sang, *'Grazie! Grazie!'* He bowed to his customers and his friends, one and all.

Nonna Rosa sighed and waddled back to the kitchen.

The dinner rolled on in a sea of laughter, pizza, pasta, salad, lemonade and wine. Vivi listened, rapt, as the story of the previous night's adventures was retold, half in Italian, half in English.

'But we still don't know how the priests came to work at the church in the first place,' said Freja. 'It was a very important part of their plan.'

'I know!' cried Roberto. 'I talked to my friend at the police station this afternoon. The fat thief, Nico, cracked under pressure! I think the police said he could not eat until he told them everything. So he blabbed!'

Freja and Tobias leaned forward. Finnegan ate Freja's pizza.

'Eight weeks ago,' explained Roberto, 'Padre Paolo — the *real* Padre Paolo — was about to catch a train from Naples to Rome, where he would become the new priest at the Church of Santa Maria in Aracoeli. But then, at the last moment, he received a letter from the bishop asking him to travel to a monastery in the southernmost tip of Argentina. There, he was needed as a teacher to a group of orphans. How could a kind man say no? He left at once.'

'*Fantastico!*' shouted Vivi. 'A forged letter from the bishop! It is very much like Bianca and Antonia in *Rome's Reward*, sending their parents on a cruise!' She reached across the table and squeezed Tobias' hand.

Tobias grinned and blinked, looking so much like Finnegan that Freja thought he might dribble on the tablecloth.

'Of course,' continued Roberto, 'when the fake Padre Paolo turned up at the Church of Santa Maria in Aracoeli at the appointed time, nobody suspected a thing. They did not know that the *real* Padre Paolo was a small man with blond hair, not a hulking monster with dark hair and a scar running down his cheek. And they knew nothing of the orphanage in Argentina. They accepted their new priest with open arms and were delighted that his friends, Padre Flavio and Padre Nico, had come along to help him settle into his new home. Three priests for the price of one! What could possibly go wrong?'

Giuseppe laughed. 'It would seem that *plenty* went wrong for the three priests!'

'But it might have gone *better* if Nico and Flavio had not been so stupid,' said Roberto. 'They were not meant to *chase* Freja and Tobias. Paolo simply ordered them to *spy* on the girl and the writer — to make sure they did not try to steal the diamonds for themselves!

If they had not chased the girl and the writer all over Rome, they would not have aroused so much suspicion.'

'Stupid! Stupid! Stupid!' cried Nonna Rosa, slamming two more large pizzas down on the table.

'Is she talking about the priests or Enzo?' whispered Freja.

Vivi shrugged. 'Don't ask.'

At that moment, a strange and colourful bird flew through the door and swooped towards them. 'Signore Appleby! My hero!'

It was Delfina Eloisa Ventimiglia, the owner of Libri e Sogni. Eufemia, the Italian greyhound, quivered at her side.

'Boof!' Finnegan leapt from his chair. He towered over Eufemia, tail wagging, dribbling on her smooth black head. Eufemia wagged her own tail and, together, they trotted out the door and disappeared. *Perhaps*, thought Freja, *they are going to find a romantic garbage bin full of food scraps for two.*

'We are *all* so thrilled about your successes,' crooned Delfina Eloisa. She waved her arm as if to indicate the empty space between her and the bar. 'You are both a crime writer *and* a crime solver! My store has been bustling all day. Your book, *Rome's Reward*, has been selling like hot *zeppole*! And now we're here to ask if you will be so kind as to autograph *all* of our books?'

Tobias looked around at the empty space. He looked at Freja and grimaced. He smiled up at Delfina Eloisa and said, 'Of course!'

Delfina Eloisa flashed a wide, orange-lipped smile, then floated to the door. 'Come! Come! The writer is here!' she called into the street, and a crowd spilt into Trattoria Famiglia, waving cameras and copies of *Rome's Reward* in the air.

Tobias pulled a pot of black ink from his pocket and a nib pen from behind his ear. For the next forty-five minutes he autographed one book after another. News of the captured diamond thieves had travelled quickly and it seemed that half of Rome wanted a signed copy of Tobias' novel. He smiled, nodded, signed and even threw in a few Italian phrases to prove his love for Rome: '*Spaghetti idiota gelati!*' he sang. '*Colosseo panini buongiorno!*'

His fans adored him! They did not even mind when he grew weary and started to jumble his autographed messages.

To Francesca, Best wishes from Apple Tobiasby.
To Tobias Appleby, Best wishes from Sofia.
To Rome, Best wishes from Rewards.
To Ugo, Best Rewards from Rome.

When the last of the fans had departed, Giuseppe let Pazzo free. The monkey scuttled along the back of the chairs and leapt up onto Freja's shoulder. He grabbed the girl by two clumps of her curly hair and rubbed his little cheek against hers. Then, making himself comfortable on the back of her chair, he started to eat the wreath on her head, one piece of fruit at a time. He plucked and nibbled and made happy little 'oo-oo-oo' sounds.

Vivi pulled her own copy of *Rome's Reward* from her basket. Shyly, she placed it in front of Tobias and said, 'I wondered, Signore Appleby, if you would autograph *my* book. Write something special, perhaps? Just for me.' Her liquorice-thick eyelashes fluttered and her olive cheeks blushed to the colour of burnt toffee.

'Oooh,' sighed Tobias. 'Special ... special ...' He pulled a second bottle of ink from his pocket, opened the book and wrote in large, loopy red letters: 'To Rome's Reward, with much love from Tobias. X.' He nodded, satisfied, and slid the book towards Vivi.

Vivi stared at it, the smile falling from her raspberry-gelato lips. 'But you have made a mistake!'

'No,' said Tobias. 'No mistake.' He pointed at the words and, for once, managed to say just the right thing. 'You, Vivi, are the absolute best that this astonishing city has to offer. *You* are Rome's Reward.'

Freja watched, open mouthed, as Tobias took both of Vivi's hands in his. 'Raspberry gelato,' he sighed. Closing his eyes, puckering his lips, he leaned in towards her.

'Oo-oo-oo-oo-oo!' cried Pazzo, and he pelted a chestnut at the writer's head.

'Ouch!' groaned Tobias. His forehead bashed against Vivi's and they both cried out in pain. Tobias flung his arms wide in surprise, toppling two bottles of wine and Freja's lemonade. Wine poured from the table into Vivi's lap.

'Oh, bother and poo!' Tobias sprang to his feet. 'I'm ever so sorry! Let me help!' He grabbed for a serviette, but took hold of the edge of the tablecloth by mistake and pulled it upward. Plates, bowls, glasses, bottles of ink, knives, forks, spoons and olives tumbled into their friends' laps and onto the floor.

Freja squealed.

Pazzo jumped up and down on her shoulder, screeching with glee.

Tobias stepped backward and tugged at his ears until Freja thought he would pull them off.

And Vivi — beautiful, wonderful Vivi — clutched her belly and laughed until she snorted.

Nonna Rosa shook her head, grumbled and cleaned away the mess. Enzo brought a new round of drinks. And finally, they locked the trattoria doors and sat down with their friends.

Giuseppe brought out a small piano accordion and played one exuberant tune after another. Enzo and his friends sang along, laughing and burping between verses. Samantha and her true love danced. Finnegan and Eufemia dashed past the restaurant window in pursuit of a large tabby cat. Nadia and Vivi arm-wrestled. Boris, Nonna Rosa and Tobias had a long and serious talk about knives. Pazzo pulled all the nuts from Freja's hair and sat on the floor, cracking them with Nonna Rosa's rolling pin.

Freja slouched at the head of the table, her tummy stretched, her eyes heavy. She looked from one happy face to the next and wondered how her life had become so full of people.

It started, she realised, with Tobias Appleby.

Crime writer. Daydreamer. Cheese Wheel extraordinaire.

Uncle?

Who knew?

But as her head sank lower towards the table, she decided that, for now, it didn't really matter. All she truly knew was that Tobias Appleby was a kind and caring man who had led her into a new life filled with many more kind and caring people. Friends. Lots of big-hearted friends. Like a large, happy family.

She had always thought that love was quiet and small, something she and Clementine shared alone.

But love was not just Freja and Clementine.

It was not Freja and Clementine with Tobias and Finnegan thrown in for good measure.

Love was a crowd.

Love hung around where there was plenty.

Plenty of laughter.

Plenty of kindness.

Plenty of cuddles, even when a mother was not there to offer her own arms.

Plenty of music and singing and dancing and eyelash fluttering and food.

And as if to prove the point, at that very moment, Nonna Rosa plonked another enormous bowl of tiramisù on the table.

'Eat, Freja! Eat!' she sang and planted a rough but affectionate kiss on top of the girl's head.

CHAPTER 38

New beginnings

Freja and Tobias ran along the cobbled street, hand in hand. Scraps of paper fell from a hole in Tobias' cardigan pocket, leaving a merry paper trail in their wake. Freja's golden curls bounced about, reflecting the sunlight as beautifully as a diamond chandelier reflects torchlight. She wore a bright white smock with cherry-red gumboots. Pinned all around the hem of her smock were dozens of green-and-grey pigeon feathers she had gathered from the balcony that morning. Finnegan dashed back and forth, one minute in front of them, chasing a cat, the next behind them, chasing one of Tobias' stray notes.

'Hurry, Tobby! Hurry!' shouted Freja, dragging on his hand. 'It was nearly an hour ago that Giuseppe saw it. I'm worried that someone will clean it out before we get there.'

The air grew damp and filled with the sound of laughter, noisy conversations, music and gushing water. They skipped around the corner and found themselves staring at the Trevi Fountain.

The girl, the dog and the writer paused for a moment to gaze up at the bright white palace, Oceanus, the Tritons, the seahorses, the rugged rocks and the gushing-sploshing-whooshing abundance of crystal-clear water. Tobias squeezed Freja's hand. Finnegan licked Freja's earhole.

'Come on!' Freja dragged them both through the crowd until they stood right at the edge of the wide blue pool.

'There!' she cried. 'And there and there!' She continued to point and shout, counting no less than seven socks floating in the water.

Tobias tugged at his ear. 'I say, old chap, is that …?'

Freja followed his gaze and giggled. 'Yes! It's a roll of toilet paper. It's all mushed up, but it's *definitely* toilet paper.'

A tall, dark-haired woman turned towards them, her mouth pulled down at the sides. 'I know! It's disgusting!' she cried. 'Socks and toilet paper in our glorious Trevi Fountain. And three days ago I saw a large woman, American I think, tossing in a tube of lipstick! Who would do such a thing? Why can't they toss coins like we have done for many, many years? It's terrible! *Terribile!*' She shook her beautiful head and flounced away.

The girl and the writer sat down on the steps and laughed. Finnegan stretched out beside them, resting his shaggy grey head in Freja's lap.

'This is my favourite place in Rome,' sighed Freja.

'Still?' asked Tobias. 'Even after being chased across the fountain by Nico?'

'Yes.' She smiled. 'Because it all turned out okay in the end.'

'Most things do, old chap.'

Freja stroked Finnegan's ears. He yawned — loudly, luxuriously — then fell asleep.

Tobias, however, could not seem to settle. He took off his cardigan, then put it back on. He ran his fingers through his messy hair. He blushed. He took a pencil from behind his ear, scratched his head and tucked it away once more. As he reached for his ear, Freja asked, 'What's wrong, Tobby?'

'Wrong?' he cried. 'There's nothing wrong … well, not so very bad … then again, it's not so jolly good … but we need to remember that things really do have a strange and mysterious way of turning out all right in the long run …'

Freja stared at him, her mouth open, her nose scrunched. 'Huh?'

'The thing is,' said Tobias, 'I have received a letter, just this morning, from Clementine's doctor in Switzerland.'

Freja's mouth felt suddenly dry.

'Poor old Clem is having a spot of bother with her treatment,' he said. 'It happens sometimes, you know. She can't see too well, which is why she hasn't written. And, well, she can't really have any visitors for a while.'

'But it's working?' whispered Freja, not really knowing what 'it' was, or what it was working on.

'Oh yes! Certainly ... well, hopefully ... It can take some time before they know, but one has to hope for the best.'

'Hope for the best?' Her eyes filled with tears, because even though the words 'hope' and 'best' had been mentioned, they were not put together in quite the right way.

'She's in good hands ... brilliant hands,' said Tobias. 'And she'll be glad to know that you are safe and sound and growing stronger and taller from all that gelato and pizza and sunshine!'

Freja thought about this for a while. 'Clementine should come to Rome! The gelato would do her good. And Finnegan could catch a cat and we could give it to Clementine and she could throw it into the Trevi Fountain.'

'Why on *earth* would she do that?' asked Tobias.

Freja threw her hands wide and mimicked the writer pretending to be Donald Dawkings, the tour guide: 'Toss in a cat and you will live for many, many years! The cat's nine lives will become yours!' She smiled through her tears at Tobias. 'Remember?'

Tobias rubbed his chin and chuckled. 'Did I *really* say that?'

'Really!' Freja wiped her eyes on one of Finnegan's ears, then giggled in a gasping sort of way.

'That's the spirit, old chap! A cry, then a giggle. Now all we need is something delicious to fill our tummies and cheer us up completely. How about a gelato? Perhaps a *raspberry* gelato.'

'I've got a better idea,' said Freja. 'Macarons at Café Vivi!'

'Perfect!'

The girl, the dog and the writer sat at the little pink table beneath the awning at the front of Café Vivi. Their knees were covered in warm rugs crocheted from pale pink and white wool. Tobias sipped an espresso and nibbled on a raspberry macaron. Freja sipped hot chocolate and nibbled on a lemon macaron. Finnegan had just gobbled a plate of sardines and three pork sausages and was eyeing off the remaining macarons in the centre of the table.

A crowd of pigeons muddled about at their feet, warbling and gossiping.

'Have you heard the news?' squawked Tobias in his best Italian pigeon accent. 'Signora Voltilini was caught stealing cherries at the market yesterday.'

'I heard it was Signora *Palumba* who was caught stealing *strawberries*!' he sang in a deeper voice.

'No! No! You are both stupid!' he cried in a third voice, not unlike Nonna Rosa's. 'It was *Signore Lazzari* who was caught stealing a *red Alfa Romeo*.'

'Cherries! Berries! Alfa Romeos! What difference does it make? They are all red!'

'But you can't eat an Alfa Romeo!'

'Signore Lazzari could. My word, that man has an appetite like no other! He'd eat the shirt off your back if you gave him the chance.'

'I don't wear a shirt! I'm a pigeon!'

Laughter, light and sweet, floated through the air. It was Vivi. Tobias spun around, knocking his cup to the ground. The pigeons scattered. Coffee splashed up the leg of Vivi's pale blue jeans and shards of pink china skittered across the cobblestones.

'I'll get it,' said Freja. She dropped to her knees and crawled around, gathering the bits of broken cup. By the time she returned to the table, Vivi had pulled up a fourth seat and was sitting between Tobias and Finnegan.

'I have some news,' Vivi said. Her raspberry-gelato lips smiled, but the happiness didn't reach her eyes. 'I am going to do some more training, to become a better chef.'

'But you're *perfect* already,' sighed Tobias.

'Yes!' cried Freja. 'Nobody makes macarons like you, Vivi.'

'*Grazie! Grazie!*' Vivi reached forward and stroked Freja's cheek. 'You are both very kind to say these things.'

'Not kind,' said Freja. 'Just honest.'

'Boof!' said Finnegan, and he snatched a blueberry macaron from the plate.

'I have been made a very fine offer,' said Vivi. 'I am to work with one of the best pastry chefs in the world, Monsieur Diderot.'

'Why, that's marvellous!' cried Tobias. 'You'll be able to teach him a thing or two, I'm sure.'

Vivi laughed. 'I hope that *he* will be able to teach *me* a great deal. Then, one day, when I return to Rome, I will make Café Vivi a place that is famous throughout all Italy for its delicious pastries.'

Tobias held a pale pink macaron in the air and stared at it. '*Return* to Rome?'

'You're going away?' whispered Freja.

'*Sì!* To France, to a little town called Claviers in Provence, for that is where Monsieur Diderot has his pâtisserie.'

Tobias' fingers closed around the macaron. A stream of fine pink crumbs fell from his hand to the table, like sand falling through an hourglass.

Vivi blushed.

Tobias dusted his hands, tugged at his ears, then fiddled with a teaspoon until he bent the handle out of shape. His shoulders drooped and his eyes looked suddenly dull, the colour of pond scum.

'Provence, eh?' he said softly. 'A brilliant opportunity. Well done. Well done.' He reached out and shook Vivi's hand, but forgot to let it go.

A little tear slipped down Vivi's face. '*Sì! Sì!* A brilliant opportunity, as you say.' She pulled her hand free.

'Provence!' cried Freja, jumping to her feet. 'In France! Huh!'

'Boof!' said Finnegan in surprise. A piece of blueberry macaron shot from his nostril.

The girl hooked her arm around the writer's neck. 'That's a coincidence, isn't it, Tobias?'

Tobias stared blankly at her. Freja moved her head up and down in large, exaggerated nods and Tobias, stunned, nodded back.

Freja smiled at Vivi. 'It's an astonishing coincidence, because Tobias and I are going to Provence too!'

Finnegan lurched forward across the table.

'*And* Finnegan, of course!'

Vivi fluttered her liquorice-thick lashes. 'To Provence? You?' Her raspberry-gelato lips stretched wide across her face and, now, the smile reached her chocolatey eyes.

Freja nodded and Tobias joined in, this time with real enthusiasm.

'Absolutely!' he cried. '*Brilliant* idea! I mean ... astonishing coincidence. Yes! We are *definitely* going to Provence. Time for a change. Rome has been an absolute hoot, but a rolling stone gathers no moss. Seize the day! Strike while the iron's hot, I say. It'll be good for young Freja's education and for my work. Who knows, I might even write a love story next, and where better to set it than in France amidst the lavender fields, the vineyards, the olive groves, the hilltop villages?'

Vivi sprang up from the table. She smoothed her pink-and-white polka-dot apron, pushed in her chair, smiled and walked to the front door of Café Vivi. But then she stopped. Dashing back, she leaned forward and kissed Freja — twice on each cheek. She patted Finnegan and kissed him once on the top of his shaggy grey head. Then, taking a deep breath, she threw herself across the table and kissed Tobias, ever so quickly, smack-bang on the lips.

Stepping back, she smoothed her apron once more, then she was gone.

'France!' cried Freja.

'Boof!' said Finnegan, and he ate the remaining three macarons.

'Raspberry-gelato lips,' sighed Tobias, standing and staggering from the table.

And together, the girl, the dog and the writer wandered along the cobbled street, through Piazza di Spagna, past the pretty marble fountain and on towards their next great adventure.

Italiano!

Here is a list of the Italian words used in this story. You will notice that many words are similar to their English mate. It is always exciting to find these twin words, because they are easy to remember and they take some of the hard work out of understanding and learning a new language!

amore	love
angelo	angel
arrivederci	goodbye
attenzione	attention
bambina, bambino, bambini	child (female), child (male), children
bella	beautiful
bellissimo	very beautiful
bravo	bravo, good
buffone	buffoon, clown
buon appetito	enjoy your meal

buonanotte	goodnight
buonasera	good evening
buongiorno	good morning
ciao	hello (also goodbye)
cioccolato	chocolate
classico	classic
complimenti	congratulations
delizioso	delicious
drammatico	dramatic
famiglia	family
fantastico	fantastic
gelato, gelati	ice cream, ice creams
grazie	thank you
idiota	idiot, fool
imbecille	imbecile, stupid
incredibile	incredible
lampone	raspberry
lunatico	lunatic
magnifico	magnificent
mamma	mother, mum
Mamma mia!	My goodness!
Mangia, mangia!	Eat, eat!
momento	moment
no	no
nonna	grandmother
padre	father
panino, panini	sandwich, sandwiches
papà	dad
pazzo	crazy, wild

piazza	square, place
piccolo	small
prego	you're welcome
scusa	sorry
sì	yes
signora	Mrs, madam
signore	Mr, sir
signorina	Miss, young lady
terribile	terrible
trattoria	restaurant
urrà	hooray
zeppole	deep-fried dough balls

Watch out for
Freja Peachtree's next adventure in

The Girl, the Dog and the Writer in Provence

COMING CHRISTMAS 2018

Acknowledgements

Travel broadens the mind. It also broadens plot options. Thank you to my mum and dad for being the first to take me travelling and for remaining the two most inspiring and enthusiastic adventurers I know.

Thank you to these three kind and clever women — Kate 'Eddie' Burnitt, my in-house editor; Chren Byng, my publisher; and Jane Novak, my literary agent. I am so very grateful that you continue to guide and support me.

Thank you to my hilarious friends. You know who you are. The love, laughter and chatter keep my heart singing, my mind whirring and the ideas flowing.

And thank you to the Great Dane. You are the hand that steers me around the mud puddles when I am daydreaming. You are the smile that welcomes me back into the real world at the end of my writing day. You are, to use Tobias Appleby's love-struck words, everything.

Katrina Nannestad is an Australian author. She grew up in country NSW in a neighbourhood stuffed full of happy children. Her adult years have been spent raising boys, teaching, daydreaming and pursuing her love of stories.

Katrina celebrates family, friendship and belonging in her writing. She also loves writing stories that bring joy to other people's lives

Katrina now lives near Bendigo in Victoria with her family and an exuberant black whippet called Olive. She dreams of one day living in Rome, where she will spend her days sitting on the edge of a fountain, gossiping with the pigeons and eating chocolate gelato.

www.katrinanannestad.com